CASTLE LAKE

CASTLE LAKE

THOMAS A. RYERSON

GREY SWAN PRESS

Publishers of Fine Books   Marblehead, Massachusetts

Grey Swan Press
Briar Lane
Marblehead, Massachusetts 01945
www.greyswanpress.com

This book is a work of fiction. Names, characters, places, and incidents are products of the author's imagination and are used ficticiously. Any resemblance to persons, living or dead, is entirely coincidental.

First Grey Swan Press trade paperback edition, July 2008

100% acid-free paper
Printed in the United States

_____

Library of Congress Control Number: 2008920761

_____

ISBN-13: 978-0-9800377-0-8 • ISBN-10: 0-9800377-0-0

10 9 8 7 6 5 4 3 2 1

This book is dedicated to Jacqueline Rosch,
wherever she may be.
(My first serious distraction 1979-1982.)

Thanks to Tina A. for
both her medical expertise
and painstaking proofreading .

A special thanks to
Charmaine Booth
Terri Childress
Jeff Crawford
Julia White

CONTENTS

Part One—October 13, 1821

THOMAS A. RYERSON

1

Meet Mr. Murdock

It was a late morning in October of 1821 and the air barely moved. The air itself was cool, a natural contrast to the warm ground. This created a thick fog which was especially strange for this time of year. The fog was "thick as pea soup" James Murdock's father would have said.

James Murdock put a weathered hand to his head and pushed his grey linen cap back from his forehead as he looked up into the sky. The fog was an excellent cover for duck hunting. He had been waiting for a perfect morning like this. Normally a hunter might want to get out to the shoot a little earlier in the day. However, for the most part, the spot on the lakeshore where James was hunting was pretty secluded and private.

James was forty-two years old but actually looked much older. His hands were very rough and cracked like shoe leather. His face was weathered from being out in the blazing sun season after season. He didn't even have to smile to reveal his laugh lines. The crow's feet of age were already there. His dark brown eyes were deep set, almost giving him a caveman appearance. His dark brown hair had transformed itself into a grey matte over the last couple of years. He wasn't self-conscious about his greying hair. It had nothing to do with his preference for wearing hats and caps. The grey linen cap he wore now was one of his favorites. His clean-shaven chin was sharp, one of his strongest features. His face was rounded--not to the extent of jowls--but full. James also had a Roman nose, which seemed to jut right out of his face. Like his chin, there was no facial hair under his nose.

James was not a handsome man. It was not one of his concerns. He was, however, a very hard worker. He believed that man had been put on earth to toil and cultivate the vast land that God had put before him and his forefathers. James didn't care that he looked closer to fifty than his forty-two years. He had no one to impress but his God. And James impressed Him by his own hard work. James felt he didn't have to impress his wife or family either, beyond setting a good moral example for them. James had been married for many years, and he and his wife, Phoebe, had two sons from that union: John was fourteen and Henry was twelve. James' aging was a natural process.

Standing in the swampy water probably didn't help his accelerated aging. His feet sank into the soft ground, and the cold water of the marsh trickled into his well-worn leather work boots. He could see from the fog that the ground was warmer than the air. By the temperature of the water in his boots, he would have to disagree. But his feet were already pretty well numb anyway. James didn't care. It was what one must endure for the opportunity of some challenging duck hunting. He was a tough man and had survived much before in life than the cold swampy water that he tolerated today. James lowered his hand from his cap to his brow and looked into the sky. He wasn't sure what he was shielding his eyes against; there wasn't really any sun. Maybe it was the moisture in the air, or more likely, just one of those things a person did out of habit.

James continued to gaze upward into the fog-obscured sky. He admired the water fowl, the ducks that he hunted, for their independence and spirit. The ducks could fly wherever they wanted to—just pick up and leave. They also had brass. They had to know that danger lay in the marsh below as they flew past. But on they flew anyway. James surmised that their independence did not come without a price.

In the distance James could hear the distinctive sounds of some approaching ducks. He had to imagine the "V" pattern in which they would be flying because he could only see about twenty feet ahead. This might allow for a well-placed shot or two. James listened intently to the sounds above which seemed to be fading. He moved a little further forward, slowing only when he realized that he was sinking in the muck.

James stood just over six feet tall and weighed a little over two hundred pounds. Yes, life had been good to him over the past ten years. All that hard work was paying off. He was able to provide his family with a bountiful supper table. James had to admit he loved his meat, gravy, and potatoes. His weight was very evident as he backed a couple of steps out of the swampy soil. He may have put on some extra pounds over the years, but he certainly didn't look overweight by any stretch. Even though James appeared older than he really was, he was still in good shape from all of his physical activity. His father would have said "he was fit as a fiddle." The fourteen-hour workdays were good for him.

James could hear the sickly suction sounds as his feet lifted out of the soft ground. As soon as his foot was free of the muck, the deep imprint that it had left instantly filled with the greenish-brown liquid, the appearance of the water in this swampy area of the lakeshore. His canvas haversack swung in rhythm on his shoulder as he stepped back.

James continued to walk back towards solid land. By rights he was on land all the time, but some of it was certainly softer than other parts. Afraid he may trip and end up on his posterior, James turned around. He trudged up to higher ground and then turned back towards the lake. The swamp water in his boots squished between his toes in his cracked leather boots. Mud dotted his trowsers, hard and dry in some places, wet in others.

James looked out over the lake, but he didn't see much other than the fog. Like the ducks he had heard above him, he could imagine exactly how the lake appeared. The water would be calm and unbroken. He had lived here his entire life, and he knew this lake. James laughed to himself why anyone in his right mind would call this lake "Castle." Swamp Lake might be more appropriate. Or on a day like today, Fog Lake.

To add to the confusion, his father, James Senior, had always insisted the lake was pronounced "Cass-steel." To his dying day that was how James' father pronounced it. James simply spoke the word as it was suggested, Castle Lake. If the pronunciation of the lake's name wasn't enough, there was also another strange matter. The lake wasn't even a lake: it was actually a lagoon, or an inlet at best.

Supposedly, many years prior to the area's settlement by the English, the lake had been cut off from Carlton Bay by a thin strip of land. Apparently, over time the strip of land had weathered away until a narrow channel had formed. Possibly, the English settlers themselves had opened the lake up to the bay. Nothing was written down, only stories passed down from generation to generation, landowner to landowner. Castle Lake led into Carlton Bay which, in turn, led out to the Atlantic Ocean. Castle Lake was only a mile inland from the Atlantic Coast.

How the lake got its name was almost as confusing as its physical history. It was commonly believed among the locals that there had once been a castle located at the north end. The castle had been long gone even before James' grandfather was born. As a teenager, James and his friends would try to find traces of where the castle once stood, but it was futile. According to the stories the castle had been called "Northbrae" and was built by wealthy family members of the original English settlers. At that time, Northbrae had been the seat of power in the district.

However, many years after the castle had been built, there was a tragedy. All the people who had lived in and around Northbrae had suddenly died of smallpox or some similar disease. Northbrae had been the only proof that the English settlers had actually even been there. When the castle disappeared, it was lost forever to the annals of time. All that was left of Northbrae were the stories.

Castle Lake wasn't a large lake by any means. It was only about three-quarters of a mile from end to end and, maybe, just over a third of a mile across. The inlet out to Carleton Bay was in the middle of the lake on the east shore and was only thirty or forty feet wide, just enough room to get a schooner through.

The Murdock family had always lived near the coast. The family had been in the area for many generations. James' great grandfather had settled on the north shore of Castle Lake, and here he had built a fine house. Since being built in the mid 1700s, the house had been passed down from father to son and had seen many improvements over the years. Even James himself had improved the property by constructing many outbuildings such as a drive-shed, a chicken coop, and also a new barn for horse training. Several additions were added to the original Murdock barn as the livestock side of the farm continued to grow. The livestock had originally begun with cattle and now included chickens, pigs, and draft horses. James had recently taken up horse training to keep himself busy in the winter months. In the midst of winter, James could usually be found in one of the larger Murdock barns which featured an indoor paddock. He really enjoyed the horses and the training process.

What James loved most of all this time of year was hunting. When it was duck season, James had no greater joy than getting out into the swamps. The cold and wet that he endured was a small price to pay knowing that he might return with a mallard or two. Duck hunting was a great way to relieve stress. He and his Labrador retriever, Cora, were a force to be reckoned with, and he figured the ducks could sense it.

The group of ducks that he had heard must have suddenly changed their course and headed out towards the bay because the noise of their honking had diminished. James wondered what may have made the waterfowl do that. He then realized that Cora was no longer by his side. Possibly she was down in the swampy area of the shore, and the ducks had somehow seen or heard her snooping around. That would be an amazing feat in this fog, but the ducks did seem to have an uncanny knack for survival.

James gripped the front of his green greatcoat. Underneath the greatcoat was a very warm but worn woolen jacket. The greatcoat and jacket had both seen a lot of action and didn't look like much, but they kept him warm on cold mornings like this. He held the heavy greatcoat tight with one hand, and with the other he steadied his Joseph Manton double-barreled shotgun, which was a little awkward to hold with his thick gloves. James had the gun imported from England the year before which had cost him quite a bit, but, after all, the hunter and his dog deserved the best.

James continued to survey the area. It was a beautiful piece of property. The land rose on a steady incline from the lake's shore up to where the Murdock homestead sat. A well-worn path led down to the lake. The lakeshore was mostly rocky except for the part where James now stood which was the swampy area--only a small fraction of the actual lakeshore and a great vantage point to hunt ducks. For this reason James never considered this area a waste of land.

James took in a deep breath, filling his lungs with the cold fall air. It felt good, clean and fresh. The wind picked up ever so slightly, and the fog drifted onto the lake. It didn't lift; it just swirled. James had to squint his eyes as he looked out across the lake.

In good weather James could usually see the distant house of his closest neighbor. The neighbor's name was William Fick. Like James, William was also a farmer. Hell, they were all farmers or fishermen down in this area. James was the one who was deviating from farming with his horse training.

William was several years younger than James. Normally, James could see the Fick property from where he stood, but today, with the heavy fog, it was different. Even though it was after 11 a.m., the fog continued to rise eerily across the ground and the water. The morning was quiet except for the sounds of many different voices which seemed to originate from the Fick property. Mixed into the lively conversations, punctuated with laughter, was the faint sound of music, but James couldn't make out anything definitive.

"Cora!" James yelled out across the lake his voice seemingly echoing off the fog. James yelled again for his dog and then relaxed when he saw the head of his beloved black Labrador trudge up from the swampy part of the lakeshore. The dog somehow managed to look guilty for not having caught any ducks. James gave the dog a reassuring smile, "Don't worry old girl. We'll get a mallard or two yet." Cora's pink tongue hung out of her open mouth as she panted.

James cocked his head to one side as he strained to listen to the sounds that drifted over from the Fick homestead. The sounds were getting a little louder now, and it seemed like a party might be going on. James wondered just what the Ficks were up to today. James and William had never really hit it off. James had all the right intentions; it just didn't go the way he had hoped.

The Murdock family had been in the area much longer than the Ficks. For some reason the property on the south part of the lake had been vacant for many years, and James had looked into buying it. He submitted an offer or two, but someone had put in a better one.

It turned out that someone was William Fick. James wasn't upset; it wasn't all that important for him to own all the property around the lake. Actually, six years prior, when William had built his house and moved in with his wife and young daughter, James was almost grateful for the company. James and his wife, Phoebe, had speculated that it would be nice to have neighbors so close by. Or so they thought.

It seemed that William was a little strange when it came to his daughter. He was quite protective of her, and when he found out that James had two young sons, William became consumed with fear that the boys would cause his daughter harm. James wondered if there was possibly some past history with the daughter. There had to be some reason for William's overprotectiveness because James thought his boys were pretty decent young fellows.

However, William was sure that "those two Murdock boys" were up to no good even though he had no reason to think that way. He formed this opinion when he first met them. William's wife, Lilly, reassured him that he had nothing to worry about: children were children.

The children were allowed to play together, but most of the time under William's watchful and mistrusting eye. But as the months passed, William seemed to lighten up somewhat. At the time the Ficks had moved to Castle Lake, William's daughter, Lorra Anne, was ten. In contrast, James' two sons were younger: John was eight and his brother, Henry, was six. James didn't understand what all the fuss was about.

Lorra Anne Fick seemed to play well with John and Henry Murdock. She and the boys were always together. They could be seen playing in the rowboat on the lake, running amongst the reeds in the swampy area, or collecting colored rocks upon the shore. In the summer they swam in the lake, and in the winter they slid on the ice. They did all the things that children were known to do.

Two years passed, and it was now the summer of 1817. One day, that summer, William couldn't find his daughter. He called her name over and over again but to no avail. He searched around his property looking in all the familiar spots where the children liked to play, and then he realized that he had looked everywhere except the barn. As he walked closer to the barn, he swore he could hear children's laughter.

Not thinking too much about it, William entered the front area of the barn and looked up to the hay mow. The giggles and the laughter were definitely coming from that part of the wooden structure.

William's old suspicions began to return, but he decided not to shout for his daughter. Instead, William headed towards the ladder that led up to the mow, where the hay and straw were both stored.

He began to climb the ladder, hand over hand, up the rungs until he took the last rung, and his eyes came up over the edge of the mow's floor. He wasn't deliberately quiet, but he wasn't making any excessive noise either.

Loose strands of green hay were scattered about at eye level and ahead of him sat some broken bales. The children were inside a circle of loose bales, and he could make out their heads and shoulders. He furrowed his brow at what he saw. William realized that he didn't see Lorra Anne's yellow dress on her shoulders. His heart raced as he got himself quickly off the ladder and up into the mow. He brushed his dark hair away from his eyes and glared at the scene in front of him.

Stepping towards the children within the broken bales of hay, he saw Lorra Anne sitting between the two Murdock boys wearing only her chemise and petticoats. Her dress sat beside her. "What in God's name is going on here?" William demanded.

Obviously the children didn't think they were doing anything wrong. They all looked at William with innocent faces. "Just a game Papa...it's called 'Underclothes.'" The twelve-year-old Lorra Anne initially spoke innocently and matter-of-factly. However, the look on her father's face began to make her think that she was indeed doing something wrong.

Both boys had their waistcoats off. John and Henry Murdock saw Lorra Anne's expression and then looked up at William Fick. They could see anger in his face. He was turning bright red.

Without saying a word, each Murdock boy grabbed his respective waistcoat and bolted from where they had been sitting. They ran over to the large double doors that led from the mow to the earthen gangway outside.

The wooden double doors were secured from the inside with a cross piece. They didn't even try to remove it. John lifted the bottom corner of the door away which created enough room for Henry to scurry through. As Henry disappeared through the opening, he pushed the door away from the frame, enough for his brother to follow. John made his way quickly through the opening. Both boys escaped down the earthen gangway and ran around the Fick barn.

Originally, they had walked casually around the lake to get to the Fick farm. On their return trip, they ran. The boys didn't speak any words to each other as they made their way home.

Back in the hay mow William stared at his daughter. He tapped his foot on the floor of the mow, arms crossed in front of his chest. The Murdock boys' hasty exit did not surprise him. They were spineless. His daughter had remained where she was, ready to face the consequences of what she thought was innocent game playing. Fear crept into Lorra Anne as she realized just how angry her father really was. "Whose idea was this game, Lorra Anne?" Before she could even answer, her father spat out, "It was those blasted Murdock boys wasn't it? They put you up to this!"

Suddenly, Lorra Anne felt guilt and shame, realizing that what she had done was wrong in some way. She put her arms in front of herself to cover her white chemise. She bowed her head and nodded in agreement and spoke to the floor of the mow in her small squeaky voice. "It was just a game, that's all."

"Put that dress back on, daughter of mine. You'll be playing no more games with the Murdock boys." He turned around and stared at the floor of the barn below him. Behind him he could hear the rustling of the hay as Lorra Anne stood up and did as she was told. When she was dressed, she spoke, "I'm dressed now, Papa."

William stepped to one side of the ladder and motioned for her to go down. She very sheepishly made her way past her father, turned, and descended the ladder. Lorra Anne fell to the ground near the bottom from sheer fear and nervousness. She got up and brushed herself off.

An hour later James Murdock could see the dust of the Fick's buggy as it tore down the concession road towards the entrance to the Murdock laneway. William had the chestnut mare pulling the buggy at a full gallop. He slowed the buggy down at the end of the laneway and then turned into it. The laneway was five hundred feet long. William got his horse up to full speed again. "Hee Haw Gitty Up!" William screamed at the top of his lungs as he sped his buggy towards the courtyard area of the Murdock farm.

By that time John and Henry Murdock had already explained to their father what had happened back at the Fick barn. They told him how they had been playing in the mow with Lorra Anne and had dared each other to take off their outer clothes. The boys explained to their father that they were both unaware what they were doing was wrong. James Murdock asked his sons how it began. Whose idea had it been? Both sons insisted it was Lorra Anne who had begun the dare with a spitting contest and had upped the ante to removing some of their clothes. James told his sons that he appreciated their honesty, but they would both have to be punished. It was at that moment that James saw the Fick buggy racing towards his farm. William was obviously still in a rage.

The Fick buggy was quite fancy. Its black paint usually sparkled. The spokes of the wheels were always kept clean. William usually drove the buggy at a reasonable speed so that it wouldn't get overly dirty. But today was not such a day. Today, dust coated the buggy and mud caked the spokes of the wheels.

The dirt-covered buggy stopped abruptly, and William almost fell out onto the courtyard. William was large and imposing, standing several inches taller than James and somewhat wider as well. Not obese, but definitely much more muscular. Although William was only three years younger than James, he appeared much younger. Some would have guessed that William might have been ten years James' junior.

William's frock coat and face were covered in dust. Streaks of moisture ran from the corners of his wind-whipped eyes. Or had he been crying? With eyes wild and teeth bared, William Fick screamed at the man before him, "James Murdock, you need to answer for the deeds of your sons. Do you have any idea what those two bastards of yours did with my daughter?"

Phoebe Murdock opened the front door of the Murdock house and witnessed the confrontation from where she stood. She crossed her arms over her plain white and brown dress. Her long dark hair fell behind her shoulders.

James stood his ground while his two boys cowered

behind him. He cleared his throat and did his best to keep his composure. He firmly believed in leading by example. "You will not swear in the presence of my sons and my wife. Is that understood, William Fick?"

William was oblivious to his audience as he spit out the words, "Do you know what they forced my poor Lorra Anne to do? Do you, Murdock?" William then looked towards the house, hoping to win the sympathy of a female. "Do you know what they did, Mrs. Murdock? They have scarred my innocent daughter."

James responded, "Now is not the time to discuss this, neighbor. You are upset and angry. You need to calm down, and only then can we talk this out like decent men."

"What do you know of decency, James Murdock? You have unleashed a pair of hellions upon my daughter. There is nothing more to discuss: neither you nor your sons are welcome on my property again." William waved both of his arms in an "X" motion to show that he was cutting off contact. The man was livid. "Do you understand me?"

James roughed up the ground with one boot as he formed his thoughts. He then looked William directly in the eyes and spoke in measured tones, "If that's how you want it, then that's how it shall be, neighbor."

"That's how I want it Murdock. And I no longer consider you a neighbor either." And that was that. William didn't say another word. He climbed back into his black buggy and grabbed the reins of the horse. "Hi ho! Giddy Up. Ha!" He turned the buggy around and returned up the laneway from where he had come.

It was now four years later and James and William still had not spoken. If they happened to see each other in Church, they would avert their gaze. The children were not allowed to associate with each other at the grammar school which they attended.

Surprisingly, from the day of the dress game confrontation, Lorra Anne began to adopt an air of superiority, and both of her parents fed into it. An only child, Lorra Anne Fick grew into a very selfish and demanding young lady. Although James didn't approve what his boys and Lorra Anne had done, he firmly believed that the whole thing was innocent and wouldn't have gone much further.

In hindsight, James was actually glad the way things had transpired. The incident probably spared his boys more serious embarrassment. Over the years since that day, Lorra Anne Fick's name became associated with several of the community's social scandals, despite her young age.

James' thoughts returned to the present. Music began to float across the lake and settled in with the fog. It was getting louder now as the party must have been getting into full swing. The music brought James out of his thoughts of the past—the sweet sound of fiddles, mandolins, and a harmonica. There was singing too, male and female voices accompanied by the musical instruments. James tried not to enjoy the sounds, as they did come from that damned Fick property, but it was hard though to resist tapping his foot.

"Cora! We have music to hunt to!" The old dog seemed to understand and looked back out across the lake. She moaned out to the lake and the music. "My sentiments exactly," James replied rubbing the dog's head. "Just you and me today, old girl," he said softly as she licked his hand.

James was home alone this particular Saturday. Phoebe had taken the boys up to visit her mother in the city of Hornerseth, a four hour ride to the north. Phoebe had left the previous afternoon and would be back Sunday evening. A new church building had been opened recently in Hornerseth and James' mother-in-law was part of the festivities. Initially the boys didn't want to go. They wanted to stay on the farm and hunt with their father, but Phoebe Murdock was persuasive. She won her young sons over with the promise of visiting some of the confectionary shops that had made the oceanside city of Hornerseth famous.

James pulled off one of his thick gloves and reached inside his canvas haversack, rummaging around until he found what he had been searching for. He looked at the object in his hand. It was a wooden whistle that he used to make duck calls. James' father had carved the whistle from a piece of local pine when he was a young man himself. James planned to leave it to his eldest son, John, some day. The whistle was simple but effective.

James walked back down towards the lake, with his gun in one hand and the whistle in the other. Cora trotted beside him. She appeared to sense that she might be needed soon. James stopped when he felt the land get soft again. He brought the wooden whistle to his mouth and blew. Out came a low-pitched moan. James crouched down and blew the call two more times.

The fog was thickening, and he could barely make out the dying reeds in the swampy area ahead of him. James settled in a crouch, his knees making cracking sounds. Once he was somewhat comfortable, he blew the whistle several more times until he heard what he had hoped for. A Mallard called back. James could hear the flapping of wings and the water being disturbed. Cora's ears instinctively shot up. James let the whistle drop to the ground. He shook off his other thick glove and then steadied the custom-made Joseph Manton double-barreled shotgun. James waited for a good clear shot, if that were possible on a day like this.

The water broke and loud quacking arose, as several mallards flew from their hiding spot among the reeds. There were three or four of them, and James could just barely make out the shapes as the birds passed overhead in the fog. Cora barked loudly and jumped up. She was excited that they were finally seeing some action.

James lined up the shot. "CRACK!" The gun boomed as the shot reverberated across the lake. James lost his footing somewhat, and the second shot wasn't as well aimed.

"CRACK!" The gun boomed again as this shot went somewhere aimlessly out into the early morning fog. The recoil from the second shot sent James falling backward, landing on the cold ground. James heard a scream, the sudden bellow of a male voice, and then the sound of oars splashing in the distance.

Cora sat attentively to see what James had shot.

Neither of them was prepared for the answer.

2

A disturbance in the fog

William Fick sat at a long log table and surveyed the scene of the celebration. Although it was only 11 a.m., William already had a full glass of ale in his hand. And it wasn't his first. The cardinal rule of drinking was never drink alone. There was no fear of that this morning because he was definitely not drinking by himself. William and his wife, Lilly, were hosting an early birthday party for Lorra Anne.

Lorra Anne's actual birthday wasn't for another two weeks. However, today was the only day that fit best into the schedules of all the invited guests. William understood that autumn was harvest time, making it somewhat difficult to settle on a day when everyone could come. So he had made some concessions and held the birthday party on this day. William had promised his daughter that on the actual day of her birth, there would be another special celebration. Lorra

Anne was quite satisfied with that solution.

The party had begun around ten in the morning. William wanted to have it early so that people could return home for their chores before dark. Some guests were traveling from as far away as Hornerseth, Evanston, and Landmark to celebrate Lorra Anne's birthday.

William and Lilly had had a grand time decorating the area around the house. White, pink, and red ribbons interlaced the wooden trellises; others adorned small trees that dotted the Fick property. A "Happy Birthday" sign hung from a large tree. William also made sure there was more than enough to eat and drink. He only hoped the weather would hold out. He didn't want to have to move the party into the small house or worse, the barn. William wanted a respectable outdoor event that would show his forty or so guests a great time. As a good host, he wanted to ensure he could accommodate all the people he had invited.

William took another drink from his stoneware mug of ale and wiped his mouth with the sleeve of his red flannel shirt and slammed the mug down on the rough-hewn logs of the table. He was a proud man from a proud family heritage and would drink anyone under the table to prove it. "More music!" he demanded. Fiddles, mandolins, and a harmonica broke into I Have Lov'd Thee, Dearly Lov'd Thee. "Now that's the spirit." William laughed. Lilly gave William a broad smile as she downed her second cider of the morning. The Fick's loved their music and their drink.

24

The day also presented a golden opportunity: William's ulterior motive for the grand party this Saturday morning was to arrange a successful marriage for his daughter. The marriage would also enhance his social standing within the community. William's cousins from up north had brought with them a prominent family friend who had contacts in the federal government. The friend's name was David Green, and he now sat at the head table with his wife, Elva, and their son Caleb. William was hoping that Caleb would be his future son-in-law.

That would definitely be a sign of success. William was going to show everybody at the party that he was the host of hosts. Not all successful parties had to be held back in the capital. William was going to show some of these "city folks" that people from the country knew how to throw a gala event, too. This was truly an event that would not be soon forgotten.

The log-hewn table where William, his family, his extended family, and his friends sat was well-worn and full of knots. It had already seen many parties and celebrations over the years. However, for this celebration a bright-colored tablecloth covered the very large outdoor table. The tablecloth, in turn, was covered with cutlery, plates, mugs, and cups each filled with some sort of alcoholic beverage. Local ale and cider were the favorites. William even let his guard down by allowing Lorra Anne and her "date," Caleb, to partake in some hard cider.

The pewter plates on the table were ready and waiting

for the roasted chicken, duck, and heaping amounts of steaming hot vegetables—plentiful helpings of potatoes, carrots, cabbage and yams. Lilly Fick scurried back and forth from the party area to the house putting the finishing touches on the food and its presentation.

Several of Lilly's own cousins assisted her with the preparations. She never asked for help, and like her husband, Lilly was very proud. However, Lilly would not turn down an offer of assistance. She and her cousins were also keeping a watchful eye on the cast iron pot that hung over an open fire just to the right side of the house. It was full of boiling water and ears of husked corn. "Not too much longer for the corn, Lilly," her cousin, Annette Norman, informed her.

Lilly was just entering the house. "Everything else inside the house is ready to be brought out, Annette. Let's feed this hungry brood," she cheerfully joked.

William gazed up at the sky and hoped again that the weather would continue to hold. It certainly appeared that it might rain. It was quite a strange morning with the thick fog and all. He couldn't even see the lake from where he sat.

However, the outdoors was the best place to hear the group of talented musicians. William tapped his fingers in time with the music pleased that everyone was enjoying the atmosphere of the party. At the table with him sat his parents, Lilly's parents, several siblings and their respective spouses, the Greens, and Lorra Anne who sat at the table's head. William scratched at his beard.

"Ah, here comes the food!" William rubbed his hands together in anticipation as large bowls of chicken, duck, and vegetables appeared in the centre of the table. The end of the table opposite from where Lorra Anne sat was left open to allow people from the other tables to help themselves to the food as well. Some folks decided instead to stand and eat or sit on the open porch of the house.

Appropriately, Lorra Anne was the first person to help herself from the bowls. She didn't take much because she knew she had to watch her waist. The large coils of her red hair bounced up and down as she moved. "This will get me started," she said.

"Ooohhs" and "aaaahhs" could be heard as everyone else at the table began to dig in. William and Lilly's parents had lent their pewter dinnerware and cutlery for the day's event. Lilly couldn't believe how fast the food was disappearing. When she came back out of the house with another bowl of potatoes, the bowl she had brought out previously was already empty. She and her cousins had quite a job to perform as they supplied the hungry guests with their late morning meal.

William glanced over at the fiddle player in the band and saw that he was licking his lips. William laughed aloud, "Come on boys, help yourselves and keep your energy levels up. We're going to need some after-dinner music as well!" William waved them to the table as he spoke. The four musicians ended their song abruptly and laid their instruments down. They hurried from their playing area over to the main table.

"You and the ladies better have something to eat too, Lilly. Or it's all going to be gone," William teased his wife.

"We've made preparations, dear husband. My cousins and I have our portions set up and ready to go waiting inside the house."

William laughed loudly and snapped his suspenders. "That's my Lilly, always planning ahead. Come join us, my dear."

"Right after the corn is served. There isn't much worse than hard-boiled corn."

William's father piped up, "There are some things worse, Lilly, but I can't mention them at the dinner table."

"Losing the crop would be worse, Father," Lilly stated. William gave his father a knowing smile. "Get yourself a second helping before it's all gone," Lilly urged.

William needed to be the centre of attention, a trait that Lorra Anne came by very honestly. "We Fick's are hearty eaters, Father," Lorra Anne reminded him.

Her father winked, "Not too hearty, Lorra Anne, if you know what I mean."

"Your chicken is getting cold, Father," Lorra Anne retorted.

William smiled and relented. "Have some more apple cider, Lorra Anne." William then felt a set of eyes on him. He glanced over to see Lilly giving him a "look." He gave his wife a quick smile. "Don't worry, Lilly, my love, this cider doesn't have too much of a kick. I won't get my daughter too fired up

28

on this the celebration of her birthday."

"It's a pre-celebration, Father." Lorra Anne quipped as she broke apart her potatoes with her fork. "The real party won't be until October 28th! That's when I actually turn sixteen."

"But we will enjoy the ale, cider, and hot food today none-the-less." William said as he banged his stoneware mug of ale on the log table. "This is a great pre-celebration."

Everybody at the party seemed to agree, and there was much laughter and some shouts. The folks at the table continued to dig into the food piled high on their plates. Lilly approved of the amount of food that Lorra Anne had placed on her plate.

Caleb Green sat cater-cornered to Lorra Anne with his parents sitting next to him. He heaped food upon his own plate having no problem with the sheer volume of food he had taken and neither did his hosts.

"Eat up, dear boy!" William encouraged, feeling that a growing seventeen-year-old, and hopefully, his future son-in-law, needed the nourishment.

"I do wish he ate like that back home," laughed Caleb's mother, Elva, as she watched her son's plate fill up. There was laughter again. Lorra Anne made eye-contact with Caleb and he with her. They both blushed.

Lilly reappeared with a large wooden bowl full of steaming hot corn. Behind her were her cousins, each with two more bowls. "Does anyone have room left for corn?" Lilly said teasingly.

Everyone said, "Yes," in unison.

"Oh, I would simply love some corn, Mother," Lorra Anne stated as her mother placed the bowl of corn on the table, "Smothered in butter, too."

"Not too much of the butter," warned her father while he smiled and wagged a finger at Lorra Anne. Lilly gave her husband a curt smile. She knew that William didn't want his daughter to get fat. Not when there was a prospective groom on hand, but on the other side of the coin, it was only fair that he cut her a little slack today.

"Please don't scold me at my birthday party, Father. I'm sure I will give you many opportunities to do so after this day. It's my party and I want to be rightfully spoiled."

"Then why should today be any different?" William teased. Lorra Anne knew her father wasn't serious. She had a good relationship with her parents. She wanted to be waited on, and they happily filled that demand. She was their life.

Lilly slid the bowl of corn into an open spot on the table. Several men, William included, snatched up their glasses and mugs of ale for fear of them getting knocked over. Steam poured from the corn, and Lorra Anne quickly reached out and grabbed the largest piece. As soon as she did, Lorra Anne realized it was still much too hot to touch. She yelped in pain as she pulled her hand back. Nobody laughed. No one would dare. Not a sound could be heard.

William broke the silence as he stabbed the offending piece of corn with his fork and placed it on Lorra Anne's plate.

He then sliced off a large slab of butter and placed it on the corn. The butter instantly melted. Lorra Anne's eyes opened wide and a smile slowly crept across her face. "Thank you, Father, I do love my butter."

Lilly tried to be understanding. She knew that Lorra Anne just wanted to enjoy the feast with everybody else. However, there were larger issues at play here. Lorra Anne needed to be seen as a cultured lady, a desirable wife to a potential husband. Although, in reality, Lorra Anne didn't really have too much to worry about. Just her looks alone would carry her.

Everyone at the party revelled in Lorra Anne's beauty. She would be sixteen in a matter of weeks, but she had already blossomed into a woman. She was five-foot-six and just a little taller than her mother. She had a lean, lithe body that was topped with fire engine red hair that flowed past her shoulders. Her hair had been specially curled so that it hung in large coils. Lorra Anne had a bright smile and sparkling green eyes to match. Her bosom didn't go unnoticed by the local boys either. The long-sleeved baby blue dress that she wore on this day accented all of her curves.

If Lorra Anne had inherited her ego from her father, she definitely inherited her looks from her mother. Lilly was a very pretty woman. She had auburn hair which rested upon her shoulders, a sincere smile, and an impressive bosom as well. She was a solid woman, but not large. William had done well to marry her.

The chattering during the meal was starting to annoy

William, so he decided it was time to summon the musicians back up for some more music. He felt like a King calling for his jesters. Lilly was pleased that all the food on the table was being eaten. "We have lots of pie for dessert, but I think I will let everyone settle with what they have eaten so far."

"It's a perfect time for more drinks!" William loudly stated. He stood up from the table and made his way back to the house to fetch the large stoneware jugs of ale and cider. He stumbled around in the house for several moments then returned with a jug in each hand. "Who's up for more?" he asked the crowd. Suddenly twenty stoneware mugs, tin cups and glasses all shot up. William let out a hearty laugh and sat the cider jug down. "Who's just for ale?" William spent the next several minutes filling the drink orders. As he poured the last drink, the musicians started to play again.

Everyone at the table and those standing began to clap in time to the music. The song was an old favorite, Blue Eye'd Mary. The fiddles in the band ensured that the party stayed lively. Lilly Fick and her cousins began to clear the table of the dirty dishes. As the head table was cleared, people from the other tables began to stand and stretch. Several men gathered by the open fire that burned underneath the cast-iron pot. Pipes were lit and smoked. The musicians continued to play. Lorra Anne also got up from the table and headed into the house.

William took a deep drink from his mug of ale. He rubbed his stubbly chin and looked north. He couldn't see across the lake because of the fog, but he knew what he was visualizing. He had purposely not invited the Murdocks. William had no guilt with that decision. There wasn't a day that went by that he wasn't haunted by the memory of the time he found the Murdock boys and his daughter in the barn together. Maybe subconsciously that was why he didn't want to have the party in the barn. William continued to rub his chin. He doubted Murdock would come even if he had been invited.

"I would like to receive my gifts soon, Father. How much longer must I languish?" Lorra Anne broke his train of thought. He turned and looked at his only child. The well-learnt girl loved to use her big words. She had obviously just peeked in her parent's bedchamber and had seen all the presents waiting to be opened.

"Just before we have our pie, Lorra Anne. I won't make you wait any longer than I absolutely have to."

"I shouldn't have to wait at all," Lorra Anne said, pouting just a little. She dragged her feet as she walked over to her grandmother for a bit of sympathy. William laughed as Lilly came up behind him. She was wiping her hands on her apron.

"Did you see all the gifts, Will? I have them stored in our bedchamber. They cover the bed and half the floor!"

"Did she ask you if she could open her presents as well?"

"As a matter of fact, she did. I told her to ask you. I can't imagine you said 'yes.' It's too early."

"I told her not too much longer. We do like to spoil that child don't we, Lilly?"

"She's the only one we have, Will; we might as well give her whatever we can. By the way," Lilly looked over the crowd of people as she spoke, "Has Lorra Anne spent much time with Caleb Green?"

"No, I don't believe she has. This would be a good opportunity for the young man to speak to her. Excuse me please." With that William crossed the lawn over to the Green family. Caleb Green was standing with his parents engaged in conversation. Caleb already knew of Lorra Anne from her visiting a mutual friend, a member of the O'Leary family. It was obvious from the first meeting that Caleb was smitten with Lorra Anne. He was just a little on the shy side. That sat well with William; he didn't think much of forward boys. Like those Murdocks.

Caleb Green was smartly dressed. He wore a very dark brown coat, a lighter brown waistcoat with off-white colored breeches. On his head Caleb wore a felt civilian tricorn. He was standing between his parents when William approached the family with a broad smile, "Caleb. Have you told Lorra Anne how pretty she looks in her new blue dress?"

Caleb blushed. His father sat his hand on Caleb's shoulder and tousled the back of the boy's long, sandy-colored hair. "I think Mr. Fick is trying to give you a hint son. Why don't you say 'hello' to the birthday girl."

Caleb glanced at his father, "What shall I say to her father?"

He grinned, "Start with 'hello' and go from there."

Caleb nodded as he thought this was an actual plan rather

that just fatherly advice. As he walked away, his father spoke to William, "Thank you for inviting us today. I know that Caleb does have an eye for Lorra Anne. She is a very wholesome young lady. Not like some of the girls back in the city. I don't know what the world is coming to."

William put a hand on the other man's shoulder, "Thank you David. The wife and I have tried to raise Lorra Anne properly. She does have an independent streak, but that will keep young Caleb on his toes." Both men laughed and they walked over to the fire pit to each enjoy a pipe.

Caleb sauntered over to where Lorra Anne was speaking to her grandmother. "Excuse me," Caleb politely interrupted. Lorra Anne stopped talking to the elderly lady and gave Caleb a curt smile. She then realized just who it was interrupting her and she quickly wrapped up her conversation and hugged her grandmother. She then turned her attention to Caleb, who hadn't moved from where he stood. He spoke with a serious tone, "How is your hand Lorra Anne? That corn was mighty hot."

Lorra Anne initially looked offended that he had caught her slight misstep at the table. She then realized that he was only saying something because he was genuinely concerned for her. At any rate, everyone at the table had obviously seen her. Caleb mistook her initial expression and was worried. Lorra Anne reassured him, "I was embarrassed more than anything Caleb. I shouldn't have been so eager to get the biggest piece of corn."

"It's not your fault. It is your birthday celebration after all."

Smoke from the open fire suddenly blew past where they were standing, and Lorra Anne waved the smoke away from her eyes, moving away a few steps. Caleb stayed at her side as she began to walk around the congested party area. The musicians in the band nodded to the couple as they passed by. Behind the musicians were a series of trellises that were usually covered in many different varieties of flowers. The flowers were long past their prime, but it didn't stop the Fick's from running ribbons in and around the wooden trellises. "The ribbon is a very nice touch," Caleb observed as they walked by.

"Bright and pretty ribbons weaved in among the dying flowers. I suppose my parents meant well, but October is such a dreary month to have a birthday. I do wish I had been born in the spring. It's such a nicer time of the year."

Caleb looked at the ground as they walked. "October isn't such a bad month. I have to admit though that the fog today seems somewhat strange. I guess you're used to it living by this bay."

"This bay is actually a lake," she corrected him.

"I won't argue with you. It is your birthday."

"My birthday has nothing to do with it. This is Castle Lake. It was incorrectly named long before I was born." Lorra Anne got a very mischievous look on her face. "Would you like a tour of the lake?"

"A tour of the lake?" Caleb gave Lorra Anne a curious glance. His forehead wrinkled up as he made the face.

"We have a rowboat down at the dock. We can go for a little ride and I'll show you the sights of Castle Lake. It will help pass the time before I open my presents."

"You know how to row?"

Lorra Anne rolled her eyes at Caleb. "Of course I know how to row. I'm a girl from the country who happens to live on the coast. I know many different things, especially how to handle a small boat."

"I didn't mean that at all," Caleb tried to redeem himself. "I don't know how to row," he admitted.

Lorra Anne gave Caleb a sly look, and she smirked at him. "You don't know how to row? Even better, I can teach you."

As they walked on the path that led down to the dock, they realized that the fog now totally surrounded them. They could hear the music and voices well enough, but they couldn't see much through the fog.

The Fick home had been built several hundred feet up from the lake. Like the Murdock property across the way, the land sloped down towards the water. However, the land on this side of the lake wasn't nearly as swampy as that at the opposite end. Down here by the dock, there were still plenty of wooden trellises. Caleb noticed that the trellises down by the lake weren't decorated with ribbons like the ones up by the house. "Your parents must have been running low on ribbon when they got down here," Caleb commented.

Lorra Anne just smiled at Caleb and let the quip pass. Her parents had encouraged the growth of many vines, flowering bushes, and weeping willows on their property. Lorra Anne wasn't that much into nature like her parents. She did enjoy the scenic property but not to the degree that her parents did. Lorra Anne thought she would have been just as happy living in the city.

Since her birthday party was on the west side of the Fick home, Lorra Anne and Caleb were now out of range of the adults. Lorra Anne ran her hand over the dying vines as they walked past yet another trellis. Lorra Anne seemed to be in deep thought, but she wasn't sharing those thoughts.

The fog was even thicker down by the lake than it was up around the house. "It's like we are in our own little world down here," Lorra Anne mused, "Almost like no one else exists outside this fog free zone that we are in."

"You have a good imagination, Lorra Anne."

Lorra Anne gave Caleb a shy smile, and it was now her turn to look at the ground. She glanced back at Caleb. He certainly was a handsome boy. There was no other boy in this area that was as handsome. Caleb cut a fine figure in his light brown waistcoat and the felt tricorn hat. She liked his long sandy hair, too.

His yellowish-colored eyes seemed to sparkle even though the sun wasn't shining. Caleb also had a charming smile. He stood several inches taller than Lorra Anne but was just about as thin. She thought to herself how they would make a fine couple. It didn't hurt either that his relatives were prominent people back in the city. Maybe she could attend a nice finishing school before she married and began a family. Lorra Anne had to think of these things; she knew she wasn't getting any younger.

They both heard the musicians begin a new song. The fiddles were very lively and loud now. They could hear laughing. "There must be some dancing going on by now! I do love the music so." Lorra Anne twirled in place as she thought about the dancing.

Caleb, slightly amused, looked at her. "It sounds like the ale and cider have kicked in back there. They are getting louder by the minute."

"Are you a dancer, Caleb?" Lorra Anne continued to spin in place.

"You're going to make me dizzy, Lorra Anne. Let's have a look at that rowboat shall we?" Caleb didn't answer her question about the dancing. Lorra Anne relented and continued down the path to the lake.

The breeze was a little stronger by the water's edge. The breeze didn't seem to affect the fog at all. It was also quite cool but not cold enough not to enjoy a little boating. Lorra Anne smiled at Caleb and skipped a little further down to the dock. As she attempted to step up onto the damp wooden structure her black dress shoes suddenly slid from under her. Lorra Anne lost her footing but quickly regained her balance before she actually fell. "Dang it!" she blurted out.

Caleb came up behind her and steadied her by touching her elbow. "It was all that spinning, Lorra Anne, dancing can't be good for you on a full stomach."

They both laughed. "The last thing I need to do is soil my dress or worse. I'm going to blame that little bit of cider that I drank."

Lorra Anne walked a little more carefully on the wet wood of the dock. She hadn't thought how dangerous her shoes could be on the old damp structure. The wood beneath her feet creaked as she continued to walk the twelve feet to the dock's end.

At the edge of the dock, a faded, white wooden rowboat was tied up. The boat, rocking lightly in the water, had the name Mercy across the stern. A rope from the bow of the boat was tied to a metal ring on the dock's edge. Lorra Anne carefully knelt down with her back facing away from Caleb, and began to untie the rope from the metal ring. Just as the rope came free from the ring, Caleb walked up to her. Lorra Anne turned her head and glanced up at him, "You climb in first, Caleb, and I'll steady the boat. Try not to rock it, or you will be having an early afternoon swim."

"Hang on tightly, then," Caleb requested of her. As she reached to take a firmer grip on the edge of the rowboat and pull it up against the dock, Lorra Anne lost her balance yet again. Caleb quickly came to her rescue and slipped over to her. He, too, squatted down as he grabbed onto her shoulder. Once she regained her balance, Caleb assisted Lorra Anne with the rowboat.

The rowboat had moved away from the dock when

Lorra Anne had almost fallen for the second time. Caleb reached out and brought the rowboat back to the dock. He then looked from the rowboat to Lorra Anne. They were both now squatting face to face. Lorra Anne quickly darted her face forward and gave Caleb a kiss on the cheek. "Thank you for not letting me fall, Caleb. Now, in you go!"

"No more cider for you," Caleb smiled. He stretched one of his legs from a squat straight out into the rowboat. He worked his other leg into the boat while hanging onto the edge of dock. Lorra Anne laughed, "You are ever so graceful, Caleb Green."

He gave her a shy smile and continued to work his way into the rowboat, finally sitting proudly on the wooden seat in the middle facing Lorra Anne. The rowboat was fourteen feet long and was three feet wide. There were four seats in the boat; one at the stern and one at the bow, and then two equally placed in the center of the boat. The oarlocks for the oars were located on either side of the seat closest to the bow where Caleb sat. The oars of the rowboat lay across the tops of the seats to one side, end to end. Caleb turned and began to lift up one of the oars. Lorra Anne blurted out most unladylike, "Let me get in first Caleb. I don't need an oar in the face."

Lorra Anne tried to be as graceful as possible. Her baby blue long sleeved dress was ankle length, and she wore several petticoats underneath it. She also wore a pair of leggings for warmth. Caleb instinctively looked away as she settled into the rowboat with him. She adjusted her dress and sat upon the seat located at the stern. Lorra Anne leaned forward towards the dock and pulled the rope into the boat, letting it fall onto the floorboard. She then shoved the boat from the edge of the dock. As the rowboat floated away, Lorra Anne moved herself one seat closer to Caleb, sitting directly across from him. "Now you may fetch the oars, one for you and one for me."

Caleb leaned over to one side and picked up an oar, carefully handing it to Lorra Anne. He then picked up the second oar. Lorra Anne maneuvered her oar against the side of the dock and gave it another good shove. She then dipped the oar into the water and moved it so that the bow of the rowboat faced out to the center of Castle Lake. She leaned forward and locked the oar into the oarlock on the side of the rowboat and motioned for Caleb to do the same.

"Okay, let the lesson begin," she looked at Caleb as she spoke. "Take an oar with each hand. You want to extend your arms forward and then cut the oars solidly into the water. Pull the oars steadily towards you. The oars will then push the water and move the boat ahead." Caleb did as he was told. However, he didn't dip the oars deeply enough into the water. When he pulled hard on them, Caleb almost hit himself in the face with his own hands as there was no resistance from the water. As well, Caleb didn't have a firm grip on the oars. Lorra Anne suppressed a laugh as the boat barely quivered in the water. She then smiled, "Hold the oars firmer, Caleb, like you held that corn at dinner time. Pretend you are going to eat the oars!"

"I can't imagine they would be very tasty!" Caleb joked.

"Let's remain serious shall we, Mr. Green?" She gave Caleb an expression of mock seriousness. "Observe." She moved over to the seat that Caleb occupied and sat down right beside him. He slid over closer to the side to allow her a little more room. Lorra Anne reached in front of Caleb in order to handle both oars at the same time. He had to lean back out of her way as she did so.

Lorra Anne grabbed the two oars and leaned forward. She dropped them deep into the water and pulled back. She used little effort and just moved her arms in a steady motion. At the end of her stroke, she allowed the water to drip off the oars. The rowboat moved swiftly and steadily ahead, gliding through the lake water. "If you hold the oars like this after your stroke, you'll prevent excess water getting into the boat and on yourself."

"What fun would that be then?" he responded, impressed how professionally Lorra Anne rowed. He was even a little envious, and this provoked his mischievous side.

Caleb leaned over the edge of his side of the rowboat and cupped a little lake water in his hand. Lorra Anne observed what he was doing, curious at first. Her semi-smile turned to a frown when she realized what Caleb had in mind. "Don't you dare be throwing water on me, Caleb Green. I don't need to smell like an old dead fish."

She leaned further past him and struck his outstretched arm. The water fell from his cupped hand back into the lake. "It was too cold anyway," he said.

With Lorra Anne's weight now on the same side of the boat as his, the other side of the rowboat lifted somewhat from the water's surface. Caleb panicked, thinking they were going to tip over. He lifted his arm up to grab onto Lorra Anne, and as he did so, he caught the oar on his side of the boat with his elbow. The oar lifted out from the oarlock and fell into the water.

Lorra Anne was not impressed by his lack of manliness and pulled away from his grasp. She slid back over to her side and the rowboat leveled out. "You're going to have to watch your tomfoolery out here, Caleb." Then Lorra Anne realized something else, "Caleb, you somehow knocked the oar into the water!"

Indeed he had. Caleb had been oblivious to the fact when it had happened; he was that afraid of tipping into the lake. The oar now floated about six feet away from the edge of Caleb's side of the rowboat. Lorra Anne lifted her oar out of the oarlock and used it to maneuver the boat over to where Caleb's oar was floating. Caleb leaned past the edge of the boat in order to retrieve the wayward oar.

"Please be careful as you fetch that; watch your weight."

"You're the one that almost sunk us!" Caleb snapped back. He reached out to get the oar and relented, "Sorry Lorra Anne, I will be more careful." Lorra Anne hung on to Caleb's arm as he grabbed the oar. Water dripped from the oar as Caleb brought it into the boat.

"Careful, Caleb, I don't need a bath." As she spoke they

both heard the low moan of some kind of wild animal. Caleb's ears perked up, "What is that?"

"Sounds like ducks, city boy," said Lorra Anne suddenly proud of her rural heritage. She craned her head around towards the bow of the boat to see if she could locate where the sound was coming from. She returned her oar into the oarlock, "Let's move closer to the sound, Caleb. Shall we try to row in unison?"

Caleb nodded and placed his oar back into the oarlock. Lorra Anne then motioned that he use his oar. Caleb cut his oar into the water at the same time she did. He was gentler on the pull-through and took more water than on his first try. Lorra Anne smiled as she made her stroke. The boat moved forwards a fair distance. Caleb glanced over to Lorra Anne and returned the smile.

Together they rowed in unison for about ten minutes and then allowed the boat to come to a natural stop. The boat slowed in the water and they listened intently. The sounds had stopped.

"Sit still, Caleb, I'm going to have a better look." As she spoke Lorra Anne carefully steadied herself and stood up in the center of the boat. She rested a hand on Caleb's shoulder and turned towards the bow of the boat. He enjoyed the feeling of her hand on his shoulder.

Caleb looked up at Lorra Anne as she surveyed the horizon like a pirate up in a crow's nest. He admired this girl and knew she had a fire in her, and what a vision. He felt goose bumps as he watched her scan the horizon. Was it the damp afternoon air or something else? Her expression was so serious.

Another low moan could be heard followed by yet another. "It's a duck call!" Lorra Anne said proudly. As soon as she said the words there was a "crack" somewhere out in the distance. Suddenly about thirty feet ahead of them a group of ducks flew up and out of the fog. Caleb's attention went from Lorra Anne up to the ducks. The movement of the wings of the ducks broke the fog. Caleb could clearly see them fly away. They had all of his attention. As he intently watched the ducks, Caleb heard another loud "CRACK" out in the fog.

Caleb heard a sudden cry to his right and, unexpectedly, the rowboat lurched. Caleb looked back where Lorra Anne should have been standing; however, Lorra Anne was no longer there. She lay on the bottom of the rowboat, her head in the center of the boat's stern seat with her bottom on the floorboard. Lorra Anne's legs were propped up on the second seat with her dress pulled back to her knees. Caleb stood up quickly to survey the scene better. As he leaped up, the boat rocked left and right.

Fear swept over Caleb and his heart jumped into his throat. There was blood behind her head where it must have struck the stern seat. "Lorra Anne! You've been hit," his voice croaked. Then, much louder, he yelled out, "She's been hit! She's been hit!" Caleb had no idea who he was talking to. All he knew was that he had to get Lorra Anne back home.

Caleb decided not to disturb Lorra Anne, thinking it may be better to leave her exactly as she lay. He sat back down in the boat and grabbed the two oars, and with his newly learned knowledge, Caleb got the boat turned around, and he began to stab at the water. The boat moved quickly across the surface of the lake. Caleb was only guessing where the shore and the dock should be. He tried to follow the sounds of the music through the blasted fog that seemed to totally envelope him. Water splashed all over the place as he just tried to get the rowboat back to Lorra Anne's home.

He could feel the moisture of the fog on his face as the boat moved ahead in the water. Just as Lorra Anne had said not long before, it was like he was in his own little world. But Caleb Green didn't really see the fog anymore. All he could see in his mind's eye was Lorra Anne's once beautiful face. However, instead of the soft porcelain like skin, the bright smile and green eyes, the left side of Lorra Anne Fick's face was now a mess of buckshot, blood, and torn skin.

THOMAS A. RYERSON

3

The party's over

The shrill sounds of the boy's screams and yells for help brought the Fick party to a sudden halt. Caleb Green's hoarse voice rose over the strains of the musicians as they played the song Absent Friends. Everyone but the musicians stopped what they were doing at once and listened intently.

The ale and cider had been flowing freely for the last hour or so. William and Lilly Fick were sitting with David and Elva Green discussing the possibility of wedding arrangements between their respective children. Then, David Green suddenly recognized his son's voice over the music. David's eyes grew large. William Fick realized that something was wrong as soon as he saw the look on David's face. "Stop the music!" William demanded.

The musicians did as they were told, and instantly the music ceased. Everyone had frozen into their last position.

Within seconds Caleb's voice could be heard out in the fog again. It was like a knife cutting through the thickness of the fog, "Help me! Please someone help me! I can't find the dock." The voice didn't sound all that far away.

The folks at the party had also heard the two gunshots. However, at the time no one thought much of it. Now, David and William both leaped from the head table. William led the way down the path to the dock. As he rounded the side of the house, people at the fire pit were already making their way down towards the dock. David was right behind William. People were beginning to realize that something was very wrong. Within moments of Caleb's initial screams, there were ten men rushing down to the dock.

William and David got to the dock at the same time. They could hear Caleb's voice clearly now. He sounded fairly close. William called out loudly, "Caleb, where are you?"

"Over here. I'm over here. Help me! I believe that Lorra Anne is dead!" Without even thinking, William instantly waded out into the cold October water. David was right behind him.

William began to visibly shake. Was it a reaction to the cold water or the news that Caleb had just given? "Caleb! Keep talking so we can follow your voice."

"I'm here. Over here!" His voice went from shouting to sobbing. William could make out the bow of the faded white rowboat. The cold water was up to his chest now, but he wasn't even aware of it anymore. His whole body was numb. Numb with fear. He grabbed the bow of the rowboat without looking inside. There was no time. He held the bow of the boat firmly and began to walk quickly back to the shore.

David came on the other side of the rowboat and also grabbed the bow. He was directly across from William with the bow between them. David didn't attempt to look into the boat either. As their bodies came out of the water, the air suddenly hit them, and both men realized just how cold it really was. William turned around and gave the boat one last tug. It shot past him and drove up onto the shore. The rowboat beached on the small rocks, ten feet to one side of the dock.

William turned, looked into the boat, and gasped at what he saw. His daughter's body lay crumpled between the two seats, her feet elevated by one and her head rested upon the other at the stern. Half of her face was covered in blood, and there was blood at the base of her head. Caleb stared at William. It was obvious he was in shock. Caleb still sat across from Lorra Anne's elevated feet. William turned to the shore and shouted out, "Lilly! Get Doctor Holt. Get someone to fetch Doctor Holt."

William jumped into the rowboat and as he did, Caleb remained sitting there, not even trying to move. David stood beside William. David too, was taken aback by what he saw. The once beautiful girl was reduced to a bloody mess on the floor of the boat.

"David, we are going to move her up to the house. Take her by the shoulders. I will take her by the knees." David tried not to stare at the bloody flesh of her cheek. Her eye was full of blood as well. He bent over and grabbed her by the far shoulder. David pulled her up so her face rested on his shoulder. William picked her up at the knees, and the two men lifted her out of the boat and began to walk, side by side, carrying Lorra Anne Fick.

At this point, Caleb, very weakened, tried to get out of the boat. He stared at the pool of blood at the boat's stern as he slowly stood up. It was right there in front of him, and he made no effort to turn his head; this was his reality now. Caleb tried to get one foot over the side of the boat, but clumsily fell onto the shore. "Caleb!" someone yelled out. They ran over to the boy and assisted him.

Caleb's father and William Fick were fully occupied with the task of getting Lorra Anne up to the house. The people standing at the shore's edge parted so that the two men could make their way through with Lorra Anne's blood-covered body. They carried her up the hill to the house.

Halfway up the hill, they were met by Lilly Fick who had come down to meet them, her light red dress fluttering as she ran.

"My God! What has happened Will?"

William and David did not stop. Lilly quickly stopped herself and turned around to follow the two men. William answered as they walked, "She's been shot, Lilly. Caleb is in shock. Has someone gone for Doctor Holt?"

"Is she still breathing?" Lilly asked her husband.

"Yes. She's in rough shape, but she is breathing. We need to get her into the house and get the wounds attended to. Lilly, has someone gone for Doctor Holt?" William was in a cold sweat as he repeated himself yet again.

Lilly walked beside the two men and her daughter. "I don't think so, Will. They are all guests here. No one will know where to go to fetch him."

"I'll leave, then, as soon as we have Lorra Anne in her bedchamber. You will clean her up."

William and David made their way up the hill, around the house, and up to the main door. Lilly had run ahead of them and had the door open. Before he entered, William stopped and said, "I'll take her now, David. Thank you so much."

David transferred Lorra Anne to William's shoulder and stepped back. Lilly reeled in horror as she saw the blood that covered David's cheek and upper chest. William paid no attention to the stains and went directly into Lorra Anne's bedchamber.

Normally, he would have taken her to his bedchamber, but the bed and floor were still covered with Lorra Anne's yet unopened birthday gifts.

As he entered her room, Lilly followed behind. She crossed over to Lorra Anne's bed and pulled back several wool blankets. William gently laid his daughter onto the bed. "Get her undressed and comfortable, Lilly. Then get those wounds cleaned up. I think the bleeding has stopped from the back of her head. I'm going to get Doctor Holt myself."

No other words were spoken as William left Lorra Anne's bedchamber. As William exited the house, Elva Green entered. William gave her a labored smile and touched her arm. "Please help Lilly as best as you can. She's going to need someone with her."

Elva entered the main part of the house and then saw some movement in a room to her left. She walked into the room and saw Lilly standing at the head of Lorra Anne's bed. Elva walked over to the other side of the bed and gasped at what she saw, without realizing what she had done. Elva glanced up at Lilly who seemed like she was now going into shock herself. William must have expected this.

Elva looked down at Lorra Anne again. The girl's face was pale, and her hair was damp. The top of her dress was also damp from both the lake water and her own blood. Lorra Anne's face was slashed open on the left side—a mass of flesh, blood, and pellets. One eye was open and white, the lid beginning to swell. The other closed. Blood began to congeal where the flow had been excessive and dry where it had been less. A red halo of blood formed on the pillow behind her head. Lorra Anne was barely breathing.

Elva spoke softly but with purpose, "Lilly. We need to get Lorra Anne cleaned up. William will be coming back with the doctor soon. Give me a hand, okay?"

Through her tears Lilly nodded. Together, the two women got Lorra Anne changed into her bed clothes and washed her face with a damp cloth.

As William left the house, he saw Lilly's three cousins approaching him from the hill. Annette seemed to be the spokesperson for group, "What can we do, William?"

"Elva Green is in the house with Lilly. Please go and give them any assistance with Lorra Anne that you are able. I'm getting the doctor." Annette nodded, pushing her own long red hair over her shoulders. She and the other two cousins entered the Fick homestead.

Several more people gathered by the log-hewn table talking about what had happened.

William spoke to the group as he crossed over to a drive-shed. "Can one or two of you give me a hand readying my horse? I'm going to fetch the doctor."

Two men broke from the group and followed William into the drive-shed. William pointed over to a buggy, and they quickly moved it out into the courtyard. William went to one end of the building and grabbed a bridle from the tack shelf. He carried the bridle with him to a barn beside the drive-shed.

Once in the barn, he crossed over to his horse's stall. William opened the door to the narrow stall and backed the horse out. As William placed the bridle around the horse's head, one of the men who had assisted with the buggy, came into the barn. "Grab the harness, Joshua. It's hanging up on the wall over there."

William led the horse over to the buggy, and Joshua followed behind with the harness. The other man was still standing by the buggy. "What happened out on the lake, William?"

"Not sure of all the facts yet, Duke," William spoke as he got the horse into place. Joshua and William threw the harness over the horse's back and William secured it. Duke bent down and held the shafts of the buggy. "I'll get the details once the doctor is with Lorra Anne, and I can afford some time."

William then secured the bridle as Joshua and Duke fastened the shafts of the buggy onto the harness. The horse moved uneasily, not used to the attention of three men at the same time. "Easy girl, it's okay," William reassured the chestnut mare.

William quickly double-checked everything. Satisfied, he climbed up inside the buggy. "Thank you for your help boys. I hope to God I'm not too long."

"Godspeed, William," Joshua said as he handed William the reins. Without delaying any further, William snapped the reins and tore off down his laneway. As William rode in the buggy, he thought how unfortunate it was that he was the only one at the party who could summon the doctor. By rights, he should have been back with his daughter.

After William had ridden away, Joshua and Duke made their way over to the assembled crowd. They relayed what little William had told them. It was clear that the party was over. No one really knew what to do. The musicians began to pack up their instruments.

A small crowd of men collected near the tables, drinking and talking. Others stood down at the dock, wondering what could have happened. David Green made his way back through the crowd and tended to his son. Caleb was now sitting on the edge of the dock with his head buried in his hands. He glanced over occasionally at the rowboat. He wished it were all just a bad dream.

David stood by his son and put a hand on his shoulder. "What happened here, Caleb? What can you tell me?" Caleb looked up at his father. David could see that Caleb had been crying. The boy was shocked to see the crimson stains on his father's shirt and coat. Caleb spoke though his tears, "I don't rightly know, Father. She just went down. It was a gunshot, but from whom or why, I don't know." Caleb couldn't take his eyes from his father's stained clothing. He knew exactly where the stains had come from.

Then, as if to answer David's question, a light blue rowboat suddenly broke through the fog. It abruptly beached itself several feet over from the Fick rowboat. A black Labrador sat at the bow of the light blue rowboat. The dog's pink tongue hung out of its mouth as if it had no care in the world. In the middle of the boat sat a rough looking man in a grey linen cap and a green greatcoat. A double-barrel shotgun lay at his side on the seat.

The rowboat had hit the gravel shore with a thud, parting a "V" in the small stones. James Murdock steadied himself and then stepped out of the wooden vessel. Cora began to bark but remained in the boat with the shotgun. Cora wasn't too sure about the group of assembled men that stood there on the shore, some of them swaying slightly from the effect of the ale and cider.

James stood at the edge of Castle Lake, "I'm James Murdock and I live across the lake." As he spoke James noticed a young man sitting on the dock with an older man standing at his side. The young man had been crying. All the men upon the shore were staring at him, watching his every move, but none of them said a word. One or two of the men cleared their throats and another man spat upon the ground.

"What has happened here? I heard the commotion from my place. I came over as quickly as I could." James had a feeling he didn't want to know the answer. He could feel the eyes of the men looking past him and at the shotgun.

"James Murdock is it?" David Green spoke up. "Have yea fired that shotgun off recently?"

David turned to face James, and for the first time James also saw the crimson stains on David's clothing. James cleared his throat and spoke, "I have. I have been out shooting ducks this morning."

David seemed oblivious to the red stains on his shirt and coat. "I believe that you bagged yourself a prey of a much different kind. Mister Murdock, would you be kind enough to peer into the rowboat beside yea. It belongs to one William Fick."

The men on the shore were taken aback by David Green's very calm demeanor. They decided to be patient and see where David was going with his line of questioning. Taylor Mitchell, a cousin of William Fick, stepped forward from the group of men. He planned to represent the Fick faction when the time felt right. Taylor was a strong looking man with several day's worth of stubble on his chin.

"What's the purpose of the action?"

"Humor me, Mister Murdock, please."

James cautiously stepped over to the faded white rowboat between him and the dock. As he walked over, the young man began to watch him, too. James stepped up to the Fick rowboat and looked it over, beginning at the bow and ending at the stern. His mouth opened when he saw the red substance all over the stern seat as well as on the floorboards of the boat below the seat. He knew then that it too was somehow connected with the stains on David's shirt. "Is that blood?" All eyes remained on James. Cora continued to bark from the Murdock rowboat.

Taylor Mitchell decided it was time to speak up, "Aye, Mister Murdock," Taylor rubbed the stubble on his chin, and his eyes narrowed. He stepped forward, and as he did, Cora began to growl. "You shot the girl in the face! You were out on the lake hunting, and shot the girl. What the hell were you thinking? Hunting in the fog?"

"It was you?" Caleb's voice broke as he continued to stare at James.

Caleb's father agreed with his son. "It had to be him, Caleb. He has to have been the only person out on the lake in this weather with a weapon. Check his gun, Taylor, see if it's been shot recently."

Taylor began to move forward, and Cora bared her teeth. James turned back to his boat, "Easy Cora. These men don't mean us any harm."

"I wouldn't go that far, Mister Murdock," a gruff voice spoke from the back of the group of men.

James turned back to the inquisition. "Yes, I shot my gun. Not thirty minutes ago. I have done nothing wrong!"

David jumped back into the conversation, "That blood belongs to the daughter of William Fick. You stand there and tell me you've done nothing wrong?"

"Not Lorra Anne Fick?" James blurted out. He was now beginning to get worried. His expression turned from concern to that of fear, "I haven't harmed that girl, have I?"

"She will probably die today," another man spoke out.

"You will hang, Mister Murdock!" yet another man voiced. The men all began to approach the shore.

James stepped back and bumped the side of his rowboat. Cora nuzzled his arm from behind to let him know she at least was there for him. James put his hands up, "Let's not get the cart before the horse here. Let's get the facts. In any case, it was an accident, pure and simple. I never meant nobody no harm!"

Caleb stood up from the dock. He was uneasy on his feet and his father helped to steady him. He took several steps closer to James. "You meant no harm sir, but I fear you have more than likely killed my future bride." Caleb glared at James with hatred. The men that were there were clearly surprised by the emotion conveyed by the seventeen year old young man. "We should cut out your cold, murdering heart right here," Caleb spat out. He edged towards James.

David cautioned his son. "Let cool heads prevail, Caleb. We are not savages." However, several of the men agreed more with Caleb and less with the boy's father.

Some of the men made approving grunts and growls, "Let's take care of the bastard right now."

Taylor sided with David. Taylor stuck his arms out at his sides to stop the advancing men behind him. "We don't know for sure if Lorra Anne Fick will die. In any case, any justice dealt will come from the law and not from a bunch of half-drunken, raged-filled men. As David said, we are civilized people here." Again, there were some grunts and growls, but the men stopped advancing. Caleb continued to stare James down.

Taylor stepped forward, and reaching out, he rested his large hand on James' shoulder. "I suggest to you, sir that you go back to your home and wait. You are not welcome here right now. You will be informed of how things unfold, be sure of that."

"It was an accident. I never meant no harm. Me and the dog were hunting ducks..." James' voice trailed off as he realized the implications of what he may have done. Had a relaxing morning duck hunt turned into some poor girl's demise?

"Go, Mister Murdock. Go before I can no longer contain

these men." Taylor didn't really think James would be harmed, but he believed the sooner James was gone from the Fick property the better it would be for everyone concerned.

"All right, then. I will be at my farm. It's directly across the lake," James turned and pointed aimlessly into the fog. The group of men grumbled and nodded. James could plainly see that Caleb was still staring him down, "I'm so sorry, really..." James returned his thoughts to his rowboat. He pushed it back out into the water and climbed into it. The boat swayed back and forth as he settled into it, grasped the two oars on each side of the boat, and began to row backwards. The group of men watched him as he rowed into the fog. James Murdock disappeared as quickly as he had appeared.

Taylor was content that James was gone. He turned to David. "There's not much more we can do down here. We should get the boat cleaned up before William gets back."

Then Caleb blurted out, "No sir! That's evidence. Leave the blood there for the sheriff to see."

"The boy makes sense." David put his arm around his son and motioned him back up the path. Then in a more reassuring tone, David added, "Let's go up to the house, Caleb, and see how she is doing. I'm sure she'd want to know you were by her side, even if for just a moment or two."

Caleb pursed his lips and then wiped his mouth with the sleeve of his light brown waistcoat. He nodded his head and walked beside his father. The group of men parted and allowed the father and son to pass through. As they did, Taylor followed right behind. The group of men then followed Taylor back up the hill to the house talking amongst themselves.

It was a much different scene now as they approached the top of the hill where the party had been held. An hour had passed but it seemed like a lifetime. Half-full mugs and tin cups sat upon various tables. Smoke curled from the smouldering fire under the cast iron pot. Caleb and David went ahead, as the group of men—led by Taylor—remained at the tables. They found their respective mugs and cups and continued to drink, discussing the events that had just unfolded.

David and Caleb rounded the corner of the house. Caleb was just about to enter the main door when his mother suddenly came out. Elva Green put her arms out and hugged her son as she sobbed. She said no words. Caleb hugged his mother back and then pushed himself away from her. "May I see Lorra Anne, Mother?"

Elva gave her son a sorrowful look, "I don't think that is a good idea right now Caleb. She is in very bad condition. We are just waiting for the doctor."

Elva could see the pleading in her son's eyes. "Mother, if Lorra Anne dies today, I want to see her one last time. That's all that I ask."

Elva glanced over at David who stood to the side of the door. He gave Elva the signal that said "Yes." Elva turned around and put her arm around Caleb's waist. They went into the house together.

At the doorway of Lorra Anne's bedchamber, Elva let her

son go. He entered into the room and caught a quick look from Lilly's cousin Annette. Annette had sent her other two cousins home, and she had taken on the task of watching over Lorra Anne and Lilly. Annette's green eyes conveyed her concern as to why this young lad was coming into a lady's bedchamber. Elva spoke, "Its okay, Annette, Caleb is my son and he just wanted to see Lorra Anne before we returned home. He and Lorra Anne were very good friends."

Annette relented and allowed Caleb into the room. Since she was a blood relative, Annette had taken charge of the situation. She sat on one side of the bed's headboard, and Lilly sat on the other. Lilly continued to stare at her daughter while holding Lorra Anne's hand. She slowly rocked back and forth. Caleb stepped a little closer to the bed and then stopped. Annette said in a soft and caring voice, "She's been sleeping ever since, Caleb. Her heartbeat seems strong, but we have no idea how long she will sleep like this."

Caleb had stopped halfway between the head of the bed and the doorway. Actually, Lorra Anne didn't look all that bad. She was pale, but at the same time, she looked quite peaceful. Annette had placed a cloth over the side of Lorra Anne's face that had been shot. The cloth, lightly stained with blood, was moving up and down very slowly. She was breathing, and he knew that was a good sign.

"Will she be okay?" Caleb asked to no one in particular.

Annette waited for Lilly to say something, but she seemed to be somewhere else at the moment. Annette decided to speak for Lilly, "We hope so, Caleb. The doctor will be here soon. I'm sure he will be able to get Lorra Anne back on the mend."

Caleb nodded and thanked Annette for allowing him to see Lorra Anne. Annette smiled at Caleb and he left the room. Elva had waited by the doorway for Caleb, and when he came out of the bedchamber, the two of them headed outside.

The other cousins from both William and Lilly's families had begun to clean up the party area. They scraped off the many plates into a large wooden barrel which sat by the tables. This would be used later for pig slop. The glassware and cutlery were gathered and washed with warm water in another large wooden tub. The cleaned dishes and glassware were placed on a table to dry and then taken into the house.

Caleb and his mother joined David at the fire pit beside the house. David had added some wood and gotten the fire active again. As they watched the dancing flames, no one spoke. Elva understood that David was going to wait for William to return with the doctor.

Just over an hour later, William returned with Doctor Holt. The only people who had remained at the Fick house by this time were the Green's and some of the cousins, including Annette. All the other guests had returned to their respective communities to spread the news of Lorra Anne's impending death. There wasn't a person present who believed that she would survive.

The Green's heard the two buggies pull up on the other

side of the house. The sounds of the horses were very clear. Caleb's ears perked up, and he glanced over at his father for some kind of sign. David said, "Let's go have a look, shall we?"

As they rounded the corner of the house, Doctor Holt was just climbing out of his black, open buggy. William was already on the ground waiting for him as he dismounted and took him by the arm and directed him into the house.

Doctor Holt, a slight man with thinning grey hair, approached Lorra Anne's bed. Lorra Anne's curley, fire engine red hair was the only part of her that radiated any life. Still unconscious, her pale skin made her appear like a porcelain doll as the doctor began to examine her.

Lilly was no longer in the room. Just as William noticed that fact, Annette came up beside him, "Lilly, herself, has taken a turn for the worse, Will. She hasn't said a word since you brought Lorra Anne in here. I have Lilly lying in her own bedchamber. Do you want me to stay a while longer?"

"Has the girl lost much blood?" the doctor said as he interrupted Annette.

"There was a fair amount, Doctor. I put the cloth over her face to help clot the blood. She was also bleeding from the back of her head, which must have occurred when she fell in the boat after the shot," answered Annette.

"I'll look in on Lilly," William said. He decided it was best to leave the doctor with Lorra Anne and keep himself busy.

Doctor Holt didn't like what he saw. The cloth that

Annette had placed on the girl's face had grafted with the drying blood and flesh. As he tried to lift the cloth away, it tore the wound open again. The flesh in Lorra Anne's cheek was dotted with little pieces of buckshot. Her left eye had filled with blood and was turning a very dark color. Her wounds seemed clean but she was deathly pale. Doctor Holt opened his black bag and took out some items including a bottle of whisky, which he used as a disinfectant.

"You have done a good job in taking care of the girl while her father fetched me," the doctor lied. The cloth over the open wound hadn't helped, but no good would come from him saying as much, and it was obvious that Annette had truly made an effort to help.

"Thank you, Doctor, I hope that I made a difference." Annette was pleased with the doctor's praise and was glad she was able to assist; however, she was still deathly afraid of what was going to happen to Lorra Anne. Annette stood off to one side so that she could observe the doctor but at the same time not get in his way.

Doctor Holt didn't want to say much more. He cleaned Lorra Anne's wounds with a cloth soaked in the whisky—two shots in the cloth and one shot for him. As he finished up, he gave the girl the once-over. He knew Lorra Anne was going to lose her eye, but that was the least of her worries. He had to get the girl conscious. Doctor Holt turned to Annette. "I'm going to try and wake her. We need to have her conscious."

Doctor Holt began to shake Lorra Anne by her shoulders

and yelled her name several times directly into her face. Annette was right beside the doctor and caught his breath in her own face. She thought that if the man's breath didn't wake Lorra Anne, nothing would. It was truly putrid.

But the continued shaking and yelling of the doctor were to no avail. Lorra Anne just lay there. Her chest did continue to move up and down—still a positive sign.

He turned to Annette, "You've done all you can do for now. I'm going to see if I can't get all of the buckshot out of her cheek and eye. You might want to leave for this part."

Annette nodded and agreed. She left Lorra Anne's bedchamber and crossed into the main room of the house. Annette caught a chill and thought it was time to start a fire in the hearth. Elva was sitting in a chair by the empty fireplace. "It's getting cold in here, Mrs. Green. I'm going to get a fire going."

"That sounds like a good idea, Annette." As she finished her words, David and Caleb came in from outside, each rubbing their hands. William entered the main room of the house from his own bedchamber and sat down beside Elva. He watched Annette get the fire ready. David saw what was Annette was doing and turned to Caleb, "Caleb, help Annette with the fire. Go fetch some wood for her."

"This way," Annette said as she walked across the room. She turned to William, "The doctor's still in with Lorra Anne. He said that he'd rather be alone to do what he needed to do."

"It's probably for the best," William spoke as he himself

rubbed his hands together. "I need a drink. David, can you fetch me the bottle of Brackla on the counter. Cups are just above the bottle on a shelf." David nodded and headed into the kitchen. He rummaged around and then returned with two porcelain cups. He handed one to William. "You're going to need this more than I."

"I agree, David. It won't cure the problem but it will help."

"How is Lilly doing, William?" asked Elva with concern.

"She's taking it very hard. We never expected anything like this, especially today of all days. I just hope to God that Lorra Anne pulls through."

David sipped his drink as he sat on a bench seat. Caleb and Annette returned with some wood. He had a large amount in his arms while Annette carried some smaller pieces. Annette walked over to the hearth and placed the wood on the floor beside the fireplace, brushed off some flakes of bark from her dark green dress, and then proceeded to ignite the kindling. Caleb assisted her and before long, a hot fire was burning. Annette stood back, "Thanks, Caleb, I couldn't have done it without you."

Caleb began to feel the warmth and smiled at Annette, who was about ten years his senior.

David swirled the drink in his glass as he thought about what he wanted to say. "William, we think we know who may have shot Lorra Anne."

"Good God," blurted out William. "I never even thought

about who may have done this. Tell me, what do you know?"

"A man from across the lake was hunting ducks in the fog. A stray shot may have hit Lorra Anne."

"James Murdock shot my daughter?"

"That was his name. He came over in his rowboat. He was concerned that something had happened. I suppose he heard Lorra Anne fall and Caleb's cries for help." Caleb shuddered as he remembered how the events had suddenly unfolded. David was surprised at how calm William appeared.

"Taylor and I told Murdock to go home and wait for the sheriff. You can fetch him tomorrow. You are going to need a good night's rest first."

"Murdock," was all William said. The fire crackled and no one spoke another word. Too much had happened and William was still emotionally raw. He couldn't think at the moment. He tried to enjoy his drink and the warmth of the fire.

An hour later, Doctor Holt appeared from Lorra Anne's bedchamber. He had removed as much buckshot as he could with a pair of fine tweezers and then had sewn Lorra Anne's cheek back together. He walked into the center of the main room of the house and cleared his throat. All eyes turned their attention to him.

"William, I have tended to Lorra Anne to the best of my abilities. I'm concerned about infection settling into her eye, so we are going to have to monitor that. She is still asleep, but I'm not too concerned as her breathing appears normal."

Doctor Holt paused for effect and then plainly stated, "I

want to remove her eye."

William Fick's thin veneer of strength finally crumbled under the weight of that news. "She's going to die anyway," he moaned. He tried to hold back tears. Annette had never seen him like this before. With everything that had already happened, this was the first time that the Green's actually appeared uneasy. They felt it wasn't their place witnessing William's emotional turmoil.

"Now, now," comforted Doctor Holt, "Let us stay in a positive mind set. She can pull through this. You have to stay grounded, William. Lilly is going to need you. Lorra Anne is going to need you."

The doctor then made some further recommendations to William about Lorra Anne's care. Annette took note as well. The doctor said his goodbyes and then went on his way. As he left, he stated that he would be back in a day or so to check on his young patient.

"We should be getting back to Hornerseth, William," David spoke as he finished off his drink. He stood up and Elva joined him, patting down her dress. David placed his empty glass on a table beside his chair. They motioned for Caleb to follow them. Caleb gave Annette a smile and left the house with his parents. William stood up and opened the door for them and followed them out to their carriage.

As David assisted Elva into the carriage, she turned and offered her sympathy, "I'm so very sorry, William." Caleb climbed into the rear of the carriage while David sat beside his wife. David extended his hand to William, "Please let us know how Lorra Anne does. Also let me know if there is anything else we can do."

"All we can do now is pray. I would ask all of you to do that for Lorra Anne."

David nodded, and with that he snapped the reins, and his two horses came to life. As the carriage pulled away, Caleb Green turned and gazed at the Fick house. His face showed no emotion. It had been such a hard day, and he felt that the worst was yet to come.

Just as the Green's carriage left the Fick property, another vehicle entered the long laneway. A dark brown buggy came closer, and William recognized his cousin, Taylor Mitchell. Taylor pulled his buggy into the spot where the Green's carriage had been only moments before. Taylor had gotten his own family settled in for the evening and came back to check in on William, Lilly, and Lorra Anne.

William took the bridle of the Palomino stallion that pulled Taylor's buggy. Taylor jumped out of the buggy and looped the reins over the hitching post where William stood. "How is Lorra Anne?" he asked while catching his breath.

"Not good, Taylor. Not good at all. She is still sleeping. She hasn't yet woken. The doctor is concerned about her flesh getting more diseased." Taylor could see that William was visibly shaken.

"What do you know of the circumstances, Will?"

William looked up at Taylor. "David Green suspects

James Murdock was the culprit. That bastard Murdock has been a thorn in my side ever since we located here. I wish I never left the city."

"You can't change the past, Will. We can only move ahead. Let's keep Lorra Anne in our prayers and hope for the best." Taylor had a good head on his shoulders for his young age of twenty-five.

"And James Murdock? What do we hope for him?" William stared at the ground and shuffled his feet. He then looked up at Taylor for an answer.

"We'll call on the sheriff in the morning. We'll let the law settle it. Vengeance won't help Lorra Anne. I'll say that there was a crowd of men earlier today who were ready to string Mister Murdock up."

"That would be too easy," William kicked at the ground again. "What am I going to do, Taylor? If anything happens to Lorra Anne it will crush Lillian."

"We have to pray, Will. Hopefully, God will show your daughter some mercy."

William stepped back and leaned against the outside wall of his house. His hands went to his head. He no longer heard anything else Taylor said. William's head was spinning. All he could see now was that day in the hay mow. As far as William was concerned, that was where the whole mess had begun.

Taylor approached William, "Is Annette still here, Will?"

William's head continued to spin. All he could focus on was James Murdock and his boys. They were trouble. Always were and always would be. Taylor shook William who stared at his cousin as if in a trance. "Is Annette still here?"

William snapped out of his lost moment. "Yes, Taylor. She's going to stay for another day or two and help Lilly and I along. Lilly is so lost to me right now. What am I going to do?"

It was hard for Taylor to see his cousin like this. William Fick was normally a very strong man. But James Murdock had found William's Achilles Heel. Taylor assisted William back into his house and asked Annette to keep a watchful eye on both William and his wife. Annette gave Taylor a look of exasperation; she felt like she was taking on more than she could handle. Taylor promised to come back in the morning and help her.

* * *

The next day Taylor returned to the Fick farm. William had now fallen deep into a state of shock. He sat in his chair in front of the fireplace and simply watched the fire crackle and burn. Taylor could hear William speaking to himself very softly, "What am I going to do?" was all he said, over and over.

Lilly was still bedridden, and Annette was realizing that she was going to need some additional help. "I can't do everything myself, Taylor. I need to be getting back to my own family."

As well as keeping an eye on William and Lilly, Annette was trying to tend to Lorra Anne. Taylor entered the young woman's bedchamber and looked at her motionless body. "Twenty four hours ago she was a healthy woman with a future..."

"Don't let the Ficks hear you talking like that, Taylor." Annette came into the bedchamber and gave Lorra Anne the once over herself.

"The doctor is supposed to be by today or tomorrow, but there isn't much we can do until Lorra Anne comes out of her deep sleep."

"I'll see what I can do about getting some other relatives to help us, Annette." Taylor left the bedchamber and walked back into the main living quarters. He spoke to the motionless figure sitting in the chair all alone, "Let's go, Will. We're going to notify the sheriff."

It took some coaxing but Taylor finally got William out of the house and up onto his horse. The ride into Roulston Corners brought William around somewhat. At the sheriff's office, William became much more animated and agitated. Taylor was glad to see the fire return to William Fick. His cousin was a fighter, not a quitter.

Sheriff Coulter was a lean man of about thirty years of age. He was very energetic and was known to get things done. He listened intently as William described what had happened the day before. Sheriff Coulter assured both William and Taylor that he and his deputy would be riding out to pay James Murdock a visit within the hour. He also offered his prayers for Lorra Anne and said that she would be in his thoughts.

Taylor and William rode back to the farm and got the day's chores taken care of. The farm work was good for William because it kept his mind off the horrifying events of the day before. Back at the house, Annette explained to Taylor how she felt guilty for not staying longer and doing more, but she did live an hour's ride away, and her own family needed her.

Taylor asked Annette to stay a day or two longer, and she agreed. Taylor himself lived forty five minutes away.

Over the next week, Taylor came out to the Fick farm and helped William with the many different farm chores.

Doctor Holt wasn't in as often as William would have liked. Both Taylor and Annette realized that the doctor just didn't know what to do at this point. He wanted to remove her eye, which was getting more and more infected no matter what anyone did. However, William wouldn't allow the eye to be taken out.

Lorra Anne was fading. On the third day she still hadn't had anything to eat or drink. Doctor Holt stated to Annette that they had to get some water into her, or Lorra Anne would die from dehydration alone. Annette left the bedchamber for a moment to fetch a glass of water from the water pump outside.

Several moments later, Annette returned with the glass of water. Doctor Holt glanced up from Lorra Anne, "We are going to sit Lorra Anne up and I will pour some water into her mouth."

"Won't she choke or drown?" Annette asked with deep

concern in her voice.

Doctor Holt gave her a slight smile, "There is a remote chance the water could fall into her lungs, but I will just pour very slowly. She just needs a couple ounces."

Annette came to the opposite side of the bed while setting the glass of water on a table by the bed. She pulled Lorra Anne's sheets back to the girl's waist. Then Annette got an arm behind Lorra Anne and began to raise her up into a sitting position. Lorra Anne was just plain dead weight, And Doctor Holt saw how Annette was struggling, so he helped her from his side. Annette thought it strange how cool and limp Lorra Anne was. Almost like a living rag doll. And just barely living at that.

"Hold her there, Annette, and tip her head back a little. Even in her state, Lorra Anne's automatic reflex will be to swallow the water."

From her position Annette was able to pick up the glass of water and hand it to Doctor Holt. He propped open Lorra Anne's mouth with a finger from one hand while he slowly poured the water into her mouth with the other. Just drips at a time. Annette knew how dry Lorra Anne's mouth was because she could see that the girl's lips were severly chapped and cracked. Annette tried not to stare at the injured side of Lorra Anne's face. Slowly Lorra Anne swallowed the water, even in her unconscious state.

The process of giving Lorra Anne several ounces of water took over forty-five minutes. When it was done, they carefully laid the girl back onto the bed, and Annette returned the bed sheets to their former position. Doctor Holt looked over to Annette, "You are a great assistant, Annette. This is going to be a daily routine until we can get her healthy."

Annette looked down on her cousin and had serious doubts whether she would ever see Lorra Anne healthy again.

The days turned into a week. Doctor Holt stopped in every afternoon at the end of his working day, and Annette became quite good at helping the doctor get water into Lorra Anne. However, he was concerned that the water may not be enough, and that the girl's blood might be getting too thick. This would compound the other problems as well.

In the meantime, William had tried to keep Lorra Anne's wounds clean. Annette was teaching him how to care for his daughter. However, it seemed no matter what they did the disease had taken over, and Lorra Anne's decaying eye was looking worse every day. She remained in her sleeping state as her body was continuously getting weaker and weaker.

William didn't understand the technical aspects of it, only that his daughter was failing. She had gone from pale to white and now to grey. Lilly had begun to take some food and drink, finally, but she still refused to come out of her own bedchamber.

At the ten-day mark, Lorra Anne Fick looked absolutely ghoulish. She hadn't moved since the accident and her body was limp. The disease now ran from her eye across her face. Her cheeks were sunken and her skin was the color of mortar but with a slight greenish tinge. Lorra Anne refused to go easily.

William knew that the end was near, and he took Annette aside and said to her, "I really appreciate the time that you have spent here, Annette, but I know you have a family too. You can return to them now if you'd like. I don't think there is any more we can do."

Another wave of guilt came over Annette. She had been a part of Lorra Anne's daily routine for the last ten days, and felt terrible for the way things had gone for the young girl. But Annette had her own family back in Landmark—a husband and three young children. Her tears flowed as she hugged William, who wasn't sure how to react.

Annette took one last look at Lorra Anne and then left to return to her family. William Fick was truly alone now. Later that evening, Doctor Holt came by to give Lorra Anne her daily dose of water. After he and William had gotten a couple of ounces into her, William told the doctor this would be the last time they would do this. Doctor Holt didn't like the idea of giving up, but it was ultimately the father's decision. William had accepted that Lorra Anne was not going to come out of this awful ordeal. Doctor Holt left the Fick farm for the last time.

It had gotten to the point where William couldn't even look at his daughter anymore. It was a horrifying ordeal for William to watch his daughter slowly slip away like this. Lilly had stopped coming into Lorra Anne's bedchamber from the very beginning. William continued to sit by the head of his daughter's bed and pray for her. He looked at the dark wooden planks of the floor as he prayed.

Just over two weeks after the accident, William was in his usual place at the head of Lorra Anne's bed, her pretty blankets pulled up to her chin. Her bedchamber was the same as it had always been; the room had never changed. Her dolls were still on a shelf, and her dresses still hung on hooks. The only thing that had changed in this room was Lorra Anne. William reached down and held her hand. He squeezed it and realized her hand was very cool. Even cooler than it had been these past fourteen days. He continued to hold his daughter's hand while he looked about her room. As he lovingly remembered the little girl he once knew, William fell asleep.

When William awoke suddenly several hours later, he realized that he was still holding Lorra Anne's hand. But that was what had suddenly awoken him. Lorra Anne's hand was now stone cold. He also noticed that her chest no longer moved.

Fifteen days after she had been hit in the face by the shotgun blast, Lorra Anne Fick died. It was October 28, 1821. It was also the dead girl's sixteenth birthday.

4

The day of reckoning

After William Fick and Taylor Mitchell had told Sheriff Coulter what had happened on Castle Lake, he and his deputy had taken a ride over to the Murdock farm. Both the sheriff and deputy questioned James, who insisted the whole thing was a terrible and unfortunate accident. The sheriff informed James that although he would not arrest the man as of yet, James was not to take any sudden trips. James insisted that he had done no wrong and he would face whatever might befall him.

At that time, the sheriff was actually waiting to see what happened with Lorra Anne. The charges he'd bring would depend on her recovery. Or eventually her lack of one.

After Lorra Anne had died, William rode up and informed the sheriff. He then made the funeral plans.

Sheriff Coulter rode back out to the Murdock farm and notified James that Lorra Anne was now dead, and that he may be facing a murder charge. The Murdock family had prepared themselves for the worst, but the news still came as a shock.

Phoebe held a hand to her mouth and looked into James' eyes. She didn't have to say the words. Phoebe didn't want to lose her husband. James took a deep breath and responded to the sheriff, "Whatever the outcome may be, Sheriff Coulter, I'm ready for the consequences."

Both John and Henry Murdock were trembling. They didn't want to lose their father, especially over Lorra Anne Fick.

"That Lorra Anne always was trouble," John blurted out. It didn't seem that he was talking to anyone in particular, just expressing his opinion.

"No one deserves to die, John. It was an awful accident. There is good in everyone." Phoebe scolded her eldest son.

John looked at the ground and shuffled his feet while he collected his thoughts, "I'm sorry, Ma. I just don't want Father to hang."

"Why would you think that?" questioned Phoebe.

Henry quickly answered for his brother, "Everyone is talking about it. They say that Father is going to hang for killing Lorra Anne."

Sheriff Coulter spoke to the Murdock boys. "I know your father didn't kill Lorra Anne on purpose. Like your mother has said, it was an accident. Just stay calm boys." It was obvious that the sheriff was trying to be reassuring, but James and Phoebe were still very nervous. Sheriff Coulter then spoke to James, "Stay on the farm James. I will be by either way and let you know what the verdict is."

"The verdict?" said Phoebe.

Sheriff Coulter smiled, which seemed strange given the circumstances. "The verdict on whether there are charges or not. We'll see which way the wind blows."

Phoebe Murdock thought this was a very strange way for a man of the law to talk. Was the letter of the law truly based on the way the wind blew? She certainly hoped not. Sheriff was a peculiar man, that much she knew. Phoebe just smiled, and to herself, hoped for the best.

Sheriff Coulter mounted his horse, and just as he was about to leave, he turned to face the Murdocks. "Mister Fick has also requested that none of the male Murdocks of this family attend the funeral of his late daughter. You ma'am are welcome to attend if you so wish." With that the sheriff rode off and back to Roulston Corners.

James and Phoebe spoke no words. They were both worried about their future.

The slow and painful death of young Lorra Anne Fick was common knowledge in the county. Her last days had been the talk of the town. Taylor Mitchell made sure that his cousin, William, had the support of the community. Doctor Holt was also quite a gossip and spoke of Lorra Anne's demise to whomever would listen.

It seemed that James couldn't walk down the main street of Roulston Corners without people stopping, gawking, and pointing at him. He then decided to simply stay home until the whole thing had been settled.

Three days after she died, the funeral was held. The order of William Fick and the sheriff didn't stop James from at least riding his horse by the church and cemetery property. It was one of the largest assemblies of people that James Murdock had ever seen in his life. He made sure that he stayed a good distance away from the proceedings. The last thing he wanted to do was cause a commotion, being well aware that he had already caused enough damage.

From his vantage point, it was clear that the wooden Presbyterian Church was packed with people. Acquaintances, friends, and immediate family must have filled every available spot in the church. These were folks who had come to pay their last respects to a young lady who once had a bright future.

James couldn't know how full the church actually was. By noon there was no more room within the church building, and a large number of people had to be content with standing outside on the front landing of the church. James had no idea that the Fick family was so well respected and represented.

The immediate family sat in the front pew. The Greens were all there as well. Lilly and William sat beside the families of Taylor and Sarah Mitchell and Annette and Charles Norman. William had been able to remain composed for the funeral ceremony. The drink had certainly helped—being half-drunk all the time since Lorra Anne's death wasn't all that bad. He could still function. That was more than he could say about his wife. She sat beside him looking quite pretty, but her gaze was blank and emotionless.

Directly ahead of William and Lilly at the front of the church was the oak casket that held their daughter. The light color of the casket's polished wood was quite exquisite, and the four golden handles shone brightly. It was a fitting memorial for their late daughter. The casket, however, was closed, and covered with fresh-cut flowers.

The Reverend Theodore Shanks, who had been the Fick's preacher back up north, had come all the way from Hornerseth to preach at her funeral. The family felt that he was the only one who could give Lorra Anne a proper burial service. The church's regular minister, the Reverend Maurice Reynolds, was initially a little put out by the decision; however, Reverend Shanks was a very fair man and asked Reverend Reynolds to say a few words before he introduced the preacher who had come from afar.

The funeral proceedings ran smoothly. Reverend Reynolds spoke sensitvely from the heart about Lorra Anne which was well-received by the congregation. He then introduced the Reverend Shanks, and Shanks in turn spoke for over forty minutes. He spoke of what he had known about Lorra Anne, her planned marriage to Caleb Green, as well as her painful and long drawn-out death. After he concluded his speech, a chorus of wails and sobs emanated from the congregation.

Reverend Shanks was a tall, lean man, and the skin of his face hugged his cheek bones. His short salt-and-pepper colored hair lay flat on his head. His eyes burned with conviction. The congregation hung onto every one of his words, and he concluded with a special prayer for Lorra Anne:

"Oh Lord above, please give this congregation guidance as they struggle with the questions of why Lorra Anne Fick was abruptly taken from her earthly domain. This young lady with so much living ahead of her suddenly robbed of her life because of another man's carelessness. We know that she is in a better place with you, oh Lord, and hope and pray that your justice is swift and righteous. Amen."

The congregation replied "Amen" with Reverend Shanks, and then murmurs of agreement spread throughout the church. Everyone seemed to agree with the Reverend's line of thinking. Off to the side, the Reverend Reynolds wondered about Reverend Shanks' intent. Was he trying to start a riot? A lynching? The people in the pews settled down, and the Reverend Shanks motioned for the casket to be taken from the front of the church.

The pall-bearers, including Taylor and Annette's husband, Charles, rose up from the pews and approached the casket. Together they removed the flowers from the wooden box and then solemnly lifted it, carrying the casket out of the church through to the cemetery grounds located behind the building.

Lorra Anne Fick was laid to rest in a newer part of the cemetery. It was a plot by the corner of the fence line. Her headstone lay upon the grass to one side, waiting to be erected later on. The grave marker was made of white sandstone and would be the newest gravestone in the cemetery.

The casket was brought out and carefully placed in the hole that had been previously dug. Reverend Shanks said some more words and another short prayer, and then that was it. The congregation walked from the gravesite and talked of what may happen next. While they walked away, two laborers shoveled dirt back into the grave. When that was done, they placed all the flowers from the church over the gravesite and then they put the stone in place. The wording on the stone was simple:

Lorra A. Fick

1805-1821

Beloved daughter of

William and Lillian Fick.

Exactly a week after Lorra Anne's funeral had taken place, James was finally arrested for her death. He went with the sheriff and the deputy willingly. James was being held at the brand new jail that had just been built at Roulston Corners. Some had joked that the jail had been built especially for him, as James was the first to ever be incarcerated there.

The public opinion was not a good sign at all; many of the locals wanted to see James hang for Lorra Anne's death. The local press had been working overtime since Lorra Anne had been shot. It was feared by the area officials that James wouldn't get a fair trial in Roulston Corners. Sheriff Coulter asked the town's judge to move the trial to the northwest, so several days later, Sheriff Coulter transported James to the nearby town of Evanston, which was about twice the size of Roulston Corners.

Once in Evanston, James was officially charged with the murder of Lorra Anne Fick. The trial was to be held after Christmas.

Now it was Phoebe's turn to experience some hardships. She and her two young sons had to run the farm while her husband was in jail. Similar to William Fick, the Murdock's didn't have any immediate family in the area either. However, unlike the Ficks, Phoebe was staying positive. She ensured her sons on a daily basis that their father would be coming back home. The three of them kept that mindset, knowing that one day soon things would begin to look up.

The same could not be said for William and Lilly. As far as William was concerned, Lilly had stopped living. Since the funeral, she barely left her bedchamber. William had hoped the impending trial might keep her occupied, but she seemed to have no interest. She summed it up for her husband, "Lorra Anne is dead. Nothing will change that fact. Nothing. Neither all the justice nor all the vengeance in the world."

William had to constantly check that she was eating food and drinking fluids. He had to manage the farm on a daily basis as well. William began to drink alcohol more and more. It was his solution to dealing with the tragedy of the loss of his daughter. Both of the families at opposite sides of Castle Lake were having a rough time.

William thought about his wife's words, but he began to form a different position on the word "vengeance." To keep himself busy while he wasn't working on the farm, William created a petition that supported the hanging of James Murdock without a trial. Sheriff Coulter had been right to move the trial, as it didn't take William long to get several sheets filled with the names of people who supported him. He rode his horse from farm to farm and was well received. After each ride he would show the petition to Lilly, who would respond with, "It's all for naught, Will. All for naught."

The shock and circumstances of Lorra Anne's death weighed on the side of the public opinion. Several weeks into the new year William presented the petition to the Evanston judge.

However the judge refused to even look at the petition saying that it was most unconstitutional. He couldn't be swayed in the least, and the trial went on as planned. It was an emotional trial, and almost everyone who had been present at the Fick party had their turn on the witness stand. The trial lasted just over two weeks and created a local sensation.

Stories on both sides were aired in the courtroom, but it appeared that James was outnumbered. It was his word against the many Fick witnesses: Caleb Green, Taylor Mitchell, Annette Norman, and Doctor Holt. Each went meticulously through the events from Lorra Anne's shooting to her death. The prosecution kept bringing home the fact that the girl died a long and painful death and that she had died on her sixteenth birthday.

William made a plea to the jury to sentence James to his death, "My Lorra Anne did not deserve to die. She was all that my wife and I had. Lorra Anne was our life. Mister Murdock has killed both of us by thoughtlessly taking the life of my daughter."

It was also an emotional time for Henry and John Murdock. The young boys watched their father in the prisoner's box. The defence thought it was a good idea to show that James was a good man who cared for his family. James trembled in the prisoner's box as he gave his only defense, "I never meant to harm that child. I could never intentionally do harm to anyone. I am so sorry that I caused Lorra Anne her death. I promise you all here that I will live with that guilt the rest of my life, as long or short as it may be."

Even though the public sympathy was with the Fick family, the judge and the jury sided with James. It was a very tragic hunting accident and the defendant showed a great deal of remorse.

In early February of 1822 the judge in Evanston gave his verdict: James Murdock was found not guilty of the murder charge brought against him. As of that moment, James was a free man. He had spent thirteen long weeks in jail.

James returned to his farm at the end of Castle Lake and carried on with his life. It felt strange being back at the homestead after the time in jail. It made him appreciate what he had before the tragedy occurred. Then, he had his life. It may have been quite simple, but it was still his life—a life of pride, a life with no regrets. While he was behind bars, James lost that. He lost his freedom to wander on his farm, lost the control of his destiny, and most important, he had lost his family. James vowed that he would never hunt again. He hung his Joseph Manton shotgun over the mantle of his fireplace and decided that was where it would stay for the remainder of his days.

However, the rumor mills of Roulston Corners kept grinding. Everyone in the town and surrounding county followed the day-to-day events of William and Lilly. The gossip had swung away from the initial support of the Ficks and their tragedy to how they could no longer deal with the state of their lives anymore. William had turned into a raging alcoholic and Lilly into a recluse.

Some of the ladies from church had stopped in to visit Lilly to see how she was coping. They were quite shocked to see bruises on her face. Lilly refused to acknowledge the source of the bruises, but it was becoming common knowledge that her husband was beating her. On a clear night the Murdocks could easily hear William and Lilly quarreling. The yelling and screaming carried well over the water's of Castle Lake. If the Murdock's could hear the fighting, so could the other neighbors. Many began noticing that William had begun to neglect his livestock in favor of operating his still.

Then on March 15, 1822, more tragedy struck. The community learned that Lilly Fick had taken her life. Doctor

91

Holt had been the first on the scene the following day, and related his story to anyone who would listen. Apparently there were lots of folks who reveled in the sordid tale. The story didn't take long to get back to the Murdocks.

Doctor Holt was reputed as telling this tale:

"While William Fick was in his barn tending to his beloved still, his wife Lilly decided to take matters into her own hands. Lilly Fick no longer saw any purpose in her living. She was well aware that there wouldn't be any more children in her life, and she was continuously haunted by the memory of her innocent daughter who had died in such an unforgiving and unpleasant manner. So Lilly got up from the safety of her bedchamber and left her house. She ventured out into the chilly March evening air, said to have only been wearing her night clothes, which I'm sure offered little protection from the cold. Lilly had decided that she was going for a walk in the moonlight."

"While William toiled away making his beloved alcohol, he was unaware that his formerly bedridden wife was now on a mission. Lilly walked purposefully down the narrow path behind her house that led to the dock. It was no coincidence that is was the exact place where Lorra Anne had been found in the family rowboat, shot. The moonbeams lit Lilly's way as she passed by the empty trellises. I imagine that her feet crunched on the semi-frozen ground beneath her. Did she wear any shoes? I know not the answer to that question."

"Then, once Lilly had reached the dock, she methodically

removed her clothing. Yes, she removed her clothing. She folded everything very neatly and laid it upon the dock. Lilly now stood at the edge of Castle Lake as naked as the day she was born. She then slowly began to wade out into the freezing waters of the lake. I'm sure the lake had only just thawed from the cold grip of winter. It had to be a terrible shock to Lilly's naked middle-aged body. The water had to have been frightfully cold. I'm sure that Lilly had been thinking about this solution for many weeks."

"Lilly had beaten herself up mentally; she should have never outlived her own daughter. There should have been a wedding and grandchildren. Lilly had to set the balance right. The cold fingers of Castle Lake's freezing waters began to rob the warmth from Lilly's body. She must have begun to feel the numbness from the frigid water. Spiritually though, Lilly had already been numb for months. As she continued to wade out into the lake, her body succumbed to that very state of numbness."

"Lilly kept walking out until the water came up to her mouth. By this time her body was in total shock. I'm a doctor and I know these things. Lilly's feet were still on the lake floor. She then let her feet go and opened her mouth, inhaling the water as she sank. Her lungs filled with the cold liquid, and she was somehow able to override all of her natural instincts to survive."

"It's been said time and time again by people that an individual can't drown themselves without gripping onto something solid. But on that bitterly cold March evening, Lilly defied all the odds. She wanted to die. She wanted to join her daughter in the world beyond. I imagine it didn't take Lilly long to succumb. After the life left her body, its naked form floated to the lake's surface. Lilly Fick later washed up onto the shore."

The Roulston Corners folk loved a good story and the Doctor certainly told a fantastic tale.

The current of the lake had carried Lilly's body from the spot where she had drowned to the lake's mouth at Carlton Bay. The Reverend and Mrs. Reynolds discovered her naked, frost-covered form while they were enjoying a morning walk along the water's edge.

It wasn't terrible enough that William Fick's wife had drowned herself in Castle Lake. She had to have also been found naked on the lakeshore by the local preacher and his poor wife. At the time the Reynolds found the body, they had no idea who it was. Lilly was face down in the water, and to them, a naked female looked like any naked female. They were forced to leave her body to the elements as they had nothing to cover her up with. It was too cold for the Reverend to leave his coat.

Once home, the Reverend rode over to the sheriff's office with the news of his grisly discovery. Sheriff Coulter took great interest in what the Reverend told him, rubbing his chin as the discovery played out. The Reverend spoke with his hands as much as he did his mouth. Sheriff Coulter then instructed his deputy to fetch Doctor Holt so he could make notes about the condition of the body. Coulter also instructed his deputy to notify the mortuary attendant.

Sheriff Coulter hitched up his horse and waited for Doctor Holt, enjoying a mid-morning smoke while he mulled over the Reverend's morbid discovery. The Reverend waited back in the office where it was much warmer. In the meantime, Coulter and the doctor would make the initial investigation, and the deputy would rendezvous back to the scene where the body was discovered a little later with Mister Bale and his "Meat Wagon."

"Let's go see what awaits us, Doctor Holt," the sheriff spoke to the doctor as he approached his own mount. Sheriff Coulter called over to the Reverend and said that he was ready to leave. The Reverend led the way while the sheriff and doctor rode behind him.

Half an hour later, they arrived at the disturbing scene. The Reverend pointed down the hill to where he had found the body. Sheriff Coulter thanked him and the Reverend rode off home.

Sheriff Coulter and the doctor walked carefully down to the lake's rocky edge. As they approached the shore, they could plainly see the naked female form.

"Let's see who we have here shall we?" with that the sheriff placed a foot on the dead woman's hip and pushed the body over. She was pretty stiff, but the sheriff "coaxed" her over onto her back for identification purposes. Even though her face was pale and bloated, both the sheriff and the doctor recognized the blank and cold stare of Lilly Fick.

"Well, Doctor Holt, what do you think?" the sheriff asked.

The doctor examined the body from a crouching position and gave his opinion, "There seems to be a lot of bruising. Strange that she is naked. It doesn't appear foul play was involved, but we should get her thawed and have a better look." Within twenty minutes of the sheriff and doctor's arrival at the scene, the deputy arrived with Mister Bale and the "Meat Wagon."

"You'll make a good deputy someday, Doctor," the sheriff laughed. He waved his own deputy down the hill.

Within ten minutes, Lilly Fick's body was loaded and on its way to the funeral parlor. There it would wait until the sheriff had some answers to his questions. While the doctor rode off to continue his rounds, Sheriff Coulter and his deputy rode their horses hard and steady to William Fick's farm. William was not surprised to see Sheriff Coulter because he had watched him and his deputy ride down the laneway. "You found my Lilly did you?"

"What do you know of your wife's disappearance, William Fick?" The sheriff wasn't exactly sure what was going on quite yet.

"Well sheriff, all of her clothes are still sitting on the dock down there, piled up all nice and neat. There is no trace of her otherwise. I can't believe that you are coming to me with anything but bad news."

"You are correct, Will, she's dead." The sheriff and his deputy walked down to the edge of Castle Lake, and when he saw Lily's clothes, he realized that Lilly had taken her own life. He would still perform a full investigation, but it looked pretty clear what had occurred.

Sheriff Coulter described to William exactly what Reverend Reynolds and his wife had found on the shore that morning. William didn't know whether he should openly weep for his wife's death or hide his face in shame for the way she died and had been discovered.

That wasn't the end of William's shame either. Because his wife had killed herself, the Presbyterian Church council refused to allow Lilly to be buried on church property. Suicides were not welcome in the Roulston Corners community cemetery. So for William there was no funeral, no respects, and no closure. The only kind regards William received was from the funeral parlor. They had taken care of Lilly and made her look respectable again. William took his wife home in a canvas body bag, which had been loaded up in the back of his wagon.

Once he returned home, William did not know what to do with Lilly's body. Why was God doing this to him time and time again? He turned to the bottle for some answers. After several drinks, William was able to come up with a plan. He felt that the alcohol freed his mind and allowed him to think with his thoughts uncluttered. William decided to bury Lilly in a secret location on his farm.

He rode out the next day after several drinks and surveyed his property. He hadn't been out too long when he found a nice quiet location where the woodlot began at the edge of one of his fields. William dug Lilly's grave by hand, and then later returned with the canvas body bag in the back of his wagon. As carefully as he could, William got the canvas bag that contained his wife into the hole. He filled the hole and then returned to his woodworking shop.

Back at his shop, he began a new project. He joined some oak planks together, and over the next week, created for Lilly, a very beautiful grave marker. William had sanded wood planks smooth, and then with a chisel, he carved an angel and two lilies of the valley at the top. In the middle of the marker, he recorded Lilly's factual information: her birth and death dates, plus an epitaph. When it was completed, the marker stood two feet wide and almost six feet tall, although two of these feet would be sunken into the ground later. William was pleased with what he had made.

When the marker was fully completed, he painted it white to protect the wood from the elements. He took the marker in the back of his wagon to Lilly's final resting place, and he carried the newly-constructed marker over to the freshly-filled grave. With a spade he dug the hole, placed the wooden marker into the ground, filed the area around it, and stepped back. William was briefly happy. He had given his Lilly a respectful burial after all.

William rode back home and continued to drink. He

reflected on how his life had changed so drastically in a matter of months. First, he had buried his only child, and now he had just buried the only woman that he had ever loved. Why was God punishing him so?

If God had turned his back on William Fick, then William Fick was turning his back on God. As William took to the bottle more and more, he began to develop plans for revenge. He had a great plan that would exact revenge on not only his God, but also on James Murdock. It would be an eye for an eye. The answer for revenge lay with Doctor Jabez Troyer.

Doctor Troyer was locally recognized as a witch doctor. He practiced witchcraft openly, and behind closed doors, he was also known to practice Satanism and black magic. Most of the people in the community just ignored him because he didn't seem to bother anybody or cause any fuss.

Doctor Troyer lived down in the swamps of Carlton Bay. His small log cabin was full of every charm, potion, and ingredient one would need to create any spell or curse required. Doctor Troyer always took his payment in trade, never for cash.

Two weeks after Lilly's death, William rode his horse down to Doctor Troyer's log cabin. He knocked upon the door and stepped back. Troyer answered the door. "I have been expecting you, William Fick. It's time to right a terrible wrong."

William entered the dark cabin where strange and pungent smells hung in the air. His stomach began to turn.

It had been said that in his prime the doctor had once stood six-foot-two. But now, for whatever reason, he was all hunched over and stood much less. His long, greasy grey hair was matted from lack of care and his body stank from an absence of any personal hygiene. William entered the cabin and closed the door behind him.

No one outside that log cabin knew what actually transpired that night. Unknown to the rest of the Roulston Corners community, a bargain had been made. It was a life for a life.

* * *

After the meeting and deal struck with Doctor Troyer, William rode back to his farm and locked himself in his largest barn. In the middle of the open area inside the barn, William created a pentagram with many special candles he had been given by Doctor Troyer. In the center of the pentagram was a wooden post that stood five feet high.

He had also placed candles on the rafters and beams of the wooden building. William had released all of his chickens and pigs housed in the barn and let them run freely inside. Strangely, as they scurried about, enjoying their freedom, they all appeared to avoid the pentagram.

Night after night, William would tie himself by the waist to the post in the center of the pentagram and scream at the top of his lungs words that no one could understand. None of his neighbors had any idea what he was doing and found the noises very unsettling.

Disturbed neighbors around that area of Castle Lake, including James Murdock, called in the sheriff. They described to the sheriff in detail about the strange and eerie sounds that came from William Fick's barn. There was fear of animalistic rituals and sacrifices. However, within the law the sheriff said there was actually little he could do. Finally, he relented and promised those concerned that he would pay Fick a visit and see just what the man was up to. Coulter realized he did have a responsibility to his community.

The next day, Sheriff Coulter and his deputy approached the main door of William Fick's barn. Coulter gave his deputy the go ahead, and the deputy rapped loudly upon it. Neither man knew what to expect. Sheriff Coulter spoke to the door, "William Fick, it's Sheriff Coulter here. I would like to know what it is that you are doing in that barn of yours. Your neighbors are rightfully troubled."

Unknown to them, William was standing right behind the door. Within seconds he responded, "What I am doing, sheriff, is nobody's concern but my own."

Sheriff Coulter took a deep breath and scratched at the dirt beneath him with his boot. He asked again, "What exactly are you doing, William?"

William paused and replied, "Black magic, sheriff. What do you make of that?" Then he roared with laughter from inside the barn. As William's maniacal laugh died down, he added, "Now leave me the hell alone!"

The sheriff looked at his deputy in disbelief. Was he hearing things? The deputy gave the sheriff a confused look and said, "Black magic?"

"William, you're not sacrificing any animals in there are you?"

"You are an ignorant one, sheriff. I'm performing black magic, not Voodoo."

"There's a difference?" the deputy whispered to Coulter.

Sheriff Coulter smiled nervously. "What exactly is 'black magic,' William? What are you trying to do? You have to know you have put the fear in most of your neighbors. They believe you are mad!"

"Mad? Oh yes, sheriff, I believe that I am. The black magic will be proof of my madness. I have nothing left, sheriff. You must know that. I have nothing!" William screamed from behind the door.

The sheriff tried to reason with William. "You have endured a great loss, Will. We in the community all know that. But you can't bring Lorra Anne and Lilly back. They are gone forever."

"Dead and buried, yes, I know, sheriff. I buried them both. They are gone, but I can redress their deaths. I shall make everything right. I will not sit idly by while the guilty enjoys his life."

"He is mad, sheriff," the deputy had never heard anyone, let alone William Fick, talk like this before.

"Will you talk to us face-to-face, William? I am tired of talking to the door of your barn."

"There is nothing to talk about, sheriff. We both know that I am doing nothing illegal. Please get off my property now and let me be."

"One last question then," Sheriff Coulter leaned against the door as he spoke.

"One last question it is then, sheriff."

"How do you plan to make up for the deaths of Lorra Anne and Lilly?" There was a moment's silence and then William responded.

"I made a deal with the devil, sheriff. How does that suit yea? I'm not breaking any laws, so leave me alone."

The sheriff had to concede that William was correct. He left William with one last thought: "William, can you please be a little quieter at least?"

The maniacal laugh began again. Both Sheriff Coulter and his deputy shook their heads. "Let's go, Heath, there is no more we can do here. We'll just have to see what becomes of it." Sheriff Coulter and his deputy backed away from the door and then turned to the hitching post by the house. Both of their horses were tied up, patiently waiting to get going again.

Nothing much on the farm had changed since the ill-fated birthday party back in the fall. The faded ribbons still hung in the trellises and on the trees. The cast-iron pot still hung over the fire pit beside the house. Rust covered the pot from lack of use and neglect. The two men of the law quietly observed how strange the scene before them was.

Resigned, the sheriff and his deputy untied their horses from the hitching post, mounted the animals, and rode off down the lane. They weren't sure whether or not they had really accomplished anything.

* * *

Several days after the sheriff and his deputy had been to William Fick's barn, William opened the door and ventured out into the daylight. He had been locked in the barn for fifteen days straight, screaming and going through his rituals. It was no coincidence that it was exactly the same number of days that Lorra Anne had languished in her bedchamber before she died.

William brought his mare out to ride. She was malnourished evident by her ribs pushing through her coat. While William had been in his barn, he had not attended to any of his livestock. He climbed up on his mare and rode her bareback. The only equipment he used was her bridle. The horse moved slowly up the laneway. William decided that today was the perfect day to pay James Murdock a friendly visit.

It was a very nice spring day at the Murdock farm. All of the doors and windows of the farmhouse were wide open. A light breeze carried through the courtyard into the farmhouse. Beside the house up on a clothes line, Phoebe Murdock had hung linen out to dry. It was time to clean everything and freshen up for the spring. Planting season had arrived--a time for everything to grow again. This was Phoebe's favorite time of the year.

The Murdock boys were in the barn cleaning the horse stalls. They were busy tossing piles of manure out beside the barn. Above them, on the second floor of the barn, their father was making repairs to the overhead pulleys.

Dark haired Henry Murdock was in a stall scraping dried manure out the corners while his fair-haired elder brother, John, worked in the main hall of the barn. The boys had released the horses out into the paddock. John happened to glance out the window of the barn as he pitched some manure. He wiped his brow with the back of his sleeve. As he brought his head up, some movement outside the window caught his attention.

John was curious at first. A figure on horseback approached. The black horse was moving slowly, and the figure on the horse was hunched over. He watched as the horse and rider got closer to the farmhouse.

Then a shiver shot down John's spine when he realized that the horseman was none other than William Fick! John could see that William's appearance was disturbing. His hair and beard were unkempt. His clothes were wrinkled and appeared to have been slept in. John noticed that William was riding the horse bareback. That in itself was very unusual.

As William got closer, John could clearly see that the man's face was gaunt. It appeared like William hadn't eaten in a month. His eyes had sunken into his head, and he was dressed entirely in black, riding a black horse. He definitely looked like he was up to no good. Behind John, Cora growled a low menacing growl, and she bared her teeth. Cora knew something wasn't right. John turned his head back to face the stalls and yelled, "Henry, go fetch Father quickly, there's gonna be trouble."

Henry walked out of the stall he was working in and sauntered over to where his brother stood. "What are you talking about John?" As he spoke the words, Henry's gaze instinctively followed that of his brother's, and his jaw dropped. William was now in between the barn and the house, in the middle of the courtyard.

John and Henry were well out of William's view. William remained on his horse and slowly moved his head back and forth as he surveyed the courtyard. Henry then did as his brother had asked. He tore down the hall of the barn. He quickly clambered up the ladder to the second level, jumped off the ladder, and ran over to where his father was working.

James turned his head and suddenly saw his youngest son, "What's the matter, Henry?"

"It's William Fick, Father. He's out in the courtyard."

James instantly dropped the tools he was using, quickly climbed down the ladder, and ran out of the large sliding door on the side of the barn. He walked quickly down the earthen ramp and into the open courtyard with Henry following close behind. John darted out from his hiding place inside the barn and joined his father and brother who now stood in front of

106

William and his sickly looking horse. James showed no fear as he walked to within ten feet of William.

John and Henry were no longer boys; they were now young men. Hard farm work toughened them, and they now stood on either side of their father, not behind him. No longer wanting to hide from William Fick, John and Henry were now there to support their father. If there were to be a showdown, they would be part of it. Then a fourth Murdock made her appearance from a distance. From the open door of the farmhouse, Phoebe stood watching but not saying a word. She was somewhat relieved that William Fick did not appear to have a weapon.

"How can I help you today, William Fick?" James Murdock kept his voice free from both fear and anger. William didn't say a word. James decided to show sympathy. "I can't say enough how sorry I am how things turned out."

William broke into crazed, menacing laughter and slapped his upper thighs with his hands. Dust rose from his dirty pants. "You're sorry how things turned out? You're sorry how things turned out?" William's drawn face contorted and his eyes looked wild, but he continued to just sit on his horse.

"I can't make it better, William. There is nothing I can do."

"Oh yes there is, Mister Murdock. There is something you can do. You can sacrifice your daughter to me!"

James gave William a very queer look. Was there something William knew? James looked over at Phoebe as if to ask her, "Are you pregnant?" Phoebe returned James' gaze

107

with a reassuring shake of her head.

"What are you talking about, Fick? I have no daughter." James was beginning to get agitated. Just what the hell was William Fick's angle?

"Murdock, I want revenge. I want to take the life of your child like you took the life of mine."

Henry Murdock then moved slightly behind his father reacting to his fear that William Fick would be returning to him for revenge; however, John stood his ground. The Murdock men then heard a gasp from the direction of the house. Phoebe could no longer contain herself. She burst from the house holding a straw broom. "You'll not touch the hair of my sons' heads before I fall first!"

William turned his head around to see Phoebe approach the horse. "As enticing as that sounds that is not part of the plan. I shall kill your daughter on her sixteenth birthday just as you killed mine."

James was originally agitated, but then he began to laugh. He realized just now how crazy William Fick really was. He had gone stark raving mad.

"I don't have a daughter Fick. I never will. I have a feeling that our siring days are behind us, Phoebe and I."

"Daughter, granddaughter or a great granddaughter, it doesn't matter, Murdock. The first female flesh of your bloodline will suffer the same fate as my sweet Lorra Anne. She will die on her sixteenth birthday, and there is nothing none of you can do about it! Nothing!" He laughed again.

Fick's insane laugh resounded, reaching to the inner core of all four of the Murdock family members.

"I made a deal with the devil, Mister Murdock! Doctor Troyer himself has it all arranged. My soul for the life of the first born female from your family's bloodline. It's done, it's a sealed deal." William Fick slapped the side of his horse's neck, and it reared up, taking every bit of energy the old horse must have had left in its poor body. Both of its forelegs flailed in the air and it neighed weakly, almost sounding similar to William's horrific and maniacal laugh. The horse landed and Fick steered the animal around. As the rider and horse headed up the laneway, Fick screamed, "She will die Murdock. There is nothing you can do!"

As he rode away, Phoebe joined her family in the courtyard, and the four of them stood there and watched Fick leave. "That's the last we will see of William Fick. I just have a feeling." James concluded.

Phoebe faced her husband with a terrified look on her face. "What if what he says is true?"

James looked into the eyes of his wife as he put his hands on her shoulders. He then smiled broadly, "You can't be serious, Phoebe. He is mad."

"It's a pretty evil thing to make a deal with the swamp doctor." Henry's voice came from behind his parents.

James turned and looked down to his son. He scowled at Henry for making Phoebe possibly worry more. "Doctor Troyer is as mad as William Fick. I won't hear any more of this nonsense." James spoke to his son John as well, "From this day forward, we don't mention William Fick's name again. Understood?"

"But Father..."

"It's nonsense boys! All of what William said. God will watch over us. Now finish your chores please." With that the two boys gave their parents one last look and headed to the barn to finish up the cleaning of the horse stalls. Cora followed the boys back into the barn, her tail wagging behind her.

Phoebe's green eyes stared into those of her husband. "James, I would be a liar if I didn't say I half believe what William said. He looked so convincing."

James stroked her hair as he spoke. "Phoebe, whatever you feel you must get past it. The boys can't worry about this. Neither can you. God will protect us. Now, not another word about it. Please." James put his finger to his wife's lips. She closed her eyes and held him. He held her too, and they remained that way for several minutes. James pulled himself back and gave her a reassuring smile, "Now what's for supper!"

* * *

Hours later, the Murdock family was settling in after dinner as the sky darkened. John and Henry had scraped off the supper dishes and then rinsed them with fresh well water. They worked diligently together in the light of the single oil lamp. The boys placed the clean dishes and cutlery on a side table to air dry, and then they began to splash water on each other until their mother gave them a glare that told them they'd better stop. They decided to play some cards before it was time for bed, and John brought a deck out and sat them upon the kitchen table.

The oil lamp that illuminated the kitchen of the house also lit the main room as well. James sat in his comfortable rocking chair enjoying a pipe, staring off into space as he relaxed in the simple process of smoking. Phoebe sat across from him in a similar chair and lightly rocked. She was working away at some needlepoint, which was one of her favorite pastimes. "Don't forget to empty the water basin boys, I don't want to find a mouse floating around in it come morning."

There were some moans as the boys dragged themselves from the table. Their father cleared his throat loudly. That was the sign they'd better just do what they were asked without any more attitude.

Each boy took an end of the wash basin. Henry walked backwards as he carried his end, and he fumbled with the doorknob behind him. The door flew open and the boys worked their way onto the back porch. John and Henry stopped at the same time as they noticed the same thing. Across Castle Lake they could see a bright light that could only mean one thing, "Fire!" they shouted.

Immediately, Cora joined in and began to bark loudly. The boys quickly dumped the wooden basin and dropped it upon the porch. Henry shot back into the house just as both his parents came rushing out, wondering what all the commotion was about.

"There's a fire over at William Fick's place!"

James went across the porch and then made his way down to ground level. He walked quickly to the lake's edge. Henry and John followed their father while Phoebe stayed up on the porch. "Can you see any better down there, James?"

"Somewhat. I think it's the barn that is burning."

"Should we go over and have a look? See what we can do to help, Father?" John asked.

"Nobody is leaving this property tonight, John."

As they watched the fire, their eyes became accustomed to the darkness and the light of the fire. It was easier to see now that they had watched for several minutes. Across Castle Lake they could make out the burning barn of William Fick. It was engulfed in flames—the orange and red fingers climbing twenty or thirty feet into the air. The three Murdock men found the sight of the fire mesmerizing. Cora bounded down to where they stood, barking some more. Henry reached down and scratched her ear as he whistled, "I wonder where Mister Fick is?"

They could see that black smoke was billowing from orange squares in the side of the barn. James shared his thoughts with his sons. "I have no doubt boys; in the middle of that fire you will find Mister Fick. I do believe that he finally went totally insane."

"I hope all the animals got out okay," Henry commented. John agreed by nodding his head. They watched the fire in silence. There wasn't much else they could do.

In a matter of six months the Fick family of Castle Lake ceased to exist. A tragic series of events took the prosperous, happy family from a joyful birthday celebration to a fiery and destructive end. The burning inferno of the Fick barn confirmed that.

THOMAS A. RYERSON

Part Two—Summer, 1888

5

Introducing Alicia Ann Murdock

Alicia Ann Murdock was an average girl. She was of average height and did fairly well in school. She had auburn hair and brown eyes and didn't like to dress too fancy. Even though her parents could afford to spend more on her wardrobe, she insisted that they didn't. Of course more of her dresses could have been store-bought, but Alicia preferred to make most of her own dresses and garments in the comfort of her home with her mother at her side. Alicia was down-to-earth and very family orientated. She didn't have many friends outside of school.

However, the few friends that she did have were important to her. Alicia was anything but superficial, coming from a family that had been in the community for generations and that had solid family values. They were regular churchgoers. The family only missed the odd Sunday here and there, and that was usually due to work on the busy farm.

Alicia's parents owned and operated a very successful horse farm. Alicia hoped that God realized that running a prosperous horse and livestock farm might deny Him her family's worship of a Sunday or two.

Alicia was respected among her peers. She was always involved in class discussions and had very well-formed ideas. Many of her fellow students thought she should be a lawyer or maybe involved in the government. Even though she may have had the brains for something like that, Alicia would never have found that type of career either satisfying or challenging enough. She preferred natural challenges.

If anyone knew anything about Alicia Murdock, it was that she loved horses. She had been raised around the animals for as long as she could remember. As a toddler, she rode ponies. By age seven, she was riding the trails along Castle Lake which connected her parent's property to that of her grandparent's home.

She was very lucky to live where she did. Her family's property encircled an entire lake! Yes, for the most part Castle Lake was hers. There was an old dirt trail that led from one of the concession roads through the woods to the west shore of the lake, but that was an unofficial road. The only people that really knew about that road were fishermen, farmers, and young couples looking for a secluded place along the water to be alone.

Most of the fishermen would just enter the lake through

the opening at Carlton Bay. As it had been pointed out by many locals and scholars, Castle Lake wasn't really a lake. However, anyone who lived near the natural feature didn't seem to care that it had been misnamed generations before.

Over the years Alicia had ridden many different horses over the same trails. Being an astute equestrian, Alicia noticed that each horse always took a slightly different approach to similar trails: no two horses were the same. Some would trot in the same place where others would canter. Alicia's horse for the last several years had been a black mare named Holly. She and Holly were the best of friends. Holly was her best animal friend at least.

Alicia was also known to ride with her best human friends and their respective horses too. These human friends were the only girls outside of school with whom Alicia interacted: Wendy Birch and Marianne Myers. Wendy was a rail-thin, red-headed girl who was always close to nature. Sandy, brown-haired Marianne had her future all figured out. She was going to marry a doctor or a lawyer and have a large family.

Alicia enjoyed the times that just she and Holly rode the trails on her family's property. However, she did like to ride with Wendy and Marianne in order to talk about certain things that she did not want to discuss with her mother. One thing that Wendy and Marianne had in common was their interest in boys--a subject to which Alicia couldn't offer any insight. Alicia would often say to her two friends, "Boys mean marriage and marriage means a family. I'm not in any old hurry to have a family. There are things I want to do with my life other than make babies and cook for some man!" Alicia was definitely an independent woman; she was also a young woman who was just a month away from being sixteen—the age both Wendy and Marianne had already hit.

It was a beautiful July afternoon when she, Wendy, and Marianne decided to go riding on the trails around her property.

Alicia was in the house helping her mother clean up after lunchtime--her two brothers, Robby and Johnnie, had returned to the fields to work with their father, Russell. Alicia and her mother, Catherine, had been small-talking about this and that and hadn't heard the two girls ride up. They tethered their horses on the hitching rail beside the house. Hearing the chatter of girl's voices outside made Alicia and her mother realize that they had visitors.

Wendy and Marianne bounded up the wooden steps that led to the porch that surrounded most of the Murdock home. The sound of the girls' riding boots on the pine planks gave them away, followed by knocking at the exterior door to the kitchen. Although this wasn't the actual main entrance to the house, it was the most popular of the house's entranceways. Everyone just seemed to gravitate to the largest room in the house that also happened to serve food. Alicia was pretty sure she knew who it was at the door as she tossed aside the tea towel onto the kitchen table and answered the door.

Alicia swung the door in and smiled when she saw it

was, indeed, her two best friends. Both girls were dressed in different colored, long, divided skirts with matching blouses. Red-haired Wendy spoke first. "Alicia, are you able to go for a ride with Marianne and I? It's been so long since the three of us have ridden together."

"I have a brand new western saddle that I'm dying to break in!" added Marianne. Her sandy brown bobs of hair bounced as she talked.

Alicia looked back at her mother, who had just finishing wiping down the large kitchen table with a cloth. Catherine Murdock dropped the cloth into a wooden bucket and threw back her long brown hair over her shoulders. She looked across at her daughter and waited for the question to be asked. Her hazel eyes sparkled as she crossed her arms.

"May I go riding for an hour or two, Mother?"

Catherine gave her a warm smile. "Yes Alicia, a couple of hours will be fine, but you will have to change first."

Alicia looked herself over and realized that her mother was right. She was wearing a yellow summer dress and that just would not do for riding. There was no way she was riding side-saddle when she was with Wendy and Marianne. Alicia didn't have to worry about riding like a proper woman around her friends. Alicia invited the two girls into the house, and they closed the door behind them. They stood just inside the door.

"Come, sit down, girls. I won't bite you." Catherine joked.

"I won't even be a minute." Alicia said as she tore out of the kitchen, through the dining room, and up the main stairs to her room on the second floor. Her mother shook her head, "That wasn't very lady-like, now, was it, girls?"

Catherine rolled her eyes and smiled. "I'm sure you two are much better mannered than my heathen child. Would you girls like a cookie while you are waiting? " They both nodded their heads, and Catherine reached up for the cookie jar. She had placed it on the top shelf in hopes that it might be out of the reach of her two boys.

About ten minutes later, Alicia returned to the kitchen where her mother was chatting with her two friends. Like her friends, Alicia now wore a similar divided skirt. This way she retained the look of a lady while still being able to ride astride. She definitely did have her lady-like moments, though they were rare.

Alicia gave her mother a kiss on the cheek and then left out the door from the kitchen to the porch. Wendy and Marianne wished Catherine a good day and thanked her for the cookies they had nibbled on. The two girls followed their friend out into the courtyard of the farm. The courtyard consisted of the open area of dirt and grass between the house, the drive- sheds, and the barn complex. The porch of the house was over a hundred feet to the barn's main entrance.

The house and barns were situated within a beautiful setting. The house overlooked both Castle Lake and Carlton Bay. The barns stood majestically on the property. Other out-buildings, drive-sheds, and chicken coops stood behind the barns.

The actual front of the house faced the lake, and the rear of the house faced the concession road. It had originally been a small, one-story structure until Alicia's grandfather, Samuel, and her father, Russell, basically built a new house directly in front of the original home. The two houses were joined by a central doorway; the original house was now the large kitchen and storage rooms. Beneath that was a cold cellar. The new house was two stories high and featured a hip roof--all four sides of the roof meeting at a peak in the center. On the top of the peak was a weathervane adorned with a horse.

Alicia only knew of the house exactly the way it was right now. This was the place where she had been born and had grown up. She skipped towards the horse barn, looking over her shoulder at Wendy and Marianne. "Are we going up along the bay or around the lake?"

Marianne replied, "Let's start by going around the lake. There are some terrific trails just off the beach."

Alicia turned around like the all-knowing, "You're telling me?" She smiled and began to pull on the large red door that led into the area of the horse stalls. Alicia was facing her friends when she grabbed the handle of the door. As she opened it, she turned and screamed.

Standing in the doorway was Roddy Fellows, the Murdock's stable boy. However, Roddy wasn't actually a boy; he was forty-four years old. Roddy was as tall as a boy, standing just five-foot-two. Roddy had thinning hair, a pointy nose, and jagged and rotten teeth. He was a nasty looking little man, and

Alicia didn't like him one bit. She liked him even less when he scared her, and she was sure that he did it on purpose. Alicia Murdock was a very jumpy young lady.

"Sorry 'bout that, ma'am, I was just going for some lunch." His breath reeked.

Alicia tried to get her composure back. She had really screamed. Her two friends behind her were quiet. They wouldn't try to embarrass her in front of the hired help. That wouldn't be polite at all.

"Are you okay, Alicia?" Her mother now stood on the porch. Alicia was mortified. Her mother had heard her from inside the house.

"I'm fine, Mother, just a little fright." Alicia walked past Roddy without saying a word. He shrugged his shoulders and left the barn to go to his small apartment located by a larger drive-shed. Alicia entered the barn and turned around to face her friends. She scrunched up her face.

Wendy spoke. "He is such a creepy little man, Alicia, why does your father keep him around?"

Alicia was still catching her breath. "He used to be a jockey back when the Mayflower was new. My father thinks he is quite a treasure."

"Someone should bury him then," retorted Marianne. The three girls laughed as Alicia walked up to Holly's stall, "Holly old girl, ready for a ride?" The horse neighed and lifted its head. "She knows exactly what I am saying, don't you girl?"

Alicia crossed over to where she stored her horse's tack

and lifted Holly's bridle off a peg on the wall. She came back to the stall and opened the door. Alicia approached the horse's head and slid the bridle on. Holly stood still while Alicia got the bridle in place and adjusted it. She then got Holly turned around and led her out into the main hall of the barn.

Marianne took the reins of the bridle while Alicia went searching for her saddle and blanket. Holly was familiar with both Marianne and Wendy and had no issue with Marianne holding her reins. "Wendy, can you come and grab the blanket please?"

Wendy went around behind Holly to see Alicia struggling with a tan riding saddle. Wendy laughed at the sight and took the checkered blanket from her friend, came back to Holly's left side, and laid out the blanket across the mare's back. Alicia was right behind her and tossed the saddle quickly upon her horse. Holly jumped as she wasn't expecting that. Marianne steadied the horse, and Alicia centered the saddle. She then tied up the girth.

"I certainly prefer you two helping me over Roddy. At any time of the day, his breath stinks of gin and cider." Both Wendy and Marianne gave Alicia a knowing glance. They knew exactly what Alicia was talking about.

"Okay, saddle secured."

With that Marianne led Holly out into the courtyard, and Alicia took the reins from Marianne. Marianne and Wendy then went to their respective mounts. Marianne had a buckskin gelding named Champ and Wendy had a bay-colored mare named Molly. The girls untied their horses and instinctively looked around for any sign of men. When none were to be seen, the three girls climbed up onto their horses in a most unladylike manner.

Alicia steadied herself upon Holly and settled into the saddle. Satisfied that everything was where it should be, Alicia pointed Holly west to go around Castle Lake. Wendy and Marianne were right behind her. "I hope you know how lucky you are, Alicia Ann Murdock, to have your own lake and fantastic trails. Marianne and I are so envious."

Alicia looked back at her friends, "Envious of my parent's property? That's not right."

Marianne looked puzzled, "Not right?"

"If you are going to be envious of me for any reason, it should be for my unsurpassed riding skills." With that Alicia broke Holly out into a full gallop. Marianne and Wendy responded like-wise. Alicia rode Holly around the lake jumping over rotten logs and watching out for rabbit and gopher holes. After about twenty minutes, they approached the swamp on the north end which was near her grandparent's home. Her grandparents, Samuel and Elizabeth, lived at the opposite end of the lake from Alicia and her family. Alicia pulled back on the reins and slowed Holly right down to a walk. Marianne and Wendy came up behind her and repeated the action. Alicia led the way through the soft soil they were now approaching, "The old Murdock swamp hole. This dang thing will never dry up."

"I don't need Molly getting into that muck. I will

be brushing it out for weeks." Wendy avoided the swamp altogether and maneuvered her mount up the hill beside the moist ground.

"Let's do some exploring." Alicia suddenly turned Holly and directed her to the southwest. She bounded up the hill past Wendy and then disappeared into some pine trees just beyond. The other two girls followed, and before they knew it, they too were inside the thick of the trees. Above them the pines provided a roof over their heads as they rode among the hundreds of trees. "It can rain for all I care," laughed Marianne, "we have the perfect cover."

"Not for long. I think I see an open field ahead." Alicia burst through the trees and into the corn field. Sitting up on top of Holly, Alicia could easily see over the tall corn stalks. If she were walking, that would not have been the case. Alicia rode across the rows of corn and slowed the horse down again. She pulled hard on Holly's reins so that Holly could trot down an actual row between the corn stalks. Behind her, Alicia could hear Wendy and Marianne laughing as she slowed her horse from a canter to a trot. The thin tips of the corn stalks' leaves and the husks bounced off the sides of Holly's plump belly as they trotted along the row of corn. Once in the actual row, Alicia allowed Holly to begin to pick up her speed. Further up ahead about half a mile away, Alicia could see the tree line of another wooded lot.

Whoosh!

Before she knew it, Wendy whipped past Alicia two

rows over to her right. Molly was in a full gallop with the corn stalks taking the brunt of the speed. To her left she could hear Marianne and Champ trying to overtake her, as well. Alicia then got Holly into a full gallop. The hooves of the horses resounded off the hard ground below them.

The three girls galloped their horses through the tall green corn field. The unofficial race was on! Wendy was still in the lead; however, Alicia was gaining.

Then suddenly the trees of the next forest were in front of them, and the girls burst back into the pines. The long needle-like branches of the trees scraped the arms of the girls as they went deeper into the wood. Wendy was well ahead when both Alicia and Marianne heard her scream.

Ahead they could see Wendy's horse, Molly, suddenly lurch to the right and lose a step. Both Alicia and Marianne thought Wendy was going down, but just like the two of them, she was an experienced rider. Wendy was able to keep Molly moving forward, slowing the horse down to a walk before pulling the horse to a stop. By that time Alicia and Marianne had caught up to her. Wendy slid off her horse, and she immediately examined Molly's fetlock.

"Some of the hair just above Molly's hoof has been scraped off." Both Alicia and Marianne had dismounted and were approaching Wendy.

"What did Molly catch herself on?" asked Marianne. Both girls looked at the area of the horse's leg that Wendy was examining. The skin had been scrapped off and was bleeding lightly. "It doesn't look terribly serious. I guess I will know when I ride her home whether she limps or not."

Alicia looked back from where they had just come. "Let's retrace your steps, Wendy, and see what could have caught Molly's leg." The girls took their horses by the reins and walked slowly back to where Wendy thought Molly had originally stumbled. They had walked about twenty-five feet when Alicia gasped, "A gravestone!"

"A what?" exclaimed Marianne.

"Why would a gravestone be out here in the woods? Did Molly trip on its edge?"

Alicia answered Wendy. "No, it wasn't the stone. Look here. There is a wire fence that goes around the grave. Molly must have tripped on the wire. It's pulled out at this corner."

"It looks really old," commented Marianne.

The girls hadn't noticed the gravestone initially because there was a tree directly behind it. Alicia circled around the tree to look at the front of the stone. It was a very weathered and grey in colour. The texture of the "stone" looked very strange, so Alicia tapped on it, expecting it to be hard. It was hard in a way, but not like stone. Alicia then figured out the composition of the marker, "It's made of wood. Funny it isn't all rotten."

Four short wooden posts marked out the four corners of the grave. They stood about a foot and a half high. Wire had been wrapped around the four posts like a fence. The stone had been well protected within the pine trees. Alicia could read the marker with just a little difficulty. Wendy and Marianne stood on either side of Alicia as she read aloud.

"Lillian Kane Fick—Born May 19th 1784," Alicia was very business-like as she read the first part. Then both of her friends gasped as Alicia read the rest of the marker, no longer so self-assured, "Who took her own life in Castle Lake— March 15th 1822."

"Good God," Wendy swore.

"You seem to have a dead person buried on your property, Alicia Murdock." Marianne plainly stated.

Alicia stepped back from the marker. "She's been gone a long time, Marianne. Over sixty years. What do you supposed is left of her down there?"

"Just dust and bones," said Wendy sounding like an expert on the subject.

"For sure her teeth are still in the old pine box," Marianne spoke almost romantically.

"Do you think your parents know about this Alicia?"

"I have no idea, Wendy. I had absolutely no clue there was a woman buried here in the first place. Not only that, she killed herself in my lake."

"It wasn't your lake in 1822, Alicia. You weren't even thought of."

"I suppose your right, Marianne. That was a long time ago wasn't it? It had to be a very cold lake in March. What would possess a woman to do that?"

"Maybe her horse died," said Wendy in a rather deadpan

tone. She went back to examine Molly's wound again. She wanted to reassure herself that it wasn't too serious.

"It had to be something really bad. People just don't kill themselves for no reason."

Alicia stuck her forefinger in her mouth. She always did this when she was heavily in thought. "Wow. I don't know what more to say. You certainly stumbled onto something very interesting, Wendy."

"We should get back, Alicia, I want to get Molly's wound looked at. I don't want it to get infected or something."

"All right, Wendy, we'll go back. I'll come out here tomorrow with my father and maybe my brothers, too."

Marianne laughed. "Your brothers? Robby and Johnnie will want to dig that poor lady up hoping to find some sort of bounty!"

"You're probably right." Alicia laughed. She gave it some very serious thought. "I will tell my father and mother at the very least."

Alicia and Marianne helped Wendy back up onto Molly. They didn't want to stress the horse's leg any more than it already had been. The remaining two girls mounted their respective horses, and they headed back around to the cornfield. This time they rode slowly so that Molly could take it easy. Once they were back into the corn stalks, Alicia had an idea. "Let's ride this particular row of corn back to my house; then we will know how exactly to return here."

Both Wendy and Marianne thought that was a good idea.

131

They rode the long row of corn quietly back to the Murdock farm, each girl thinking about what they had just discovered. The row of corn ended at the most southern tip of Castle Lake. A small stand of trees stood between the corn field and the lake shore.

Alicia made a mental note of where she needed to catch the row of corn to return back to the gravesite. The girls rode out of the wooded area and had the horses trot to the water's edge. The dock was nearby. "I'll bet this is where Lillian Kane Fick drowned herself," Alicia said solemnly. It was only about five hundred feet or so from this point to the door of the house. Alicia shuddered.

She said goodbye to her two friends and then returned Holly to her stall. Alicia took the saddle and blanket off Holly and placed them back into the tack box. She then removed Holly's bridle and hooked it on a peg above the tack barrel. Alicia shut the barn door behind her and went into the house.

It was like her mother hadn't even moved in the hour or so that Alicia had been gone with her friends. Catherine was in the same place, except this time she was busily cutting up vegetables on the dark plank kitchen table. As Alicia removed her riding boots, Catherine wiped her hands on a towel and picked up a metal serving tray. She turned towards the kitchen counter. As she did so, Catherine could sense that something was troubling her daughter. "What is it, Alicia?"

Alicia thought for a moment. "We found something out in the woods, Mother, something I never expected to find. It was very strange."

Catherine wanted to make a joke, make light of her daughter's serious mood, but at the same time Catherine could see that something had visibly upset her eldest child. She stopped halfway between the counter and the table. "What did you find Alicia?"

Alicia answered the question with a question. "Have you ever heard of a Lillian Kane Fick?"

Catherine gave the question careful thought. She then shook her head in a "No" motion and replied, "No, Alicia, I have never heard that name before. Who is she?"

"I don't know who she is, Mother, but I do know that she is buried out in our woods."

Crash!

Catherine dropped the metal serving tray she had held in her hands. The thin steel echoed loudly off the oak floorboards. "Someone is buried on our property, Alicia?" Right away Alicia was confident that this was also a new fact to her mother. Catherine almost fell into one of the hard wooden kitchen chairs. "How do you know? What did you see?"

Alicia scurried over to the kitchen table and pulled up a chair beside her mother. She placed a hand on that of her mother's. "It goes back a quite a long time, Mother. The grave marker says that Lillian died in 1822."

Catherine looked relieved until Alicia added. "The marker also says that this woman took her own life right out there in the lake. How is it we never knew about this?"

"The stone says that, Alicia?"

Alicia nodded her head. "Yes, Mother. It says that Lillian took her own life in Castle Lake. And it's not even a stone. It's made from wood. I don't know how it has survived all of this time. Marianne and Wendy..."

"Marianne and Wendy know too?" Her mother sounded mortified.

Alicia squeezed her mother's hand again. "It happened a long time ago, Mother. Wendy actually found it. Her horse, Molly, tripped on a low wire fence that had surrounded the marker for over sixty years. The woman's death happened before even you were born." Alicia tried to look reassuring. Catherine then burst out laughing.

"Alicia. This happened even before my mother was born."

"You know what I mean, Mother." Alicia smiled. She was just trying to make her mother feel a little safer, to reassure her that this wasn't an event that had just recently occurred. Some woman didn't drown herself just outside the door of their house and was then buried in their woods out by their cornfield.

Catherine squeezed her daughter's hand in return. She stood up. "How is it, Alicia, that we have never come across this before?"

"I was actually going to ask you and father the same thing," Alicia shrugged her shoulders as she spoke. "I suppose we've just never been in that part of the woods before. The marker is partly hidden by a pine tree. It seems to be a very strange place to have buried a person, but maybe that was the point."

"What was the point, Alicia?" Catherine spoke as she rubbed the side of her cheek. It was a nervous habit that she had.

"Maybe the grave wasn't supposed to be found. Maybe it was a terrible secret."

"Well, I can't imagine that it was foul play, or there wouldn't be such a marker there. Doesn't that sound reasonable?"

"Yes, Mother. That part makes sense. If it was foul play, there definitely wouldn't be such a descriptive grave marker." Alicia repeated her mother's action and rubbed the side of her own cheek.

"I found it strange that the marker said how Lillian Kane Fick died. Almost like whoever buried her wanted the world to know this lady took her own life. I know that things like this can happen, but certainly not so close to home."

Catherine wanted to steer the topic away from suicide. She brushed her apron with her hands and gave Alicia a pitiful look. "Well, Alicia Ann, we need to make supper, and I seriously need your help. We will tell your father all about your find when he gets home, and we will go from there."

Alicia gave her mother a smile and then walked over to her. She then treated her mother to a hug. "To what do I owe this honor? I thought Alicia Murdock was too old now for hugs."

"I make exceptions for you, Mother," Alicia said with a

big loving smile that only a daughter could give her mother. Alicia bent down and picked up the metal serving tray that her mother had dropped.

* * *

Hours later after supper, Alicia decided to go for a little walk. She gave her parents each a kiss and then left the house out the side door of the kitchen. Her yellow Labrador retriever came up the steps of the porch and licked her fingers.

"That tickles, Brewster! I don't think you'll like the taste of homemade soap." Alicia spoke to her canine companion of many years. Brewster continued to lick her fingers anyway.

Brewster had been in Alicia's life forever. She was only a year or two old when the dog was born. Brewster's coat was a combination of cream with yellow highlights. He was a beautiful dog. He barked and Alicia laughed, "Let's go look for fossils, Brewster, shall we?"

With that the dog bounded down the porch steps and towards the lake. Alicia remained on the porch and followed it around to the side of the house that faced the lake. She walked by the main door of the house, which was rarely used. It was a fancy multi-paned glass affair with a wooden frame made from oak. Alicia walked down the wide steps of the porch and out onto the lawn. She crossed over the well-manicured grass and made her way to a gravel path that led down to the edge of the lake.

As she walked down to the dock, the gravel pathway that led to the lake became a little wider. The shore of the lake consisted of small rounded stones of many colors. Alicia continued down the slope to the lake, where Brewster had already reached. His huge, pink tongue hung out of his mouth as he stood on the rocks of the shore. Brewster loved the water. He turned his head back to see Alicia coming along, so he jumped into the calm lake and began to swim out.

"Brewster!" Alicia called out to him. But it was no use. Brewster was thirty feet out in the water already. As Alicia went to walk up on the dock, she accidentally tripped upon the ground. She quickly regained her balance and looked down to see what she had stumbled on. It turned out to be a simple piece of driftwood. The piece of wood was about eight inches long and two inches thick. Picking up the wood, she yelled out Brewster's name again. He stopped out in the lake and paddled around to face her.

Alicia jumped up upon the dock and walked to the end of it. She then wound up her arm and threw the piece of driftwood as far and as hard as she could. The piece of wood landed about halfway between her and the dog. Brewster's interest had been peaked, so he started to make his way back towards her to see what Alicia had thrown. Alicia laughed and called out for him again. She watched as Brewster dogpaddled closer and closer to the driftwood. Before she knew it, Brewster had scooped it up in his mouth. He was bringing the prize back to Alicia, who was delighted. "Good boy, Brewster, Good boy!"

Brewster swam toward shore with the wood in his mouth, and when he finally got into shallow water, Alicia smiled as she watched him paddle toward her. She jumped off the dock and back onto the stone covered beach, but as Brewster got closer to Alicia, the wood began to look a little strange. It was longer than she remembered and much narrower. It was also whiter than she recalled. Brewster, now out of the shallow water trotted proudly towards Alicia. She bent over and held out her hand. Brewster then dropped the wood into her hand and suddenly began to shake all of his fur free of the lake water. Alicia put her hand up to protect herself and fell on her bottom in the process. She laughed as Brewster continued to shake. As she laughed, Alicia picked up and examined the wood Brewster had brought back to her. However, it was not the same wood she had thrown into the lake. It wasn't actually wood, either!

She was holding a bone. The bone of a skeletal arm and hand which had been broken off at the elbow. Suddenly the fingers and thumb of the skeleton hand began to bend all on their own, seemingly trying to grab Alicia's own hand. She instantly threw the bony hand away from her and watched in horror as it fell onto the gravel of the lakeshore.

Brewster looked proud of himself. His pink tongue still hung out of his mouth. Alicia could swear that he was smiling. Did dogs actually smile? Brewster wanted to be petted, but Alicia was still in shock. Brewster didn't seem to care or realize that he had brought her back a hand instead of a piece of driftwood. Then Brewster was gone.

She looked all around her, and he was nowhere to be seen. Or was that him back out in the water? Alicia could just make out a shape which was about the right size of Brewster's head. Alicia stood up from where she had fallen and called out the dog's name. She brushed away any dirt that may have stuck to her bottom from when she fell. As she did so, she looked down to where she had thrown the hand and realized that it too had now disappeared.

Her attention returned to the shape in the water. It was getting closer and closer to Alicia, but it wasn't a dog at all. The shape was human which she could clearly see as it got closer and the head, shoulders and torso emerged from the lake. Then Alicia realized it was a woman wearing a grey dress which was in shreds. Her face was grey, eyes sunken in. Seaweed crowned her head and hung from her shoulders.

Alicia tried to move but she couldn't. She was stuck. The woman was now right in front of her. Alicia's two feet were cemented to the bright colored stones of the lakeshore. Castle Lake had turned against Alicia Murdock. The grey woman's arm rose from the side of her body and pointed at Alicia. The arm was missing everything from the elbow down. Alicia figured maybe if she returned the hand back to the grey lady, she wouldn't hurt her. The dead lady from the lake would hopefully forgive Alicia for taking her bony arm in the first place.

Why did she assume the lady before her was dead? Was it

because her skin and clothing were grey, and she was mostly a skeleton? Fear swept across Alicia as she bent down and tried to locate the hand. Where was it? It had to be there; it just had to be!

Alicia used both of her hands as she waded into the cold water. She didn't even realize that she was now able to move from where she had stood before. Alicia kept walking, unaware that she was getting deeper and deeper into the lake which was so cold, way too cold for this time of year. It was freezing. Alicia was up to her waist now, searching for the hand. She looked up from her search and suddenly there was the face of the grey lady again.

It was a face with no face. Where her eyes had been were now only empty sockets from which water poured out. The nose was just two holes with a disgusting membrane over them. The membrane sucked in and out as the grey lady breathed. Then the mouth of the grey lady opened to reveal all her rotting black teeth. When the grey lady's mouth opened Alicia heard Brewster bark. Brewster!

Alicia turned her head to try and find Brewster. As she turned her head back towards the grey lady, she could feel a hand on her head. Suddenly, Alicia's head was being forced underneath the freezing water of the lake.

Weird. The water under the surface was very clear, and Alicia could see the skeletal legs of the grey lady. Alicia could now see Brewster, except now Brewster had become a skeletal dog. Alicia realized that she could no longer breathe. Her lungs were just about to explode, and skeletal Brewster wagged his skeleton tail. Alicia's head remained trapped under the water.

Alicia tried to scream, but as she did, the water entered her mouth and flowed down into her lungs. She could feel her lungs fill up with freezing water and explode. The last thing she saw was the skeleton dog and the grey lady covered in seaweed.

Alicia suddenly woke up in a cold sweat. She pushed herself up from her sleeping position as though she were drowning. However, Alicia wasn't drowning. She was safely in her bed with her down-filled comforter wrapped around her waist. The summer moonlight streamed in through her window, its white fingers stretched out across her blankets and the floorboards of her room.

It had been a nightmare--a terrible, awful nightmare. Alicia was foggy. Her head was thick from sleep. Her mind still whizzed from the scary and realistic dream. As she came around from her slumber, Alicia then realized an awful fact: her dog, Brewster, had been dead for over six months. What made her think of Brewster out of the blue like that? "Be rational, Alicia Murdock," she thought to herself. Alicia figured the dream was a combination of her adventure earlier that day with Wendy and Marianne as well as finally dealing with the loss of Brewster. It was the first dream of Brewster that she had recalled.

Alicia lay back down on her bed and pulled the down comforter up to her chin. It was summer, but it was, however, a very cool evening. She stared up at her ceiling. How she did miss Brewster. What a strange dream and it had seemed so real. Alicia was sure that she was drowning. She had the sensation of being pulled under water by that dead woman. A dead woman she had never and would never meet.

At least that's all it was, a dream. For Alicia Murdock did not believe in ghosts. Ghosts were not sensible nor did they have a place in the real world. Alicia was no longer a kid either. In fact, in just over four week's time she would be sixteen!

6

August 8, 1888: A prelude to a sweet sixteen

"Alicia Ann!" Catherine Murdock stood on the porch in front of the main entranceway of the house. She had her hands on the railing for support as she shouted for her daughter. Then Catherine thought she would try a different tactic. She leaned forward, her waist pressed against the railing, and cupping her hands around her mouth, she yelled a little louder, "Alicia Ann. It's supper time!" There was some movement down on the dock. Yes, that seemed to be the form of Alicia down there. Alicia could never get enough of the outdoors or of Castle Lake.

Alicia's slender arm reached up and waved back to her mother. Catherine returned the wave and was satisfied that her daughter had heard her. She turned around and headed back into the house through the multi-paned, glass front door.

Catherine could just imagine Alicia laying down there on the dock with her head propped up with a hand as she held a book with the other. Catherine closed the door behind her and walked down the main hallway to a connecting hall that led to the kitchen through the dining room.

Since the house had been expanded almost twenty years before, the kitchen was very spacious and welcoming. Cooking for her family here was a pleasure. The centerpiece of the kitchen was the black cast-iron cooking stove which had a large oven in the center and two smaller ovens on either side. Catherine could have a roast cooking in the main oven, bread in one of the smaller ovens, and buns yet in another. On top of the stove were six burners. They were removable round plates that could be taken off to allow the direct heat of the wood stove on the pot or pan. Catherine could feed her entire family from this stove. And there was enough of a family to do that with the extended Murdock clan, which included her husband Russell's parents, Samuel and Elizabeth Murdock, who lived across the lake. Samuel's younger brother, James, lived with them, as did their father, John Murdock. John was eighty-one years old this year and was Russell's grandfather. The Murdock family had lived by Castle Lake for generations.

Catherine knew that any time she was either near the stove or thinking about supper her two sons would always appear out of nowhere. Today was no exception. "What's for supper, Mother, I'm starved."

Catherine turned her head to the large doorway that led from the dining room, and standing there was her fourteen-year-old son, Robby. Right behind Robby was eleven-year-old

Johnnie. Both boys had light sandy-colored hair; although Robby's was a little longer and darker at the roots. Robby parted his hair in the center and slicked it back, while Johnnie kept his closely cropped. "Something smells good in here," Johnnie said, speaking to no one in particular.

Both boys were dressed in similar canvas trousers with red cotton suspenders and cotton blue and white checkered short sleeve shirts. Even though they were three years difference in age, their clothes were similar because Johnnie was given all of Robby's hand-me-downs. Johnnie didn't care because, to him, clothes were just clothes, and it didn't really matter where they came from. Of course, unless they were Alicia's hand-me-downs.

"You two smell like the barn! A combination of cows, pigs, and chickens. Maybe you should wash up before you help me."

"I don't smell like no chicken, Mother." Robby said defensively.

"You do smell like an ol' piggie, though," laughed his brother while pointing.

"Actually, I don't smell nuthin' but home cookin'," Johnnie replied with a smile.

"You don't smell *anything* but home *cooking*," corrected Robby's sister. Alicia entered the kitchen through the side door. She was carrying a well-worn book under one arm. The door clicked shut behind her. "And I certainly smell something! I smell two boys who have been either working hard or playing

145

harder in the barn. And I have a feeling you were playing."

"What do you know? You're a girl! Everybody knows boys do all the real work," Robby spoke with mock-authority.

"Everybody? Would you like to plan and cook supper young man?" His mother put her hands on her hips and softly smiled. "You don't think making supper for this brood is real work?" She held her hands out in front of her to imply she was referring to Robby and his brother.

Robby made a face as his mother turned. "Come on Johnnie. Let's wash up before we have to cook or something worse."

The boys left through a back door to the porch. This door was at the side of the house which faced the concession road. They turned and went down the steps to where the well water pump was located. A very workable hand pump was at the sink in the kitchen, but, obviously, the boys didn't want to wash up under the critical eyes of their mother and sister.

Alicia walked over to a side table in the kitchen and put her book down. She stretched her arms, pointing them towards the ceiling, and turned to face her mother. "I fell asleep down there while I was reading."

"Must be a very interesting book," her mother joked.

Alicia missed the punch-line. "It's a school textbook. I want to get caught up before I go back."

"You should enjoy your summer, Alicia. It might be your last." Alicia gave her mother a strange look. Catherine understood and laughed. "I meant that you will be going back to school for another year, and then after that, you will probably work for a spell and then marry."

"I won't be marrying any time soon, Mother. I was put on this earth to do more than make babies."

Her mother gave her a knowing look. They had this same conversation many times before. "Is that all I am to you, Alicia Ann Murdock? Just a baby-making machine?"

"No, Mother." Alicia rolled her eyes and put her own hands on her slender hips. "You know what I mean. A young woman has so many more opportunities these days than when you were my age. I want to live some life before I settle down."

Catherine chuckled at her daughter. "You know so much don't you, Alicia. I sometimes wonder about you getting too much school and knowledge."

"I never get too much school or too much riding, for that matter. Maybe I could open a horse riding school for ladies. I'll bet there would be a call for that. Then I would have the best of both worlds."

"There's no money in either," a male voice boomed from behind. Both women glanced over to see Russell Murdock enter the room from the dining room. He had a newspaper rolled up in one hand. Alicia came by her bookish tastes honestly. They were from her father; there was no doubt in that. Alicia's father gave both of the women in his life a broad smile. He then walked up to the stove in the center of the kitchen. "What's for supper? Something sure smells good."

"Just like a man," Catherine sighed.

Like his daughter, Russell also had a scholarly look about

him. He did not give the impression of being a farmer or a horse trainer. Russell stood just under six feet in height and was of a medium build. He had a strong looking chin that gave him a confident air. When he laughed, Russell's bushy, dark brown hair shook to and fro with his head. As well, he sported a well-trimmed moustache. He also wore glasses, which were perched toward the tip of his nose, and he looked over them as he spoke.

His arms were muscular, a result of working on a livestock farm his entire life. Russell walked over to the side table where Alicia had placed her book. He set the newspaper beside the book and then picked up the book. "*Geometry for Beginners,* that sounds really nice and dry. Does it taste like a soda biscuit?"

Alicia rolled her eyes, "Believe me, it is dry. But I can't imagine it would taste very good." As she talked, she pushed her shoulder-length, auburn colored hair behind her shoulders. Alicia's hair had a lot of body as a result of her constant brushing. Her father would kid her that she brushed her own hair more than that of her horses. Alicia liked to look her best, which Russell also teased her about, saying that her favorite subject in school was herself. Alicia insisted that if she were being vain it was not for the attraction of the opposite sex. Any vanity she had, she hoped was a deterrent to ward off boys. Alicia had no interest in boys other than as platonic friends. She would say that again and again. Her parents had to admit that from the way she acted, Alicia was probably right.

"Come on, Alicia. Let's see what we can rustle up for our hungry men. Wash up, please."

Alicia dragged her feet as she walked from where her book lay to the kitchen's hand pump by the small wooden wash basin, located in front of a window in the kitchen. Through the window, she could see her two brothers at the outdoor pump. They each had a wooden bucket and were splashing each other with the fresh well water. Alicia rolled her eyes. She pumped the handle of the indoor pump until the water began to flow and poured an inch or two into the basin. Alicia rubbed the oddly-shaped bar of homemade soap and stabbed her hands into the cold water of the basin. Content that her hands were clean, Alicia dried them on an over-sized grey and white tea towel that lay beside the basin. Underneath the counter that supported the basin, Alicia found her cooking apron. She stepped back and flung it open and tied it around her waist, facing her mother.

"Let's do what women do best, Mother. Let's cook for the Murdock men."

Catherine shook her head and rolled her eyes. "Alicia, you are certainly going to be a challenge for some young man one day."

"Well, Mother, someday can take its sweet time getting here."

* * *

The fluffy little ball of fur yelped several times. Catherine cooed to the little dog and tried to settle it down. It was going to be a great surprise.

"Russell, do you want to go and wake Alicia. I won't be able to keep this little guy quiet much longer."

Russell gave his wife a smirk. He rounded the corner and shot up the wide flight of stairs to the second floor of the house.

Several moments later, Alicia came around the same corner and entered the dining room. Alicia was still wearing her night clothes. She looked groggy and was wiping away "sleep" particles from her eyes. "Father said that you wanted to speak with me?"

"Actually, I didn't Alicia, but this little critter did." Catherine lifted her apron up to reveal a black-and-tan Welsh terrier that was sitting in her lap. The little pup began to yelp when it saw Alicia.

"He's mine?" Her eyes danced with excitement.

Her father came into the dining room just as Alicia asked her question. "It's the least we can do when we wake you up early on a Thursday morning," Russell said to his daughter.

"I know he's an early present, Alicia, but the Hammonds said they wanted the little guy picked up by this morning. It was the last pup of the litter to go."

"This is the best present ever, Mother!" Alicia was suddenly very excited. A broad smile covered her face, and she gave her mother a toothy grin. Alicia forgot all about being a young lady as she fell completely in love with the pup. Alicia wouldn't be sixteen for a couple days but didn't mind the gift was early since it was a new puppy.

"Was he the runt of the litter?" Alicia picked the puppy out of her mother's lap and sat herself upon one of the comfortably padded chairs that surrounded the dining room table.

"I have no idea, Alicia." replied her mother. "He was the last one in the box. He is a wee thing though, isn't he?"

"He'll grow big and strong soon enough, Mother." Alicia cradled the puppy on her lap and bent over to kiss his little pink nose. As she did so, her tussled hair fell forward and into the pup's face. Automatically, the pup began to chew on her hair. "Look, Mother, he likes me!"

"Well, he likes your hair at least." Russell watched his daughter revel in the excitement of receiving the early and furry birthday gift. The pup's little pink tongue darted in and out of his mouth as he tried to chew her hair. Alicia moved her finger over to the pup's mouth and brushed her hair away from his busy and sharp teeth. Alicia rubbed the tip of the pup's wet nose.

Alicia then saw some movement in the dining room doorway and looked up. Both Johnnie and Robby had just entered, lured awake by the smell of bacon that wafted in from the adjoining kitchen. At the same time, the pup suddenly seemed to pick up the scent.

"No fair! Why does Alicia get a puppy?" Johnnie rubbed his eyes as he tried to wake himself up.

"Johnnie, you are aware that your sister will be sixteen

in three days?" Russell couldn't believe that Johnnie would forget his sister's birthday.

"Oh yeah. Happy birthday, Alicia. What's cooking? I'm so hungry I could eat a horse."

"I am definitely not serving you horse, John Henry Murdock. You get fresh cooked bacon like the rest of us."

"Charlie too? Does he get bacon?"

Her parents, as well as Johnnie and Robby, all looked at Alicia and in unison replied, "Charlie?"

The puppy looked directly at Alicia and cocked its head. His ear fell to the side. "He likes 'Charlie'! See how well he responds to the name."

"Why Charlie?" her father was almost afraid to ask.

Alicia looked up at her father as the puppy played on her lap, "No reason, really. He just looks like a Charlie."

"He's no Brewster that's for sure," stated Robby.

"Brewster would have eaten Charlie for breakfast. Never mind the horse."

"Johnnie. Robby. That is enough. Are you trying to hurt Alicia's feelings?" Russell gave each of the boys a playful whack on the back of their heads. He seemed to smack Robby a little harder than he did Johnnie.

"Hey now. What was that for?" Robby questioned.

"Robert Samuel Murdock," his father began, "I don't think it's fair of you to compare Charlie with Brewster. We had Brewster for almost fifteen years. You have to give little Charlie here a chance."

"All I'm just saying is he's no Brewster and he's not. Ouch!" Russell gave his son another swat on the back of the head.

"The puppy isn't replacing Brewster," Catherine stated. "He's a different dog altogether. We just know how much Alicia likes animals."

"Yes, she likes you two monkeys well enough." Russell laughed as he spoke to his sons.

"I suppose he is kinda cute. Can I have a puppy on my birthday?"

"One puppy and one birthday at a time, Robby. Let's go see how that bacon is doing."

"It smells pretty good to me, Mother."

"Like boys have any sense of taste." Alicia rolled her eyes at her two brothers as they left the dining room and followed their mother into the kitchen. Charlie suddenly leapt from Alicia's lap and fell into a ball of fur on the hard floor. He scrambled up quick enough and scurried into the kitchen where all the good smells seemed to be coming from.

"Looks like the kitchen is the place to be, Alicia," Russell pursed his lips and put an arm around his daughter. "It's not too soon for a new dog, is it? We thought since you were having some bad dreams recently about Brewster, maybe a new puppy would help you through it." Russell gave his daughter a concerned fatherly look.

"I can see this puppy is going to need some training." Catherine's voice carried out from the kitchen.

Alicia jumped up from her comfortable chair and headed

into the kitchen. Russell followed so that all five Murdocks and the tan and black ball of scraggly fur were all in the kitchen. The pup was jumping up on Catherine's legs as she turned the bacon in the large frying pan.

"Charlie! Bad puppy."

"I'm sure we are going to be hearing that a lot for the next little while."

"Don't worry, Father, I will get him trained. If I can train a horse, I can train a puppy."

"Time will tell," her mother laughed. "Now, someone head outside and fetch some eggs. It's time for the Murdock bunch to get serious with breakfast."

"Come on, Charlie. Let's go visit the hen house." Alicia glanced over to her mother who was giving her one of those "looks." Alicia quickly added, "Once we get properly dressed, of course." With that Alicia scooped up the puppy and headed up to her room to dress.

* * *

Later that evening, Alicia lay on her bed and watched Charlie sleep. He was curled into a ball like a kitten. She poked at the puppy now and again, waking him up. She would then cease so that he could fall asleep again. Alicia giggled to herself as the puppy repeatedly got himself comfortable after being awakened. He was too little to get mad; he would just make the best of it and go back to sleep.

154

Alicia was unaware that her mother had stopped at her open doorway and decided to watch her mischievous daughter as she teased the poor puppy. After about ten minutes, Catherine spoke up.

"How would you like it if a big puppy kept poking at you and woke you up when you were trying to have a nap?" She smiled so that Alicia knew she wasn't too serious.

Alicia rolled over to face her mother. "He's had a hard afternoon of playing. I want to make sure he sleeps through the night."

"Probably wouldn't hurt to have some newspapers on the floor in case the little guy has to go during the night. Just make sure it's one your father has already read."

Alicia had to laugh. "I know. If Charlie ever soiled an unread paper, it might spell the end of him!"

Catherine picked at the paint in the doorframe. She glanced over at the sleeping puppy and then Alicia. "It's probably a little late to ask, Alicia, but did you have any kind of party in mind for your birthday?"

Alicia gave it some thought, twisting her fingers in the down-filled comforter. "I don't think that I want a traditional party, Mother. Maybe have Marianne and Wendy over for a little bit but no cake and streamers. I think I'm getting a little old for that childlike stuff."

A big smile grew across Catherine's face, and her hazel eyes sparkled in the light of Alicia's oil lamp. "Childlike stuff, eh, Alicia. Obviously, you weren't down in the dining room when this little chap over here made his debut. You want to talk childlike...It's your sixteenth birthday, Alicia, and it's snuck up on your father and I. We should have planned ahead better."

Alicia gave her mother a smile that defied her young age. She was a sharp girl. "I'm good, Mother. I don't need a big party. I don't need to impress anyone."

Catherine was impressed by her daughter. The maturity she could show at such a young age. "Don't stay up too late, Alicia. I'll see you in the morning. Good night."

"Good night, Mother." Alicia then climbed out of her bed and walked across the cold, hardwood floor. She gave her mother a tight hug and then returned to her warm bed and comforter. "I think there is a new ice age coming, Mother! It's cold out!"

Catherine smiled and closed the door to Alicia's room. She walked across the hall and into the master bedroom. Russell was already on his side of the bed, deeply engrossed reading the paper. Catherine reflected as she got ready for bed herself. Having children certainly did have its rewarding moments. Her daughter's hug on a cool evening was certainly one of them.

Part 3—August 11, 1888

7

Apparition rising

The gravestones at the Roulston community church cemetery were not very well-tended these days. Even more so for the gravestones which were located at the back of the cemetery grounds, which were some of the oldest in the cemetery. Some of the gravestones were actually wooden markers that had tin name plates nailed to them. Many of these old types of wooden markers were half-rotted with the tin so rusted they could barely be read. Not too many people made their way over to this area of the cemetery anymore. While the newer parts of the cemetery expanded a little more each year, the older area just seemed to continue to decay. The only visitors to the old section seemed to be dogs looking to relieve themselves and revel in the odors left by previous animals. The gravestones at least served some sort of community service.

The gravestones that really stood the test of time

were the ones made from granite, which were the most expensive. Gravestones made of marble also wore well over time. The white sandstone markers along the rear fence line of the cemetery, though better than the wooden ones, did not stand up very well.

In the far rear corner of the churchyard cemetery were two very old sandstone markers. Both gravestones had sunken several inches into the ground over the years. One could no longer read that one of the stones had been manufactured by Richard E. Douglas. The gravestone next to it had tilted to one side. Years of punishing weather had taken their toll on these two gravestones until it was just about impossible to read what had been inscribed into them. If a person were very patient and used a finger to trace over the aged words, this is what the older of the two gravestones read:

Lorra A. Fick
1805-1821
Beloved daughter of
William and Lillian Fick

The newer gravestone simply read:

W. Fick
died 1822
aged 40

Moonlight streamed across the hundreds of gravestones in the cemetery. A light breeze stirred across the tops of the trees that lined the fence and also dotted the cemetery property. The waving branches of the pines and poplar trees created eerie shadows across the stones and wooden markers. A racoon, a skunk, and a badger poked in and around the various stones, each unaware of each other perhaps, but not unaware of something strange and unearthly that was beginning to occur. All three animals stopped their respective poking and began to listen. Their ears quivered and then, without any warning, each of them tore out of the cemetery—back to the safety of their individual lairs.

The three animals had all sensed the same thing. At exactly 12:01 a.m. something began to happen over one grave in the cemetery. It was almost as though a timer had gone off that set something in motion. Something sinister. Evil. Something or someone had predestined this unearthly happening. Sixty-six years before, the clock was set. A deal was a deal, after all.

A dark and ominous fog-like shape began to rise above the area directly in front of the gravestone that belonged to "W. Fick." The shape expanded and grew to the full length of the grave and was about seven inches thick--about the size and shape of a coffin. The shape began to change form—the shifting mist took the form of...a man! This entity—this fog-like spirit that was William Fick—hovered over the grave for several minutes as if it were trying to get its bearings.

Then it slowly began to move, floating directly over the

grave next to the one from which it had come. Hovering over the grave of Lorra Anne Fick for several moments, it began to move slowly—and then faster and faster—until it floated out of the cemetery's old section. The spirit did not fully understand its connection to Lorra Anne Fick as it floated across the cemetery grounds.

It weaved in and around the granite, marble, sandstone, and wooden grave-markers and approached the stone foundation wall of the church building. William's spirit changed course and floated along the edge of the foundation wall and along the path from the church out to the concession road, and the more it moved it began to gain the power of reasoning. It began to think! The first thing it wondered was if it had the ability to actually float through the foundation wall. William Fick would have to test that possibility out at some point.

William's spirit sensed that he definitely had a purpose. Like his internal timing mechanism, he also seemed to possess primitive navigational instincts, like migratory birds flying to some innately sensed destination. He knew where he had to be. He crossed the concession road and continued beyond the road and over the field, moving south. William's spirit crossed over several fields full of various crops and some more concession roads as well. He wandered through several residential properties, investigating whatever he came across. Although time was not a factor in its meanderings, William's spirit definitely had an objective.

He had been traveling for over an hour when he recognized

the landscape that he was now passing over. Floating along the ground and between the rails of a fence made from logs, he came upon a barn complex—a group of smaller barn buildings built around a large barn. The large barn looked familiar, but at the same time it didn't.

William's spirit floated across the courtyard of the farm and closer to the house situated there. He thought, too, that he recognized the house, particularly the front. Making his way back to the stone foundation wall of the large barn, William's spirit took a deep breath and then passed through the stone wall. He felt nothing. As he effortlessly made his way into the main floor area of the barn, he realized that he had just passed through solid rock.

William Fick's spirit rationalized that he needed to enter into one of the animals in the barn. He needed to do this to complete his task. Trapped for so many years beneath the ground, now he had the freedom to do whatever he wanted. But he knew that he was not a free spirit; he had an inner nagging sense of purpose—a sensation of the need to complete a mission.

Because of his mission and his sense of purpose, William's spirit understood he had to have an actual body. He had to have a living form in order to do what he had to do. He decided that the best thing to do was float around the barn until he could possess a proper host. Entering into an animal seemed like the obvious place to start. William's spirit was thinking and rationalizing more. He knew that he had to be responsible for a death, and he was to cause the death in a most horrible way. It wasn't as simple as entering into the body in question and killing the person.

Causing the person in question to commit suicide would have been quick and effective. But William's spirit sensed that this was not part of the original plan—the plan set in motion so many years before at Doctor Troyer's log cabin. William's spirit remembered Doctor Troyer very well.

Once inside the stone foundation walls, the spirit noticed that this barn was comprised of many different-sized stalls located up and down both sides of the main hall. As he floated up the main hall, he observed that the stalls were all occupied by horses of many different colors and sizes. Interestingly enough, the horses seemed to sense that he was there. As he passed by each stall, the horse within the stall made a little neighing sound. Not a whinny, but a sound that clearly showed they knew they were no longer alone. William's spirit thought this was strange. Since rising from the grave, the horses were the first creatures that detected his presence.

What would be a good animal to inhabit? The horses were definitely a viable option. People had to ride the horses to get from place to place. William's spirit kept this in mind as he floated to the end of the horse barn and from there into another section.

William's spirit was now in an area that was divided into many large pens. The pens were full of pigs. As he floated over the pigs, he realized that the animals were separated in the pens by their sizes. The pigs didn't impress William's spirit as an option as he floated around the barn. He decided to see how high he could go within the barn.

He simply willed himself up, and up he went. Up he floated, high in the barn above the pigs below. The pigs didn't pay any attention to his presence like the horses did.

As he floated up, he was struck by the realization that his scope of vision was three hundred and sixty degrees. He could see everything at once. The fingers of the moonlight worked their way between the cracks of the barn walls. The odd window also let in some light, but it was like he didn't need the light. He could see everything.

The ceiling of the pig barn became the floor of the next level. In this level there were hundreds of baby chicks secured within a large, wooden pen. At the moment they were all sleeping in one corner of the pen, bunched up on top of each other. Their natural body heat was keeping them warm in the cool evening.

He rose even higher through another ceiling and up into the rafters of the barn's ceiling. Bales of hay and straw were piled up on either side of the loft. There he noticed several doves cooing in a nest in the corner of two adjoining rafters. He made his way over to the doves. The doves didn't react to his presence either. Was it possible they couldn't see him? William was a spirit after all. Could the doves sense his energy? Obviously, like the pigs below him, not all the animals were aware of his being there.

As he floated back down, he heard an owl in a far-off part of the barn. Whoo! Whoo! The owl's call resonated through the upper area of the barn. Little brown wrens hid in small nests along the beams and crosspieces holding up the roof. A bird might have some advantages, but William's spirit wasn't sure how viable it would actually be for the task. He kept moving, deciding to return to the main level of the barn.

As he lowered back down towards the floor level, he saw some rats walking on the edge of a support beam. The rats were fat and waddled as they made their way carefully along the narrow beam. They didn't seem to be in any sort of hurry. Then a peculiar scratching sound caught his attention. William's spirit observed a squirrel zipping up the side of another beam. Who would have thought there was so much life in a barn at this time of the morning? Ah, the sweet sounds of life!

He floated further down through the floor, passing again by the hundreds of baby chicks still nestled in their pen. The floor of the second level became the ceiling of the first. Back on the bottom level now, he floated past the pigs and into another section of the barn.

In this part of the barn milking cows were tethered in open stalls. The stalls had low sides with open ends at the hallway. At the rear of this section were similar enclosed pens with calves and their mothers. The mother cows lay with their backs to the wall while their calves slept safely in front of them. William's spirit didn't see the cow or calf being particularly useful either.

There was a door at the end of the milking area of the barn. William's spirit figured that behind the door were either more animals or an exit. He decided he needed to discover all of his options, so he passed through the solid timber door. It was indeed into another section of the barn.

This area of the barn complex was inhabited by cattle and like the pig's section, it was all open. But unlike the pig's section, all of the cattle were allowed to wander within their large area and were not separated. Most of the cattle lay on the floor sleeping while some others took advantage of less competition at the hay rack.

At the end of the cattle barn was yet another door. William Fick's spirit glided over the head's of the sleeping cattle, and passed through the door, which led outside. He surveyed this area which surrounded the barn complex; some out-buildings dotted the perimeter of the barn. He felt that he needed to check everything out, so he entered into a white-washed building that turned out to be a coop, full of free-range chickens. Passing through this building, he found himself in another similar building that was full of egg-laying, nesting chickens.

There was just one more building to investigate. It was a little larger than the two chicken coops. Unlike the other buildings, the entity had traveled through, this out-building had a chimney. Soft fingers of smoke floated out the top of the chimney and into the night air.

William's spirit passed through the wall into the building, and he realized that this place actually belonged to a person.

He had done enough exploring already to realize that this was a very good option for him. An animal would work, but another person would be of greater advantage, so he began to explore the inside of the building, searching for an occupant.

Embers smouldered in the small open fireplace. On a kitchen table lay some half-eaten food. Clothing was strewn all over the floor and on some of the furniture. In the corner of the large room was a bed. And in the bed was the form of a man, snoring and clutching an empty bottle.

William's spirit floated across the room and rose up just above the bed. The disheveled man slept on top of the covers of his bed fully clothed. He had probably passed out there after a drinking binge. Some things never changed.

He had passed through inanimate objects easily enough. However, William's spirit had no idea what may happen, or what he would feel, when he attempted to enter into another living being. Now was the time to try.

William's spirit floated directly over the sleeping man and then lowered. The living form of the man was quite different from moving through inanimate objects. William's spirit immediately felt the warmth of life as he spread into every fiber of the man. Only then did he realize how cold it had been while he was in his fog-like state. He enjoyed the warmth of his new host.

William Fick's spirit ceased to exist as a cloud. He had now returned to his original form—that of a human being. It had been a long time since the spirit had been inside a body with life. He had his own consciousness, but now also shared the one of the man he was in. But he, William Fick, could influence the man's thinking. This was all quite new to him, and he allowed himself to relax in his new form. Like his host, a man by the name of Roddy Fellows, William fell into slumber.

* * *

"God-damn you bitch horse. Settle down or I will really wallop you!" Roddy Fellows snarled at the black mare like it understood every word he said. It wasn't a bad horse at all. Roddy was just a nasty man with a short fuse. Working with horses was all he knew, but at the same time he hated them because he had never made it successfully as a jockey. He never blamed his bad temper, his antisocial drinking, or his womanizing. Roddy Horace Fellows blamed the damned horses.

Today though, Roddy Fellows didn't feel like his usual self. He had gotten a severe chill over the night, and it seemed like there was nothing he could do to get warm. It was the middle of August; however, it was still the morning and it was cool. But not cool enough to make Roddy feel as he did now. He swore that he felt like the walking dead. Maybe it was not getting enough sleep. He was definitely hung over.

Roddy had to wake up at 6 a.m. every morning and get the barn and horses prepared for the day. He had to make sure the animals all got their proper amount of food and exercise, too. It wasn't just the popular horses that the family used for pleasure, either. Roddy had to get all of the horses ready-- the work horses, the breeding horses, and the mothering mares, as well. His job was to make sure that they were all well taken care of.

Roddy was a very small man but the perfect size to be a jockey. However, his previous lifestyle had ensured that his jockey days were long behind him. The Murdock family was fair to Roddy, and he tried to do his job as though he really cared. Roddy was an employee, but he did have a lot of freedom to do the required work as he saw fit.

Roddy was paid a monthly salary and his lodgings were free, so he had a decent lifestyle. Often Roddy would ride into the town of Roulston and have a drink or two at the local drinking establishment. He knew that he represented the Murdock's, who were quite respected in the community, so he would never get too drunk in public. He brought his gin and cider home with him to do his serious drinking. Once his chores were all done, then he would break the bottle open.

Roddy secured the black mare in her stall and closed the stall door behind her. He wiped his hands on his pants and felt that he was ready for a coffee with a little fire added for extra effect. Suddenly, Roddy felt another chill run through his entire body, similar to the chill he had gotten this morning. It was a very strange feeling. He had never experienced this feeling before. Now it seemed that every fiber of his body was cold. Definitely, this was time for another special coffee.

Roddy also had to do something about the taste in his mouth. He ran his tongue around the inside of his mouth and over his teeth. The foul taste was everywhere. He imagined it was like the flavor of week-old maggots. How would he even know what that tasted like? Roddy's breath was disgusting on a normal day; what made today any different?

The spirit of William Fick had now fully settled into his new host. Both William and his host were each feeling new sensations. But it would have to be said that William had the upper hand. William had taken control. It was an entirely different feeling than he had experienced in his out-of-body form. The body that had once been Roddy Fellows only hours before, now belonged to William Fick. Every minute he enjoyed his new host, the less it was the actual Roddy Fellows. They had a shared consciousness, but William would eventually take that over, too. It was so amazing to be able to touch and hold again. Doctor Troyer had come through in spades, William Fick was alive. He now had feeling. Roddy turned back to the wooden stall door and shook it hard to ensure it was locked. The door moved back and forth and so did the arms of William Fick, the living entity.

This was so much better than floating around. This meant that he could no longer float through walls or float up to visit with the wrens again—a small price to pay to have life, to have all five senses working. William looked around at his surroundings and realized now that he didn't recognize this barn at all. When he had floated through it early in the morning, everything had felt new to him. But there had been a barn here years ago.

He knew the property though. This place was where he had to come. His sense of direction had been good but slow. William walked out of the barn and into the courtyard. On the left was an open area that led down to the lake. Ahead of him, about a hundred or so feet, was the house. On the right was a laneway that must have led to the concession road. His attention turned back to the house. It was his house. William had recognized it earlier this morning in his spirit form. Some major alterations had been made: a second-story building was added onto the original house that he himself had built. That had been years ago when he had first settled onto the property. As well, a railed porch had been built all the way around the structure. A huge stone chimney stood at the end of the house that faced the road. He approved of these changes. They made the house look much more like a completed home than when he had lived here. The additions definitely complemented what he had already built.

William had walked twenty-five feet from the barn towards the house when he suddenly changed course and headed towards the lake. The willows had grown in very nicely and gave the property a very stately look. The fire pit and the cast iron pot were gone. William laughed to himself remembering the flack he had taken when he first erected the fire pit and pot beside the house. How his wife had argued with him. Hmmmmmm. Whatever happened to that wife of his? Something about the lake gnawed at him.

He could see across the lake; it was so beautiful this time of morning. It was so quiet right now. Where was everybody? Would he recognize anybody? He had no idea of how much time had actually passed. Not that it really mattered. William looked up at the front of the house. It was a full two stories with a large dormer window built on the roof. When he had lived here, there were just the three of them. This new and improved house would hold a lot more people. That was for sure. William, however, was only interested in one of those people.

Would anyone recognize him for the person he really was? Of course they would recognize the body he was in. He assumed that much. But the people here probably wouldn't recognize the spirit within the body. William turned from the lake and walked up the five steps of the main entranceway of the house to the porch. He went up the steps and then turned back towards the lake again, leaning on a section of the railing. Behind him sat two rocking chairs. One could sit and relax. From this vantage point, William could almost see the entire lake. This had become a very beautiful property.

William took a deep breath of the fresh morning air. Down at the lake, he could see that the dock was still there. Like many things here, it was the same but somehow just a little different. A small white rowboat tied up to the dock rocked gently back and forth by the waves of the lake. Even from here

William could hear the boat softly bump onto the side of the wooden structure. The boat reminded him of something, too. Something very dire from the past.

William looked out beyond the dock and the little boat. In the distance he could make out the Murdock place. He remembered that. Or, perhaps, did he already know that. What were William's thoughts and memories, and what were his host's? William's head was a confusing place right now.

William wiped his mouth with the back of his hand as he squinted his eyes for a better view. Maybe he would take a jaunt down to the dock. But there was another thought in his head. William had a mission to accomplish. It was like something that had been pre-set in his brain, and now he was just following orders. William was just about to go back down the stairs when he heard a woman's voice.

"Roddy?" the voice spoke from behind him. William knew that he should respond to the name he was being called. He didn't recognize the name. It wasn't overly familiar to him. Or was it?

"Roddy?" the voice seemed a little agitated now.

William turned around to see Catherine Murdock. He recognized her, although he assumed that was a newer memory. One of those many shared scattered memories with his host.

"Yes, Mrs. Murdock?"

"Roddy, why are you up on the porch? You know you shouldn't really be up here. This is reserved for the family only."

"I'm sorry, ma'am. I just got caught up in the beautiful

view of Castle Lake. It is really wonderful to see it from up here on the porch."

Catherine gave Roddy a confused look. Never in all the time Catherine had known Roddy had he ever complimented the view of the lake. She patted down her apron and then tugged on the sleeves of her off-white blouse. She had her long brown hair pulled back in a pony tail. Catherine seemed concerned, as this was out of character for Roddy. "You look pale, Roddy, are you feeling all right? Is there anything I can do?"

William gave Catherine a polite smile. "I feel fine, Mrs. Murdock," he lied. "Just sometimes it just feels really good to be alive. To be on this earth, right now. This is just one of those moments, I suppose."

Catherine wasn't so sure that Roddy felt well. She had never seen him this animated and apparently sober at the same time. "Roddy, do you remember what today is?"

William scratched at his short, greasy, thinning hair and thought about it. He made a face that clearly said, *I have no idea*. "I seem to have forgotten, ma'am. I guess these are the things that come with age." He gave her a sheepish smile.

"Roddy, today is Alicia's sixteenth birthday. We are going to have a surprise party for her. Do you remember that?" Catherine wasn't sure what to make of this.

William nodded implying that he understood. The name itself wasn't very familiar to him, however, the age certainly was. "Yes, Mrs. Murdock, I remember that now. I need to make some preparations don't I?" This was something that William assumed he needed to do. If there were a birthday party, there would have to be preparations.

"I just want to make sure that the property is extra presentable today, Roddy. So please make sure that the horse barn is very clean and that all the soiled straw is out back in the paddock. Break up any obvious spider webs. Also, put out of plain view anything that is just sitting around collecting dust. I would also like some of the farm equipment that's out sitting on the front lawn moved back behind the barn." Catherine figured that was enough instructions for Roddy to handle at the moment.

"Yes, Mrs. Murdock. I can do that on top of my other duties. I will have this place looking good for Alicia's birthday. A very special day, the sixteenth one is."

Catherine gave Roddy a curt smile and then motioned him to remove himself from the porch. William nodded again and walked back down the steps, across the courtyard, and back into the horse barn.

William was now having a serious case of *déjà vu*. This whole scenario was much too familiar. Cleaning up and preparing the farm on the day of a daughter's birthday. Suddenly, William got a vision. He stumbled back into the barn and fell onto a wooden barrel, using it as a stool. William put a hand to his forehead. He broke out into a cold sweat. The horses neighed as they heard him enter the barn. They hoped they were about to either get brushed or fed.

William sat on the barrel and thought about what was overcoming him. He had been in this similar situation before. He had no idea how long ago, but he remembered getting the farm all ready for a celebration. It was this farm and it was for a sixteenth birthday party—a sixteenth birthday party that had gone wrong. Terribly wrong. It was the first day of the end of life as he knew it.

Suddenly, it hit William Fick. Doctor Troyer's plan now came back to him. The memories flooded through his brain. William now knew what his mission was. He also knew who his target was. Today was the day that William Fick would set right a wrong that had been committed so long ago, "An eye for an eye."

There would be a celebration today. But William didn't think that the Murdock's would be quite as enthusiastic as he was. It would be he that celebrated, not the Murdock family.

THOMAS A. RYERSON

8

A morning ride

"It's just terrible about what's been happening back home over the last month," exclaimed Nora Rogers in her shrill and thin voice. Nora was Catherine's sister and was down Roulston way early to help celebrate Alicia's birthday. She had made the trip from Hornerseth to the Murdock farm for the day. That was a pretty serious effort for Nora, who hated to tear herself away from the big city. However, as usual, Nora had to get her sister up to date with all the titillating city news.

"So what's been happening, Nora?" Catherine was just putting some baking into the oven so that most of her attention was on the black cast-iron stove. There was, however, still a little piece of her attention that was actually listening to her sister.

"You haven't heard, Cathy? Oh my. It's the talk of the city. Someone in Hornerseth has been killing prostitutes in the middle of the night." Nora's curly red hair bounced back-and-forth as she talked. She was a very animated conversationalist.

"Prostitutes?" questioned Catherine. She thought it might be uncaring, but she always voiced her opinion. "Someone is killing prostitutes, and that is seen as a problem?"

"The killings are brutal, Cathy. It's just terrible. And I mean, prostitutes are still people, too. They have feelings and families. And, Cathy, the way they are being killed, that's the tragedy."

"What's the tragedy?" asked Alicia as she came in from the dining room, missing the initial part of the conversation. Her mother instantly changed the subject, turning around to face Alicia. Putting her hands on her hips, Catherine proclaimed, "My, my, Alicia, don't you look smart! Turn around for your Aunt Nora."

Alicia groaned, but she did as she was asked. She had dressed in a light brown, long, divided skirt. She matched the skirt with a white blouse and covered her shoulders with a darker brown, pleated riding jacket. Alicia was going riding today. If serious company had been present, then Alicia would ride side-saddle. However, Aunt Nora was not serious company, so today she would be riding Holly astride.

"You do look charming, Alicia. You would fit right in with the people of society back in Hornerseth." Her aunt then inquired. "You are going to attend the Hornerseth Girls Finishing School, are you not?"

Catherine had a surprised look on her face. How quickly

Nora could change a conversation. First, Hornerseth was a city full of prostitutes who were being brutally killed, and then, in the next breath, the city was suddenly a place of great society. Catherine was glad that she and her family lived near Roulston. The nearby town with a population of nearly five hundred people was perfect for her and her young family.

"I'm not exactly sure, Aunt Nora. I have one more year here at the grammar school, and then we will see. I've all the time in the world to decide. However, no big decisions today! It's my birthday, and right now I am going riding with Holly!"

"With no breakfast under your belt?" her mother voiced with real concern.

"I had some thick-cut bread smothered in butter when I first awoke, Mother. I will have a proper breakfast when I come back. I promise." With that Alicia kissed her mother on the cheek and said goodbye to her Aunt.

"Happy sixteenth, Alicia," Nora added, not sure if she had already wished her niece a happy birthday when she had arrived a little earlier in the morning.

"Thanks again, Aunt Nora," Before she left the house out the side door, Alicia slipped on her high riding boots. She tied them up and then headed outside. Back in the house, Nora and Catherine picked up the conversation from where they had paused when Alicia had come into the kitchen unexpectedly.

Alicia bounded down the steps of the porch and also skipped the hundred and fifteen feet to the barn. Alicia

Murdock loved to ride. Horses were in her family's blood. She entered the barn through the side entrance and walked up to Holly's stall. The barn was very well-lit for the late morning. All the barn door-toppers were open, which allowed a great amount of light inside. Alicia called her horse's name so that the animal wouldn't be startled. The other horses in the barn neighed when they heard Alicia "talk" to Holly.

Holly came to the door opening and gave Alicia a little "neigh." Alicia smiled at her horse, and then crossed over to where she stored the horse tack. Alicia lifted a halter off a peg on the wall above her tack barrel. The tack barrel which sat by the hall's edge was actually a large wooden barrel that had been cut in half. It was a great place to store all of her grooming equipment. Above the barrel, several bridles and halters hung on wooden pegs

"Come on, Holly," Alicia said with a soothing voice. She entered the stall, and patted the horse's forehead. Alicia slipped the halter over Holly's head and then guided the mare around through the open stall door. The black mare ventured out into the hall. Alicia closed the door of the stall and then picked up the cross-tie straps.

Alicia secured the mare in the cross-ties. She ran the leather straps from the mare's halter to a steel ring located on the posts on either side of the main hall of the barn. This way Alicia could brush the mare while she was standing still. She patted the back of the mare's neck and continued to sooth her. The mare was usually calm, however, Alicia wanted to ensure that she really was. An accident could easily occur. If Holly were suddenly startled or unsure while strapped in the cross-ties, she could rear up, buck, or even flip herself over. Alicia believed that a little precaution was worth the effort. It could save fixing up a big mess afterward. Holly was a good-natured animal, but Alicia knew that accidents did happen.

Alicia walked around behind the horse and dipped her hand back into the wooden barrel. She took out a wire brush and turned back to Holly. Alicia liked to groom the horse herself. Roddy was good for the more menial jobs, but when it came to brushing her horse, Alicia preferred to be the only one that did it. Of course she allowed both Wendy and Marianne to help her at times.

The black mare whinnied as Alicia began to brush her. The secret of brushing a horse was doing it "neck to butt." That is where Alicia started. She worked the brush under the horse's mane and worked down her long, sleek neck. She worked past the mare's neck and began to brush her barrel. Alicia stopped at this point and pulled the loose hair from the coarse brush. She continued at the flank and then over to the croup near the horse's rear. As she brushed over the croup, she could hear the horse get restless, like something strange was afoot. Alicia stopped and listened. She couldn't hear anything out of the ordinary, but Holly was certainly beginning to act strangely.

As Alicia brushed just over the point of Holly's hip, there was suddenly a loud and unexpected bang! Then without any warning, Holly kicked back and up. The wire brush flew from

Alicia's hand, and the horse's hoof just missed the girl's forehead by a mere an eighth-of-an-inch. Alicia fell back against the wall of the main hall of the barn. The horse continued to fuss within the confines of the cross-ties.

Alicia was suddenly sitting on her bruised bottom on the floor of the barn. "Easy, Holly. Easy, girl." Alicia spoke with an unsteady voice from her present position. Even though Alicia's voice wasn't firm, it was enough to relax Holly. The horse settled herself down after the initial shock of being startled. Alicia looked up and realized that the noise had been caused by the slamming of the overhead door of the hay mow. There was no breeze in the barn. What had caused the door above to mysteriously slam down like that? Holly became restless again. Just what exactly was upsetting her?

Then Roddy Fellows entered the barn. Was it coincidence? He was a weasel of a man, and Alicia didn't think much of him. Alicia could spot an insincere person a mile away. Roddy acted like he was actually concerned. "Miss Murdock, I heard the commotion from outside and came as soon as I realized you might be in trouble. Are you okay?"

Alicia gave Roddy a forced smile. "Yes, Roddy. Holly got a scare. I'm okay. Please help me up."

Roddy bent over and took Alicia's forearm. His leather work gloves were rough upon her skin as he pulled her up. Once she was back on her feet, Alicia leaned against the wooden wall of the hallway and tried to clear her head. Roddy stepped back from her. He looked even weirder than usual. Funny, he didn't reek of liquor like he normally did. That was certainly out of character for him.

Alicia decided to cut the brushing short. She needed to ride. "Please fetch my saddle and blanket, Roddy."

He gave her what she thought was a phoney smile and obliged her. He walked to the opposite end of the hallway to where she stored her saddles. Alicia unhooked the cross-ties and tossed the leather straps back into the wooden barrel. She then quickly changed Holly's halter. The halter was good for leading and brushing the horse, but Alicia would need to use the bridle to actually ride the horse. Alicia suddenly needed to get out of the barn. She desperately had to get some fresh air.

Alicia hung the halter back on a peg and picked up a bridle and reins. Alicia expertly slid the bridle into place and adjusted it. She then led the horse out the side door. The sun reassuringly streamed across her face, and already Alicia felt better. She led Holly away from the barn and towards the lake but remained in the courtyard proper. What was keeping Roddy? "Some stable boy," she thought to herself.

Alicia was just about to give a very un-ladylike shout, when Roddy appeared in the doorway and came up to her and Holly. He held the saddle and a blanket. Alicia took the blanket from him and sat it gently across the mare's back. Roddy then tossed the saddle up onto the mare. He came around to the opposite side of the horse and buckled up the girth, pulling on it to assure Alicia it was secure. He gave her a gesture that implied the girth was done up properly and Alicia was ready to go.

185

"Thank you, Roddy. That will be all for now...wait!" Alicia turned her attention back to Roddy, "Please clean out Holly's stall, as well. Thank you." Alicia was curt but not rude. She respected Roddy Fellows; she just didn't like him. Alicia held onto the reins and crossed over to the horse's side.

Alicia maneuvered her foot into the stirrup and grabbed onto the pommel of the saddle and pulled herself up, mounting astride the horse. She noticed much to her disgust that Roddy was still watching her. Many men believed that a woman who rode astride might "damage" herself. Alicia would have none of that. Damaged or not, she was going to ride Holly the way she wanted to, with one leg firmly planted on either side of her. Roddy smiled from where he stood, "By the way, happy sixteenth birthday, Miss Murdock."

"Thank you again, Roddy," Alicia snapped the reins and Holly came to life. Alicia got Holly into a trot leaving the farm and headed north towards the lake. They rode down a path beyond the house and past the collection of flowering trees that her parents had planted years before. She then trotted Holly down the hill and underneath the huge willow trees. Before she knew it, Alicia was at the stone-covered shore of Castle Lake. The dock jutted out into the calm water.

Alicia decided to go west around the Lake and wind up at her grandparents' house across on the other side. Some time ago, Alicia had been informed that the house where her grandparents lived had been the original Murdock homestead. The house where she was born had been purchased by her grandparents as a wedding gift to her own parents. That was well over seventeen years ago, as she was born ten months after her parent's marriage.

She was actually born in her mother's bedroom, which was across the hall from her own room. She didn't know the exact history of her parent's property, but did know that it had passed through several hands over the years. Alicia was interested in knowing who had lived on the property before she had come along. She liked history and discovering new facts.

Like the gravestone that she, Wendy, and Marianne had found back in July. That was real history. Right in her own backyard. Alicia recalled when she had brought the topic up to her father, Russell. It was news to him! Alicia's own father didn't even know about the gravestone out in the woods.

Two days after she and her two friends had originally discovered the grave, Alicia rode back to the location with her father. Together, they rode down the row of cornstalks that she had mentally marked. Returning to the spot this time and finding the gravestone was a fairly easy task.

She and her father had taken their time getting out to the gravestone. They trotted their horses all the way up through the corn, just relaxing and enjoying the ride. Alicia gave her father a heads up that they were approaching the area and to be on the watch for the wire fence. Both father and daughter were careful not to catch the fence with their horses like poor Wendy had several days before. Wendy's horse, Molly, was healing up very well, thankfully.

Once Alicia was able to point out the actual gravestone, she and her father dismounted from their horses. She walked up to the "stone" with her father and he had a closer look. Her father was also amazed at what good shape the wooden "stone" was still in. It was over sixty-six years old after all. Russell didn't recognize the Fick name either.

He now explained to Alicia that when he was a young man, the farm on which they lived had been a rental property with a high turnover. In fact the original house became run-down and uninhabitable, until Russell's own father, Samuel, bought the property. Once Samuel Murdock had purchased the property, he and his brother, James, as well as her father, Russell, set about expanding and renovating the house.

As her father read the grave marker, he was also taken aback by the peculiar wording, "Took her own life in Castle Lake—March 15th 1822." He was also perplexed as to why someone would go to all of the trouble of putting that particular information on the marker. Was it a warning? Her father promised Alicia that he would ask his own father about it.

"Don't pester me about it though, Alicia, I will have to ask your grandfather, Samuel, about it when the time is right. He is a particular man. Okay?" Alicia agreed to let her father ask his own father on his own accord.

Russell then did the math in his head. He figured out the age of his grandfather, John Murdock, at the time that Lillian Fick had committed suicide in Castle Lake. Unlike Lillian

Fick, John Murdock was still very much alive. "Alicia, when Lillian Fick died, my own grandfather, John, was only fifteen years old."

"That's almost the same age that I am now, Father," Alicia mused.

Russell Murdock had planned to ask his father about the grave marker. However, a little later on, Catherine had decided that she wanted to let the whole affair go. "Alicia's had some terrible dreams, Russ. Let's just let it pass for now. If Alicia mentions it again, we'll go from there."

Russell agreed with his wife. Alicia was having nightmares over the discovery of the grave marker. Maybe it was best not to mention and see what became of it. Amazingly enough, Alicia had forgotten all about it.

That was until today. A full month after she had made the discovery, it just suddenly hit Alicia out of the blue. "Father never did ask Grandfather Sam about that grave marker, Holly. I'm going to have to remind him," she confided to her horse.

Alicia now brought Holly up from a trot to a canter. They were traveling about fifteen miles an hour. The terrain here was interesting. There were logs to jump and also rocks to look out for. The rocks were small and Holly could easily lose her footing. From where she was by the willow trees, Alicia could clearly see her grandparents' home. But since Holly couldn't canter on water, they had to take the long way around Castle Lake.

Then a little ways ahead, Alicia could make out a huge

oak tree which had fallen across the path. The path on which she rode Holly ran parallel with the shoreline of Castle Lake, and the fallen oak tree was a challenge! Alicia and Holly would jump the welcome obstacle. Alicia clicked her heels on the horse's sides and brought Holly up to a quick gallop. She yanked on the reins and Holly jumped over the tree effortlessly. Alicia and Holly landed perfectly. But then something went terribly wrong.

As horse and rider landed from the jump, Alicia's saddle felt like it suddenly let loose. The saddle lurched to one side, and Alicia felt herself rolling over with it. Had the girth come undone? How was that possible? Roddy had secured it himself right in front of her. But for whatever reason, the saddle continued to spin right around so that within seconds, Alicia was upside down and underneath the galloping horse. Holly continued to gallop at full speed on the path. There was no way now that Alicia could get Holly to stop. Alicia had let go of the reins when she began to roll over. How could this have gotten out of control so quickly?

Then Alicia's head hit the ground below her with a sudden thud as Holly continued to run. Alicia didn't stop with the fall though. Holly was dragging her along the ground upside down. Why wasn't the saddle letting go? Then, as if to answer her question, the saddle released just enough so that half of Alicia's body was now being scrapped along the rough path. The small sharp rocks and other objects along the dirt trail tore into her back, as her head continued to bounce off the surface of the trail. Alicia craned her head up to see what was going on. It was then that to her horror Alicia realized her foot was caught in the stirrup of the saddle. Somehow the saddle wouldn't fully release from her horse. Something had given just enough to loosen the saddle but not make it fall off entirely.

Alicia's head and body continued to bounce off the rocks of the shore. She prayed there wouldn't be any more logs to jump. Her back began to burn and she imagined that her clothing had been stripped away. It felt like the earth was digging right into her bare flesh. Her arms burned as did her hips. To add to the dilemma, the horse had also been spooked by the strange sensation of Alicia dragging on the ground behind her. Holly was wound up as fast as she could go.

Alicia's body began to feel like it was being pulled apart. Then, just when she thought she couldn't take it any more, God showed some mercy. As quickly as the accident had occurred, it was over. Bouncing her head off another rock, Alicia finally broke free of the stirrup. As her foot let go from the saddle, Holly's hoof stabbed into the side of Alicia's leg. The leg had to have been broken. Alicia's body rolled several times and then stopped in a heap. She lay in the dust of the dirt-and-gravel path. The saddle had also fallen off, landing in the middle of the path about ten feet ahead of Alicia. Her horse, Holly, continued to run on.

Alicia Murdock was seriously hurt and bleeding upon the stones on the shore of Castle Lake. Would her family's birthplace also be her place of death? As Alicia lay there motionless, she wondered how she might be found. Then Alicia heard a very familiar sound. She looked up to see that it was the snorting of Holly's snout. It appeared now that when the horse had broken free of Alicia, she had come back to investigate. Holly snorted again as she "examined" Alicia's bruised and battered body.

Alicia looked up into the sky. Her vision was beginning to blur. She felt weak and her body was going numb. She could hear crows circling over her. Or were they buzzards? The last thing Alicia Murdock saw was a large dark figure loom over her.

And then it all went black.

2

Reverend Sweetwater

Reverend Egerton E. Sweetwater had preached at the Roulston community church for over fifteen years. He had seen a lot of changes over that time; many parishioners had come and gone. Sometimes they left in a wagon to a new community, and sometimes they left in a pine box to be buried in the churchyard cemetery. Either way, the Reverend was always there to see them off.

The times, however, were definitely changing. The modern world was making his job a lot harder. People were either getting caught up in recreational activities or busying themselves with too much work. The Reverend Sweetwater just continued to do what he did: preach the gospel as best as he could and serve his flock. He had never thought of moving. He liked the Roulston community and also the church in which he served.

The church was grand. It had been built a year or two after he had arrived in the area. At that time the town of Roulston was known as Roulston Corners and was half the size it was now. Before he had come to Roulston, the Reverend Sweetwater had preached out west in the larger cities. He felt he needed a change and decided a trip to the east coast would help.

Roulston seemed like a community in need of solid spiritual leadership, and the Reverend Sweetwater knew he could deliver that. He did enjoy his work and he truly believed in what he preached. His message was for the good of the entire town and the surrounding county.

He looked out the multi-paned window of his manse office. From his seat he admired the impressive white clapboard structure of the church which stood about two hundred feet away from the manse. The church's most prominent feature was the tall steeple with the bell located inside the top. He liked that. The steeple even had stairs on the inside so he could make his way to the belfry and ring the bell from there if he wished. If he didn't, he could just tug on the rope at the bottom of the steeple. At any rate, he had a great view of the surrounding area from the top of the steeple. On a clear day, he could even see Castle Lake from up there.

However, on this particular day, Reverend Sweetwater had writer's block. He had some good ideas for tomorrow's sermon, but at the moment, he wasn't exactly sure where to go with it. Maybe a long walk would help. It seemed like it was a very nice day out, so a walk might be just what he needed to clear his mind of the pressure of having the actual sermon written before he had to give it. He laid his fountain pen down and reread the last words he had scribbled, "Ye shall be judged."

He would come back to that in an hour or two once he could get his mind on track again.

Reverend Sweetwater pushed his chair back from his desk and stood up. He gave a long, deep stretch and then made his way out to the foyer of the manse. The manse was one of smallest houses he had ever lived in. It was a good thing he didn't have a family to speak of. He assumed his three cats didn't count as such. The two bedroom house served its purpose, however, and that was all that mattered. It was a place for him to live and from which he could write his sermons. In his letters he had described the house as quaint.

The Reverend made his way to the front door of the house. He slipped on his boots and an overcoat. The day was quite nice, but he still had to look respectable. He was a pillar of his community after all. He picked his wooden walking stick out of the cane holder and then lifted his black hat off the hatrack. He opened the front door and stepped out into the early afternoon. The sun had been shining in through the frosted glass of the front door, but it was even nicer out than the Reverend had thought. A light breeze blew as he walked down the brick walkway to the concession road. He decided to walk towards the water and directed himself that way.

It was nice to get out and just walk for the sole purpose

of walking. He wasn't going anywhere in particular, and he wondered how long it would take him to walk down to the Atlantic coast. As he walked, the Reverend saw a buggy approaching. A well-dressed man and a woman nodded at the Reverend as they rode by in their buggy. The Reverend tipped his hat.

The road began to slope down towards Castle Lake on the right. That's what he would do. Instead of going all the way to the ocean's coast, he would, instead, take a little jaunt down to the lake. Good thing that he had his walking stick. Up ahead the Reverend saw a well-worn dirt path that deviated from the concession road. He knew that the path cut through the woods of the expansive Murdock property and led down towards the lake. He had journeyed down this way many times before. There were interesting things to see. There might be racoons, badgers, and maybe even a skunk or two. That was one of God's creatures he could do without!

Before he knew it, the Reverend had been walking along the path for forty minutes. He walked down a hill and approached the shore where the path and Castle Lake met. As he came carefully down the incline, the Reverend saw what he thought was a peculiar sight. Up ahead by the lakeshore, it appeared that a large black horse was standing all alone out in the open. Then a motion to his right caught the Reverend's attention. Coming up long the shore from the opposite direction was a short man who, like the Reverend, also appeared to be walking towards the horse.

As he walked closer to the animal, the Reverend could see that it was actually nudging at something on the ground. It was some kind of brown bundle just lying there. Then the Reverend could clearly see that the bundle wasn't a bundle at all. It was a girl who lay on the rocky shore of the lake. She must have fallen off the horse. The short man was also approaching the girl. Was she sleeping? Was she dead?

That particular thought shook the Reverend. The short man got to the girl first. He began to bend over her, and the Reverend was suddenly concerned for her safety. "Hello there! What is your business here?"

The short man turned towards the Reverend. "What is your business here, sir? Oh...Reverend Sweetwater. I didn't realize it was you." Roddy rose and then stepped back six feet from the girl on the ground.

"Roddy Fellows?" The Reverend recognized the man as Russell Murdock's stable boy. In all the years that the Reverend had known Roddy, the man had never stepped foot inside his church. But Reverend Sweetwater certainly knew who he was. There weren't many strangers in this area, pretty well everyone knew everyone here. It was a very close knit community.

Russell Murdock and his family were regular church-goers, and only missed a service on a rare occasion. More important to the Reverend, Russell Murdock's tithe exceeded the annual average of most of the other parishioners.

The Reverend turned his attention to the situation. He walked up to the girl crumpled upon the lakeshore. He could see that she had taken a pretty bad fall. Blood marked the sides of her cheeks. The Reverend's glance went from the girl to Roddy.

"What's going on here, Roddy?" As he spoke, the girl began to stir. She moaned and rolled over. It looked like she was having a hard time focusing on what she was seeing. He continued to lean over her and said, "Alicia Murdock? Are you okay? What happened?"

"She's had a fall, Reverend. I can take care of it from here."

The Reverend turned and looked squarely at Roddy. Instinctively, he didn't trust him. Roddy approached the Reverend, who stretched his hand out in a motion to stop Roddy.

Strangely enough, Roddy stepped closer to the Reverend and made exactly the same gesture with is own hand. Before he could react to Roddy, Roddy placed his hand directly on that of the Reverend. No sooner had Roddy touched the Reverend's hand, when the man suddenly jumped back like he had been shocked. The Reverend recoiled in surprise at how cold Roddy's hand was. A severe chill then overcame the Reverend, and he momentarily lost his footing. Roddy grabbed the hand of the bulkier man in order to steady him.

At the same time, Alicia began to get herself up from the ground. She sat on the shore and rubbed her brow. She turned her head and looked at Roddy and the Reverend standing in front of her, seemingly holding each others hands. It looked quite bizarre. "What's going on? Where am I? Roddy? Reverend Sweetwater?"

The Reverend turned to face Alicia. "You've obviously

had a pretty bad fall from your horse, Alicia. This is your horse, right?"

"Yes, that's my Holly. Reverend, my leg hurts something awful. The saddle fell off of Holly as we rode." As she spoke, the Reverend realized that Roddy was still hanging on to him. The Reverend then pushed Roddy away from him.

Free of the Reverend's hand, Roddy shook his head, rubbing it at the same time. He suddenly looked bewildered. "Alicia?"

The Reverend decided it was time to take control of the situation. "I've got it from here, Roddy. Why don't you return back to the Murdock farm and notify Alicia's parents? I will take Alicia to the manse with me and see to it that she is okay."

Roddy continued to stand in place and shake his head not saying a word. Instead, he glanced over at the Reverend and stared at him for a minute. He then did as he was asked. Turning around, he headed back around the lake.

"You've got a good friend there, Alicia."

"Roddy?" She looked somewhat confused.

"No," laughed the Reverend, "Your horse. Holly? I imagine that she stayed with you the whole time you've been lying here. I'm not so fond of that Roddy fellow. I know I shouldn't say that. Hopefully, God will forgive me." Then under his breath the Reverend added, "and also for anything else I may do today."

The Reverend walked closer to Alicia and extended his hand. "Can you get up Alicia? Is anything broken?"

Alicia pushed herself up further into a sitting position. She stretched her legs out slowly. She knew that she was bruised, but nothing actually felt broken. Alicia was quite surprised; she was sure that she should have been in much worse shape than she was. Alicia checked her arms for scrapes and cuts. Her ankle was very sore. All of her clothing seemed to be intact, as well. Her thick riding jacket had protected her back and arms during the whole ordeal. "Holly is a good friend. I don't know why the saddle fell off. Roddy did a shoddy job securing it, I suppose."

The saddle was on the ground about ten feet from where Alicia sat. The Reverend crossed over to it as Alicia continued to examine her body, reassuring herself that she was, indeed, all right. The Reverend bent down and looked the saddle over. He lifted the girth up. "I don't know much about saddles Alicia, but I would have to guess this leather strap appears to have been cut almost all the way through."

"That's very peculiar," she commented, "Roddy and I are the only two people that handle my tack. Why would the girth have been cut?"

"I'm sure Roddy has the answer. Alicia, I think we should head back to the church for now. I don't trust Roddy at all." The Reverend lifted up the saddle with both hands and carried it over to where Alicia sat. He carefully placed it beside her so she could inspect the saddle for herself.

"It's been cut all right. Shouldn't we get home to my parents and let them know?" Alicia remarked.

"Roddy could be up to something. I'm glad I got here

when he did. I believe that God wants me to take you back to the church. Please?"

Alicia Murdock was a girl who had her own mind, but at the same time, she wasn't going to question a man of God. "Can I ride Holly to the church?"

"That will be up to Holly. Can you stand?"

The Reverend leaned over behind Alicia. He lifted her by the arms of her riding jacket and didn't make any actual skin contact. Alicia slowly stood up and put both arms straight out like she was balancing, except that she was on both feet. She appeared to be steady. "I'll need some help. Holly! Come here, girl."

The horse gave a little whinny and came to Alicia as she was instructed. Alicia rubbed the horse's cheek and then steadied herself. The Reverend cupped his hands and Alicia put her foot into the cup. She threw one hand over the horse's mane and hung on to her neck, easily pulling herself up onto the horse. The Reverend handed Alicia the reins, and Alicia decided to ride side-saddle in front of the Reverend. Her bottom was sore, and her head ached like nobody's business, but all-in-all she was in better shape than she originally thought. Her head was still cloudy though. The Reverend began to walk back up the path towards the concession road and Alicia followed behind riding Holly.

Reverend Sweetwater picked up his walking stick and slowed his pace so that he was beside the horse's barrel. He glanced up at Alicia and made sure that she looked secure and comfortable. The chill that he had gotten since touching Roddy was beginning to spread across his body, and the good Reverend wasn't feeling like himself at all. "We can come back later for your saddle, I'm sure it won't be going anywhere down here."

"Okay, that sounds good. I'm glad that you happened to find me lying there, Reverend. I wouldn't have felt too safe had Roddy come upon me."

"I agree, Alicia. It was God's will that I found you. I was going to walk to the coast, but instead, something told me to take this path to Castle Lake. What do you recall?"

Alicia turned her head and looked down at the Reverend. He was a tall man, standing six-foot-one at the very least. His dark hair was longer than it probably should have been but was hidden under his black hat. Like his hat, his hair was also black. He was a stocky, middle-aged man with a good sized belly. Alicia found him to be an interesting speaker, and mostly enjoyed his sermons when she wasn't daydreaming. Alicia conveyed what she remembered, "Holly and I jumped a tree trunk that was in the way of our path, and when we landed, the saddle slipped around her belly. I could have been easily killed. God was watching out for me."

"That he is, Alicia. That he is." Before long they were at the concession road. At the road they turned towards the church. "How are you feeling, Alicia?"

"I'm feeling all right. I am thirsty, though."

"I will get you a nice big glass of cold water as soon as we get to the manse."

"The what?" She blushed after realizing she said "what" to the Reverend.

He chuckled at the oversight. "The manse is the house beside the church. It's where I live. There is a water pump in the kitchen there."

"There's a big old water pump by the side of the church, too. Isn't there?" Alicia knew there was. She just wasn't too comfortable with the idea of going into his house. Her head was foggy, but going into his house alone with him just didn't seem right. She shouldn't be in the house unless her parents were with her there. She was also nervous about riding side-saddle, and bareback to boot. She didn't want to slip off and hurt herself even more.

"Are you worried about coming into my house alone, Alicia?" It was almost as though he were reading her mind.

She looked down at him and blushed a little more. "We won't be alone, my girl. God will be there. You have nothing to worry about. I can promise you that." As he said the words, the Reverend was formulating a plan. He had to make it look like an accident. The Reverend returned her gaze and gave her a reassuring smile. Alicia felt a little better. "Some birthday," she thought to herself.

Within ten minutes, the tall steeple of the church was visible in front of them. Suddenly, Alicia had a very random thought. "Is it possible to go up inside to the top of the church's steeple?" Her youthful curiousity was getting the best of her.

"Of course it is, Alicia. It's a beautiful view. You can see many of God's beautiful creations from there. Would you like to go up and have a look?"

"Oh yes!" Alicia was suddenly excited. She forgot all about her misadventure and became preoccupied with the thought of going up the wooden tower. She imagined what the view would be like. "How tall is the steeple?"

The Reverend gave it some thought as they entered the lane onto the church property. "It has to be at least thirty or forty feet, Alicia." "Just perfect for a little leap," he thought to himself.

Alicia continued to stare at the steeple. It was amazing how this church had been here all her life, and she never once thought about what it would be like to go up to the top.

"I don't know if you can manage the steps okay, Alicia. There are a fair number of them, and they are rather narrow."

"Oh I know I can do it, Reverend Sweetwater. My fall wasn't that bad!"

"Pity," thought the Reverend to himself. Then aloud he said, "Pass me the reins, Alicia and I'll get you secured to a post."

Alicia did as she was asked and passed the reins to the Reverend. He took them and led Holly to one of the hitching posts that dotted the area designated for parking buggies, carriages, and horses. He looped the reins in and around the metal loop that hung from the three-foot wooden post. As he secured the knot, a face that should have been familiar to him came around the corner. The Reverend wanted to recognize the man, but his own memory was suddenly getting foggy. His brain was a single-minded entity now. He had a mission, and he was going to complete it.

"What cha' be doin' Revrend," spoke the fifty-year-old man with a thick Scottish accent.

The Reverend's facial expression didn't change. He didn't smile or frown. It was somewhere in the middle. He tried to figure out who was standing in front of him.

Alicia piped up, "Hi, Jeremiah! Cutting the grass?"

"Ah, I mite git aroun' to it. I mite nut. I have too mach ta do. The Revrend gives me too mach work donna ya, Revrend?" Jeremiah Kenzie smiled to both the Reverend and Alicia. Alicia had known Jeremiah all her life. For a long as she knew him, he had worked at the church—cutting the grass in the summer months and shoveling snow in the winter. He also did all the maintenance work around the church and the manse.

"Being kept busy is very good though. Idle hands are the devil's plaything. Isn't that right, Reverend?" Alicia looked down at him for approval. The Reverend continued to just look confused, however.

"Yah look like yah've niver seen me before, Revrend. Ah ya cummin' down wit sumthin' then? Yah look a mite pale ya do." Jeremiah scratched his red matte of hair. He also had a matching beard and moustache. Jeremiah looked very unruly but was actually a very down-to-earth and friendly man.

"Jeremiah. Yes, I'm all right. Just in a bit of a shock. Alicia here had a terrible spell down on the lakeshore." The Reverend put his hand to his chin as if in deep thought and then came up with a great idea. "Jeremiah, would you be able to fetch the doctor for me?"

"Yah be needin' Dockta Fenney, do ya?" Alicia was still sitting on top of Holly. She got Jeremiah's attention when he realized that she wanted to dismount from the horse. Jeremiah walked up to Holly and extended his arms. Alicia slid down the side of the horse and into Jeremiah's strong grip. He took most the momentum as Alicia landed solidly on her two feet.

"I fell off of Holly, Jeremiah. I am feeling much better though, Reverend..."

"None-the-less, Alicia, I don't want to assume anything. I'm sure Jeremiah won't mind taking a few moments just to fetch the doctor for us, will you?" He gave Jeremiah a look that said "get the doctor."

"Course nut, Revrend. No issue. Ah go git tha dockta fi ya. If it be meanin' that Alicia be takin' care ov. No issue at ill." He nodded to both Alicia and the Reverend and headed to the drive-shed located between the church and the manse. They watched him open the main door of the shed, enter and then after several minutes, ride out on a sorrel-colored mare. He waved to them both as he encouraged the horse on, tearing off down the concession road.

"Now, Alicia, shall we have a look at that view?"

"Do we really need the doctor, Reverend?"

"Oh yes, Alicia. You had quite a fall. I want the doctor to make sure that you are okay. You have to be careful with head injuries. Would you like to lead the way?" He held out his hand pointing towards the church entrance like Alicia was royalty. She scrunched up her face.

"Maybe we should just wait for the doctor then. Make sure that I am indeed okay." Alicia walked to the church steps and turned around. She sat on the second step and stretched out her legs. Her one knee did hurt when she did that. Her head and ankle continued to throb a little. She was also starting to get some strange vibes from the Reverend. He just didn't seem like himself.

When Jeremiah mentioned that he didn't look well, Alicia thought the same thing to herself. She did have a hard fall, so she just wanted to relax. As she stretched her legs, she pulled her skirt down. Her attention was spent on fretting with herself, and she didn't even notice the Reverend disappear around the corner of the church. Alicia then heard some rustling. She looked out across the landscape. The land was higher here, and she could make out where Castle Lake should be. Just over the ridge. She couldn't see her house, but she knew where it was. Then a thought hit her. Where was her family? What did Roddy do when he returned to the farm? Roddy had acted strange, too. Was everybody around her going crazy?

Then, as if to answer her question, the Reverend returned from around the corner. His demeanor seemed about the same as it was before, except instead of his walking stick, the good Reverend was now carrying Jeremiah's scythe!

He rounded the corner quickly and immediately had Alicia trapped within the railings of the steps. Alicia reacted quickly, abruptly standing up, and backing herself against the doors of the church.

Unfortunately, Alicia had forgotten there was still one more step to go. She tripped backwards, falling firmly on her bottom on the landing just in front of the church's main double doors. As she landed, her head bounced off the center of the hard wood of the oak. She was also rudely reminded from a searing pain in her backside that she had already bruised this part of her body when she had fallen off Holly.

"Are you mad?" Alicia blurted out as she lay sprawled on the church landing. The Reverend continued to advance on her, and she maneuvered herself back, almost like a crab. She used her hands and the balls of her feet until she was firmly up against the doors. The Reverend looked mad, indeed! His eyes were wild and his hands shook as he held the sharp scythe at his chin level. His demeanor had really changed now for the worse.

He began to ascend the steps. "You'll understand, Alicia Murdock. You will understand soon enough. The Ficks will have their revenge." The Reverend began to lunge the scythe at her in short, stabbing motions. Alicia pushed herself up, turned quickly on her heels, and entered the church building. She latched the door shut behind her just as the Reverend got to it. Alicia now stood in the foyer of the church. She decided that her best option was to go up. She quickly looked around the foyer and scanned the door to the steeple on her right. The latch on the main church door began to open.

Alicia darted over to the door on her right and shut it behind her quickly. It was dark inside the stairwell to the top of the steeple. A little of the natural light from above filtered its way down, but it was still very hard to see. As her eyes adjusted to the darkness, she noticed some loose pieces of lumber piled in a corner under the stairs. Alicia grabbed a walnut plank about three feet long and jammed it under the doorknob of the steeple door, wedging it into the wooden floor of the steeple stairwell. Alicia then kicked the bottom of the plank towards the door and secured it tighter under the doorknob. The plank gave just a little as the Reverend suddenly threw his entire body weight upon the door. He then began to pound on the door with his hands. He sounded like a child having a tantrum.

The door buckled some but the walnut plank remained firmly locked in place. "Alicia I just want to talk to you. It's a message from God. You have to trust me."

"I trust my instincts Reverend Sweetwater," Alicia yelled to the Reverend with great effort. All the excitement was beginning to take a toll on her. Then as suddenly as he had begun making all the noise beating on the door, it was now eerily quiet. Alicia knew that he didn't leave. "What was he up to now?" she thought to herself.

She carefully and quietly moved towards the door. Alicia thought about peeking into the keyhole to see if he was still there. She began to bend down and move her face towards the keyhole, and when her face was about five inches from the door, there was suddenly a deafening crack!

Splintered wood splattered against her in the face, and the cold steel blade of the scythe almost touched her nose. An inch or two more and Alicia Murdock would have been seriously injured or worse!

Alicia pushed herself back from the door, and she turned and scrambled up the steps. The only way was up. The steps were steep and narrow, built in a series of five or six steps and ending at a small landing in the corner of the steeple. From that landing the steps turned and followed the wall up to the next corner. Each set of steps brought Alicia about four feet higher inside the forty foot steeple. She would get to the top of the steps to the landing, turn left, and hurry up the next set of stairs to the next landing. As she raced up the steps, Alicia's divided skirt whipped back and forth at her ankles. It didn't prevent her movement though. She reached the top of the steeple in no time.

As she made her way up the last few steps to the top of the belfry, Alicia almost struck her head on the large brass bell that hung low from the steeple's center. "That's all I need to do," she thought to herself. She went around the bell to the far corner of the steeple. She turned so her back was wedged into the corner. The wall was four feet high and had an opening of about two-and-a-half feet at the top, just under the edge of the roof. Alicia turned and glanced out the opening at her world below. In the distance she could make out her home by Castle Lake. There was her house with its two chimneys and the large barn complex. How she longed to be there now. The sounds of splintering wood brought her back to her harsh reality.

Down the steps below, Alicia could hear the Reverend continually hitting the door blow after blow. Then the tone of the blows changed. Alicia turned around from the window and looked down the stairwell. There was a square opening in the middle of the steeple that allowed Alicia to see all the way down the center of the stairs. Light flowed in below from the opened door. She could see pretty clearly to the bottom of the steeple now. The door below had been totally destroyed.

Alicia jumped back as she saw the Reverend boldly walk through the jumble of broken and shattered timber and begin to ascend the stairs. He still held the scythe in his hands. "Isn't he getting tired? I sure am," Alicia thought to herself.

Alicia knew she had to somehow bring attention to herself. God only knew how long it would take Doctor Feeney and Jeremiah to return. How long had Jeremiah been gone already? Alicia looked up at the bell. Of course! She grabbed the wheel of the bell's headstock. Alicia pulled down on the wheel and then let it go. The clapper inside the bell began to swing. She continued to pull down on the wheel and release it until finally the bell began to sing. The sound of the bell in the top of the steeple was almost unbearable, but it didn't stop her. The bell was her only hope. "Stop that right now!" screamed the Reverend from down below. She could hear his voice in between the piercing peals of the bell.

Alicia looked out the window of the steeple and saw that two horses were approaching from the direction in which Jeremiah had left. She now pulled even harder on the wheel—the sound now resounding ten-fold from inside the top of the steeple. Just as Alicia let go of the wheel for the last time, she saw the head of the Reverend coming up the steps. Then she also saw the top of the sharp scythe.

The Reverend stopped on the steps, realizing that he wasn't going to get a clear shot at Alicia because of the low-hanging bell which was still swinging back and forth. From where he stood, he could clearly see her ankles. It was better than nothing. He extended the scythe underneath the moving bell and swung it several inches above the floor of the top steeple landing.

The tip of the scythe just missed one of Alicia's ankles. She saw him stop on the steps, wondering what he was up too. Alicia swore she felt something brush the top of her foot. She stepped back as she saw the scythe swoop under the bell again. She pushed herself away from the bell and back into the far corner of the steeple.

The bell was still swinging on its own momentum but was slowing down on each swing. Alicia glanced out of the steeple again. Doctor Feeney and Jeremiah were riding up to the church steps. They both looked up at her wondering what had transpired while they were gone. Alicia filled them in quickly. "Help me, please! Reverend Sweetwater is trying to kill me!"

she screamed down to them.

"Jump, Alicia Murdock! Jump to your death. It's the only way out!" The Reverend walked up the rest of the steps so that he too was on the landing of the belfry with her. She could see his sneering face just over top of the bell. He slowly approached her.

Inspiration came to Alicia. She lurched forward and grabbed the bottom edge of the bell; she pushed as hard as she could, and it swung into the Reverend. It hit him in the chest and sent him reeling into the opposite corner. Alicia swung herself under the bell and continued forward with her hands out in front of her. She slid over the edge of the landing and fell head over heels down the steps.

Alicia continued her forward motion with her hands stretched out as she dove down the steps. As she fell, Alicia tried to grab onto anything—a stair or railing—but she was out of control. She tumbled down the narrow stairwell, and she had traveled down two sections before she was able to stop herself by sticking a foot out and catching it on a railing spindle. Alicia landed in a ball against the wall on one of the steeple's landings.

As she came to her senses, she realized that the Reverend was beginning to make his way back down the stairs. He was swinging the scythe back and forth as he maneuvered himself down the narrow steps. It took all of Alicia's strength to push herself up and descend the steps, stumbling as she did so.

As she leaped from the last step at the bottom of the

steeple, the Reverend threw the scythe down the center of the stairs in a desperate attempt to hit her. It did little more than make a clattering noise at the bottom of the lowest landing. Alicia was safely out and made her way into the foyer of the church and burst out the double doors.

Alicia ran full tilt out of the church doors and right into the arms of Doctor Ramsey Feeney and Jeremiah. "He's still after me!" she screamed as she tried to get through the two men. They weren't letting her go, though. Doctor Feeney and Jeremiah held onto Alicia and turned back down the stairs. They each had an arm and more or less carried Alicia to the waiting horses. "Get her into the house and bolt the door!" said Doctor Feeney to Jeremiah. The doctor was a medium-sized middle-aged man and must have figured he could take on the Reverend, who was older and heavier

Jeremiah did as he was told. He took Alicia's hand and held it tightly. He pulled her across the area between the manse and the church. "I knew there wosn't somethin' rite 'bout him taday!" declared Jeremiah as they made their way into the church manse building. They entered through the front door and made their way down the hall and into the kitchen. They crossed to the far side and then rested against some cupboards. The Reverend's cats peered around the doorway to see just who was in the kitchen. Alicia and Jeremiah were both out of breath. Alicia slipped from Jeremiah's hand and collapsed on the floor.

"Alicia!" Jeremiah fell to his knees at the girl's side. He

knew there wasn't much he could do, so he just tried to comfort her as best as he could. Jeremiah wondered if the Reverend would try to get them in here.

Back outside, Doctor Feeney stood in front of the church and waited for the Reverend. His long hair had fallen from where it had been slicked back. He quickly tried to put his hair back in place before the Reverend got there. Once he was satisfied with that, the doctor put up his fists. He was now ready for a fight.

Then the cavalry entered the scene. Of sorts. Doctor Feeney heard the hooves of approaching horses and glanced over his shoulder. He saw several horses and a carriage entering the church property. The rider of the horse yelled out. "Doctor Feeney! Look out behind you!"

The doctor turned just in time to see the Reverend coming towards him with the scythe raised above his head. The doctor immediately turned on his heel and bolted towards the cluster of men. On the two horses he recognized Russell Murdock and Sheriff Dereham Harris. In a very regal carriage sat Colonel Barrington W. Bostwick. The doctor scurried up to the carriage and turned around just in time to see the action. Sheriff Harris' grey moustache was twitching. Apparently, it always did that just before he shot.

"Hold it, Reverend. One more step and you'll get to meet that God of yours." Sheriff Harris remained on his horse, but his handgun was pointed directly at the Reverend. The Reverend didn't seem fazed in the least. He continued to approach the men while still wielding the scythe. "One more step, Reverend, last warning."

The Reverend didn't stop. CRACK! The shot rang out and hit the Reverend in the lower shoulder. He stopped and reeled. He took a step back and shook his head. The Reverend looked at his assailant and began to walk towards him again. CRACK! The second shot was a little lower than the first. The Reverend stopped dead, gave a puzzled expression, and then fell straight back onto the ground with a deafening thud. Dust rose as his body hit the dirt. The scythe fell beside him, just off to the side. Sheriff Harris and Russell Murdock dismounted from their respective horses, and Colonel Bostwick worked his way out of his carriage.

The Colonel walked directly over to the Reverend. He then leaned over the man and said, "Why, Egerton? Why?" Colonel Bostwick extended his hand to see whether or not the Reverend's heart was still beating.

Suddenly and with no warning the Reverend's hand shot up and grabbed the hand of the Colonel. The Reverend hung on tight, lifted his head slightly, and softly spoke, "Barrington. She must die today, and you must do it."

His body then went limp. The Reverend was either dead or unconscious. However, his hand still clung onto that of the Colonel. Colonel Bostwick roughly shook the Reverend's hand free, and it fell back onto the large man's chest. Colonel Bostwick felt a sudden chill come over his body.

"Where is Alicia? Where is my daughter?"

"She's rite here, Mista Murdock." Russell turned around to see Jeremiah Kenzie with his arm around Alicia. Russell burst from the spot where he stood and ran over to his daughter. Russell embraced Alicia as Jeremiah let her go. She fell into her father's arms. Their eyes made contact, and Alicia gave her father a faint smile. She knew that she was going to be okay now.

Russell Murdock held his daughter tightly, "Roddy told us that you had an accident with Holly, and then left with the Reverend to the church. That didn't seem right to us at all. I fetched the sheriff and Colonel Bostwick here came with us for support. I'm sorry I took so long."

Alicia hugged her father and spoke into his ear. "That's all right, Father, you're here now and I'm safe."

"Let's get you home." With that Russell put his arm around Alicia and walked her back towards the sheriff and Colonel Bostwick.

THOMAS A. RYERSON

10

A dream or a memory?

"The Ficks will have their revenge," Alicia's voice was weak. She was delirious, sounding like she was perhaps just coming out of a fever.

"Quiet, my dear, you're okay, now. You're safe, now. You're home." Catherine Murdock realized that her daughter had been put through a terrible ordeal, both physically and emotionally. Alicia had feared for her life twice already today. Catherine continued to pat her daughter's forehead with a damp cloth.

Content that she had her daughter as comfortable as she could get her, Catherine decided it was time to let the girl sleep. She sat the damp cloth back into a white porcelain basin which was perched upon a nightstand. Catherine smiled and looked into Alicia's dark brown eyes. Alicia was fighting sleep, but it was a losing battle. It was obvious her body needed rest. Alicia seemed oblivious to her mother who stood beside her at the head of the bed. Catherine tucked the down-filled comforter around Alicia's neck. It was going to be another cool evening, and Catherine did not want her daughter getting a chill. Some sixteenth birthday Alicia was having.

As she watched her daughter sleep, Catherine mulled over the words that Alicia had just spoken before she had fallen asleep. There was that name again, "Fick."

It was the name that Catherine had heard the previous month when Alicia and her friends had discovered the grave marker out in the woods. At that time, Catherine had asked her husband to downplay the whole event. Alicia had just had the terrible nightmare of the female skeleton in Castle Lake, and Catherine and Russell didn't need their daughter's already overactive imagination working overtime. Catherine was also afraid the nightmare might evolve into a reoccurring one, and she didn't want that, either. So Catherine thought it best to nip it in the bud right then and there.

Although Russell had promised his daughter that he would try to find out more about Lillian Kane Fick, behind closed doors, Catherine had asked him to drop the whole affair. Catherine explained herself and Russell understood and agreed. The two of them made light of the discovery and Alicia eventually stopped asking about it. Whether Alicia actually forgot about it, or just stopped asking at the time, neither were sure.

At any rate, Russell and Catherine had no knowledge of

the Ficks or why the woman had been buried in their woods in the first place. At the time Catherine and Russell figured it just wasn't that important.

Now, a month later, the Fick name was rearing its head again. Catherine couldn't help but wonder if there was a connection between the grave marker out in the woods and what had happened to Alicia today. There had been two attempts on the young girl's life.

Once they had come back to the farm only hours ago, Sheriff Harris examined Alicia's saddle more closely. Upon further inspection, it was obvious to the sheriff that the girth strap of the saddle had been cut almost all the way through. The cut was intentional because the strap had been cut evenly and close to the edge, so that only about an eighth of an inch of leather remained. The girth strap may not have even broken if only Holly had stayed in a trot, but once the horse began to exert herself, Alicia's safety was definitely in question. Roddy insisted over and over again that he was innocent.

Regardless, the sheriff did not believe him, and Roddy was locked up for now. The Reverend's ill intent had been much more obvious. There was no doubt he had tried to kill Alicia with the scythe. There would be questions soon enough, but for now he was recovering back at his manse under supervision.

Both Catherine and Russell were equally surprised when the sheriff wanted to question Alicia. They implored that she was in no condition, and he would just have to wait. It had already been one hell of a day for Alicia. And the day wasn't even over yet.

Alicia's ordeal with the Reverend Sweetwater combined with the apparent intentionally-caused fall from her horse was enough to convince Catherine to cancel the surprise birthday party, even though party wasn't going to be anything too grand—just a little something to let Alicia know how loved she was.

But now with the day's events, Catherine knew it would be just too much for her daughter. Catherine would host the party again in a week or two when Alicia was feeling better. Alicia's two best friends, Wendy and Marianne, understood the situation. They couldn't fathom why someone would want to bring harm to Alicia in the first place. They both gave Catherine a hug and reassured her that they would be thinking of Alicia in their prayers.

Also, Catherine's sister, Nora, and some other guests had left, too. The only people that now remained were Alicia's immediate Murdock family. They were all downstairs on the main floor, assembled in the parlor. However, they were no longer here for a party but for moral support. Catherine's two sons were out in the barn doing their chores.

Catherine's train of thought was suddenly broken when she heard a commotion from downstairs. Voices were loud and getting louder. She wanted some quiet for her daughter, who had finally fallen into a deep slumber.

Catherine glanced back at Alicia once again and then backed out of the room. Alicia's new puppy, Charlie, was balled up in the covers at the foot of her bed. His little pink nose was buried under his back paw. Catherine felt silly, but it was still comforting to know that someone, if even a puppy, was with her daughter while she slept.

Catherine left Alicia's room and quietly shut the door. She walked the ten feet across the hall to the top of the stairs and descended to the main floor. As Catherine walked down the steps, she thought how painful it must have been for Alicia to tumble down the steps of the church steeple.

"I am not a crazy old man! There is truth in my words. I had forgotten, it was so long ago." Catherine instantly recognized the voice of Russell's grandfather, John Murdock. It was his commanding voice that had carried up to the second floor several minutes before.

At the bottom of the steps Catherine turned to her right, and saw the Murdock family assembled in the parlor of the house. They were all in the room except for Russell's uncle, James, who was attending a horse auction in the nearby town of Evanston.

Catherine walked across the main hall of the house and into the parlor which was gaily decorated with Queen Anne style furniture. As she entered, John Murdock gave her a warm and reassuring smile. He was pretty spry for his eighty-one years. He had lived a long, good life. However, today John's usually well-kept, short grey hair was matted and his matching moustache hadn't yet been trimmed. He looked very disheveled even though it was only mid afternoon; it appeared that John had just awakened, "How is our girl doing, Cathy?"

Catherine walked up behind the chair in which Russell sat. She placed her hands on his shoulders and gave her husband a reassuring squeeze. Catherine then looked over to John, "She's sleeping now. Some bumps and bruises, but nothing too serious. Doctor Feeney says she will be fine with some rest."

"She is one lucky girl," spoke Elizabeth Murdock, Catherine's mother-in-law.

Elizabeth's husband, Samuel, agreed, "We are just content that she has survived this ordeal unscathed for the most part." Samuel and Elizabeth Murdock sat side-by-side on a purple colored settee. Samuel was the only clean-shaven Murdock man in the room. Across from Samuel and Elizabeth, sat Russell, and behind him stood Catherine.

John was standing in front of the fireplace mantel in the parlor. This was also the largest fireplace in the house. Over the mantle was a painting of John's own father, James Murdock. John stared at the painting like he was either reflecting or remembering.

Catherine broke the silence. "Yes, her scrapes will heal, and before we know it, our Alicia will be as good as new. Charlie is watching over her as she sleeps."

"Who the hell's Charlie?" John turned and blurted out.

Catherine gave John a warm smile. "It's just her puppy, Grandfather John. The one she got for her birthday." John Murdock then nodded his head in understanding.

"Did I interrupt something? You were all talking when I

came in."

Russell turned his head slightly to speak to Catherine. "My grandfather was just enlightening us with a family yarn that none of us here have ever heard of before. It's the story of a family curse." Russell glanced back over at his grandfather with an unbelieving look.

Samuel Murdock spoke up. "All these years Pop and I've never heard of any of this. I knew of the Fick name in passing but not like you are suggesting."

"Does this have anything to do with the grave out in the woods?" Catherine divulged, "Only moments ago, Alicia said something about the Ficks as she fell asleep."

All heads in the room suddenly turned and stared at Catherine. She felt a little flushed as three generations of Murdock men gave her their full attention. John softly spoke, "What grave in the woods, Cathy?"

Catherine looked down at Russell, and he spoke for her. "Grandfather, I didn't want to make a big deal about it at the time, but last month Alicia and her friends discovered a grave out in the west woods. The grave is over sixty years old and is of a Lillian Fick."

"Lillian Kane Fick," Catherine corrected.

Samuel couldn't believe he was just hearing this now. He spoke to his son. "Why didn't you say something when you found the grave, Rusty?" Rusty was the family nickname for Russell. Samuel then shot his own father a look, "Pop, why am I only now hearing about curses, graves, and ghosts?" It was obvious that Samuel Murdock was getting quite agitated. His wife put her hand on his upper thigh to try to reassure her own husband.

"Okay, everybody. I will come clean with the whole story. It's only just come back to me in the last couple of hours. But first, I need a stiff drink. Okay, Sammy? Rusty, do you have anything to drink with a little kick? You will all want to partake with me. What I have to say will rattle your skulls."

Russell adjusted his glasses and then scratched at his moustache. He was lost in thought. So much had happened already today, what with Alicia, and now the story that his grandfather had just begun telling before Catherine came into the room. He was reminded of her again as he felt his wife's hands still on his shoulders. She spoke from behind him, "Your grandfather wants a stiff drink, Russell. We should have something that will fit the bill, don't we?"

"Yes, Catherine, there will be something in the pantry," Russell said, but he was still somewhat oblivious. His mind was reeling, and he had to get something off his chest. "Grandfather, what you were saying moments ago was like a ghost story that gets passed down from generation to generation. It has no actual merit. This is the real world, after all. It's near the end of the nineteenth century."

John Murdock slapped the top of the mantel with his hand. The resounding sound snapped everyone to attention. "Not another word till I have my drink. Do you have whisky, Cathy? I think a strong whisky will help calm my nerves."

Samuel rubbed his chin as he thought. "If a drink is what it's going to take to get to the bottom of this 'ghost story,' then a drink it will be." Samuel stood up from the settee. His wife followed suit.

Catherine smiled and motioned everyone to follow her. She released Russell's shoulders and turned around on her heel, exiting the parlor through the main hallway. She passed through the dining room and into the spacious kitchen. The table in the kitchen was large enough to seat all of them and more.

Catherine entered the kitchen first and John followed. Then Russell came into the room and began to pull the wooden chairs from around the table. He motioned for his grandfather and his parents to take a seat.

As Samuel and his wife, Elizabeth, sat themselves in the wooden kitchen chairs Samuel commented aloud, "These chairs don't appear to be anywhere as comfortable as the ones back in the parlor."

John grinned and spoke as he, too, sat down, "I need you to pay attention, son, can't have you getting too comfortable and dozing off on me."

Catherine busied herself at the kitchen counter putting some cookies and biscuits on a plate while Russell stood off to her side. She then turned and faced everybody seated at the table. "Who else here needs a hard drink?"

"Just a coffee would be fine for me," said Elizabeth in her soft voice. Elizabeth tugged at the back of her dress which had bunched up as she had sat down.

"I'll have a whisky too, dear," Russell said from where he stood.

"A cider for me please," added Samuel. Like Elizabeth, Catherine thought that a coffee would satisfy her, as well.

She turned to Russell, "Can you get a fire in the stove please, Russ?" He nodded and crossed over to the stove. Beside the stove was a tin box that was full of kindling and tow. Russell reached down and took a little of the stuffing-like tow and dry kindling out of the box. With his other hand, he opened the front door of the stove, placing the tow and kindling inside. Russell reached over to the brick mantel of the kitchen fireplace and picked up a small tin box. He opened up the box and from it took a wooden match from the many inside. Russell replaced the tin box on the mantel. He then struck the match on the mantel's side and brought the flame to the kindling. As the fire started inside the stove, he opened the rear damper and closed the front door. "It will be ready in a minute or two, Cathy."

Catherine nodded her head as she poured two shots of whisky into a set of foggy-colored liquor glasses. Russell stepped over to where she was and took the glasses from her. He handed one glass to his grandfather and set the other one at his place at the table. Then planning ahead, Russell set the decanter of whisky close to his place setting.

Catherine put the plate of cookies and biscuits in the center of the table. "Can you also get the cider from the cold room, please?" Catherine smiled as she made her request.

"You've got him trained well, Cathy. Can you give me some pointers for his father?" Elizabeth laughed at her little joke.

Russell returned from the cold room with a jug of cider and placed it on the table by his father. He also got a stoneware mug and placed that beside the jug. It was now Samuel's time to make a joke, "All of this for me? I shall enjoy it immensely."

"You drink all of that, Samuel Murdock, and you will be walking home!" Everyone at the table chuckled.

John Murdock took a good-sized sip from his glass of whisky. The liquid burned his throat, but it felt reassuring all the same. Russell sat at the table and had a sip of his own drink. He drank it a bit slower than his grandfather, letting the liquid sit on his pallet first before he swallowed it. Samuel lifted the heavy cider jug carefully and poured himself a good glassful in the white, stoneware mug.

Catherine got the coffee pot and coffee together. "Do you want a hand?" Elizabeth offered. Catherine laughed to herself, as she was almost done with what she needed to do.

"Thanks for the offer, Lizzie, but I'm okay. You relax. I need to keep my mind busy right now. Catherine used the hand pump in the kitchen and pumped some fresh well water into the well-used coffee pot. She placed some fresh ground coffee in the metal center cylinder and then placed that into the coffee pot. Catherine picked the pot up and walked back over to the stove, putting the coffee pot on the burner where the hot fire was now burning. She added some small pieces of dry pine from the pile beside the fireplace. Catherine opened the front of the stove and pushed the wood pieces into the burning kindling. It wouldn't take long at all for the coffee to boil now.

"About ten minutes, Lizzie, and we will be enjoying a great cup of coffee." Catherine Murdock finally sat at the kitchen table, cater-corner from her husband. She pursed her lips and spoke. "So, John, what did I miss while I was upstairs with Alicia?"

"He had some crazy talk about ghosts and demons!" Samuel blurted out.

"I said nothing about demons, Sammy. Not a damn thing."

"But ghosts?" asked Catherine carefully. "So do you believe that grave out in the west woods has some bearing in what you were saying when I interrupted you in the parlor?"

John Murdock stared at the liquor in his glass. He swirled it around as he thought about the parlor conversation. John looked across the table at Catherine and Russell. "Rusty, Cathy, what do you know of Lilly Fick?"

Russell took another sip from his drink and then crossed his arms in front of his chest. "Well, Grandfather, now that you ask, the gravestone of Lillian Fick did mention that she took her own life in the lake just outside my door." Then a little anger seeped into Russell's voice, "You'd think that a woman who may have committed suicide a little more than a couple hundred feet from my front door might have been common knowledge. But apparently not in the Murdock household!"

Catherine held his arm as he talked. She, too, was upset that they had never known of the body buried on their property.

"So Alicia and her friends found the grave, did they?"

Russell lifted his hand and pointed at his grandfather. "Yes, Grandfather, your sixteen-year-old great granddaughter found it. Really fine dinner conversation for her and her friends, don't you think? Do you know the nightmares she had because of that?"

"Actually, Rusty, I didn't know. I didn't know because you never told me about it. If you had, I may have told you this story a month ago." Russell Murdock knew that his grandfather was correct with that line of thinking. Russell had kept the discovery of the grave from his grandfather on purpose, for Alicia's sake.

"We're not looking for blame, Grandfather John. We are looking for answers," Catherine wanted to hear the story.

Against his better judgement, Russell added, "Why didn't I know the grave was there in the first place, Grandfather!"

Samuel Murdock echoed his son's sentiments, "Yes, Pop, Rusty's right. After all of these years of living on this property, even I never knew about a grave in the woods."

"Boys, Boys. I knew that Lillian Kane Fick was buried on this property somewhere, but I had no idea where. And frankly, I had forgotten. I was fifteen years old when she died. I was just a year younger than Alicia is now. After Lillian Fick's husband was burned alive in a barn fire, my own father James said we were never to speak of it again. So we simply didn't.

231

The story got lost with the passage of time."

"Her husband died on this property, too?" Russell took another drink from his glass. The coffee began to percolate. Catherine excused herself and got up from the table. She walked over and got two, off-white porcelain coffee cups from the cupboard. As she did so, the four that remained at the table helped themselves to the treats on the plate.

Catherine took the coffee pot off the stove and carried it to the table, setting it close to Lizzie. Catherine got the brown sugar and cream and placed them beside the coffee pot. She put the two cups down and then took her place back at the table. She and Elizabeth fixed their coffees the way that they liked them.

Once Catherine and Elizabeth had their coffees prepared, and the clinking of the spoons on the insides of the cups had subsided, Russell asked his grandfather again. "Okay, Grandfather, exactly how many people have died on this property?"

John looked across at his grandson. "Three."

Samuel whistled. "And we've never known about this before, Pop?"

"Sammy, like I said. I never intentionally kept this from anyone. My own father asked my late brother, Henry, and I never to speak of it again. I simply became disassociated with the story over the years. But it's all flooding back to me now."

Then at that moment everyone in the room seemed to understand and appreciate what John Murdock was trying to say. Russell relented. "I'm sorry, Grandfather. I didn't mean to get angry with you. It was just such a shock. And now what you say..."

Samuel Murdock was silent as he nibbled on a cookie. He nodded his head in agreement with his son.

John took another drink. "I had no idea the Ficks would ever raise their miserable heads again. But they have."

Russell decided to cut to the chase. "How does all of this affect Alicia?"

"Oh, Rusty, it affects her very much. Very much." John played with the rim of his glass. "There is something that I never told you. I never told you because, as I already said, I frankly forgot all about it. It was a very long time ago."

"Say what is on your mind, John." Like Catherine, Elizabeth was now also ready to listen without prejudice.

Russell finished his glass of whisky and decided that he had a taste for another. He looked over at his grandfather, "Ready for another drink?"

John smiled and finished the tiny amount of liquor left in the bottom of his glass. He then handed it to Russell. Russell topped it back up from the decanter on the table and slid the glass back over to his grandfather. "We're all listening now, Grandfather John."

John rubbed his stubbly chin. He looked across the table at the four family members waiting to hear what he had to say. The whisky he had already consumed was going to make this process a little easier. "Where to start?" he murmured.

"At the beginning?" stated Elizabeth, as she placed her hands on the table with her cup of coffee in the center. Elizabeth was a schoolteacher and had a very pragmatic approach to everything. Her light brown hair was pulled back into a bun, and a pair of fashionable glasses sat on her nose. She definitely looked like a teacher.

John took a deep breath. "At the beginning it is, then. Before I answer your questions about Lillian Fick, I want to ask you all something. Do any of you here know the history of the property that we are on right now?"

Samuel answered flatly, "I know that three people died on this property and that one of them committed suicide and is buried here, too. Is there more?"

"Now, Samuel," Elizabeth lightly scolded her husband. "Your father is going to explain things. Please give him a chance."

"I'm sorry, Pop," Samuel said as he rubbed the bridge of his nose. "I bought this farm just over twenty years ago from the Parr family. I was never told who owned it before the Parr's did."

Elizabeth spoke up again, "Before the Parr's owned it, the farm was just a rental property, I believe."

"That's correct, Lizzie," John took a sip from his glass. The two women finished their coffees and poured themselves each another cup. "My father always wanted to own all the property around Castle Lake, but it never turned out that way. I can't remember the details." John stared down at his glass as if speaking to it. He went into a deep reflective mode. "As I said earlier, when I was just a little younger than Alicia, this farm we are on now was owned by one William Fick. He was the husband of Lillian Kane Fick."

"Oh, my God," Catherine murmured under her breath. She then spoke a little louder. "That's why Alicia said the Fick name. There's more to this than just the gravestone that she discovered. There has to be."

Catherine, it seemed, was the first one buying into John Murdock's story. None of the other three judged her though. They continued to listen.

John looked up from his glass of whisky and cocked his head, "Do you remember exactly what Alicia said before she fell to sleep, Cathy?"

Catherine thought. "It was something to the effect of the Ficks seeking their revenge. I assumed she was just rambling with memories of the gravestone. What is the connection, John? How would Alicia know the Fick name other than the gravestone that she and her friends found back in July?"

John looked past Elizabeth to the far wall of the kitchen. "The answer is hanging over the fireplace up on that wall." John was looking at the shotgun that used to belong to his father. It was now a family heirloom and had been around ever since anyone could remember. Samuel and Elizabeth had presented Russell and Catherine with the gun as a housewarming gift when the couple had first moved into their home, seventeen years before.

Russell, Catherine, and Samuel all looked up at the same place on the wall. Elizabeth craned around to see what everyone else was looking at. "That old gun?" questioned Elizabeth, looking at the antique shotgun that hung over the mantle of the kitchen's fireplace.

"Yes. The gun," John was staring at the weapon. The memories were really coming back now.

"That gun used to hang over our own mantle until we gave it to Rusty and Cathy. It's always just been around. I don't even know if it still works or not, Pop."

"I don't know either, Sammy. But it wouldn't surprise me. The Joseph Manton double-barreled shotgun was the best money could buy back when it was new. That danged gun is probably over seventy years old."

"Okay...so what's the big deal about the gun?" questioned Russell. He scratched at his bushy head of hair. Catherine gave him a sharp glance as she didn't approve of Russell's "bad habit." Not even in front of family. Catherine thought it was unsightly to see her husband scratch at his head.

John Murdock continued to stare at the gun hanging over the fireplace. "In a nutshell? That there gun shot and killed the sixteen-year-old daughter of William and Lillian Fick."

Catherine and Elizabeth gasped at the same time, "Sixteen?" Both men cocked their heads curiously.

John Murdock definitely had their attention now. He carried on with his story, "The young lady's name was Lorra Anne Fick. She would be well over eighty years old today, if she were still alive."

"The gun killed Lorra Anne Fick all by itself?" said Elizabeth. As soon as she said the words, she realized how dumb she must have sounded.

"No. Not by itself. It was fired by my father, James Murdock."

"Your father was a murderer?" blurted out Russell. He scratched his head again and paid no heed to his wife. Everyone looked at John and then to the gun and back to John, again.

"He was no murderer. It was an accident. My father regretted that day for the rest of his life. The court cleared his name. I remember now like it was yesterday."

"Tell us, Pops. Don't leave us in the dark."

"If I remember right, Sammy, the girl didn't die right away. She didn't die from the wounds so much as from the disease caused by the wound. I believe she died in this very house." Everyone remained quiet, thinking about how terrible it must have been.

"So, how exactly does this relate to Alicia?" Catherine asked. Her gaze went to the ceiling of the kitchen as she thought about her own daughter sleeping upstairs.

John took a deep breath like he was holding in a huge secret. "Lorra Anne Fick not only died in this house...she actually died on her sixteenth birthday."

Catherine gasped again and this time put her hand to her mouth, "Oh, my God."

"The whole thing is making some sort of sense now," said Elizabeth.

John took a drink from his glass and carried on with his story. "Life went downhill for William and Lillian Fick after their only child died. I remember that they lived miserably after the funeral of young Lorra Anne. William took up with the bottle in a bad way and began to fight continuously with his wife. It was rumored that he would beat her. Then, one night, Lillian Fick decided she had had enough of her husband in particular, and life in general. She went down to Castle Lake, and she drowned herself."

John pointed in the direction of the lake and dock as he spoke, "Right down the hill at the end of the dock. The church would not allow a person of suicide to be buried in hallowed ground, so William was forced to bury her out in the field, which I assume eventually, became the west woods. Then William Fick, himself, had had enough. It was said that he tied himself to the timber supports in the original barn here and set the barn on fire with him inside. But before he burned himself alive he did one thing..."

Samuel, Russell, Elizabeth, and Catherine hung onto John's every word. "What was that?" Elizabeth almost demanded.

"William Fick cursed my father, and the Murdock family."

"Here is where the ghosts come in. Right, Pop?"

"Yes, Sammy, this is where the ghosts come in. Apparently, before he died in the impending barn fire, William Fick had gone to see the local witch doctor, a man by the name of Troyer. The story goes that William Fick gave his soul to Troyer in exchange for the life of the first Murdock girl who lived to see her sixteenth birthday. Simply put, William Fick cursed our family."

Yet another gasp escaped from the mouth of Catherine Murdock. Her hazel eyes got extremely wide. She grabbed onto Russell's hand. Russell could feel that she was growing cold. Russell and Catherine looked at John Murdock like he was crazy. Samuel and Elizabeth, too, were also shocked at what they were hearing.

"You believe this?"

"Take it or leave it, Rusty. I give you the facts. And the fact is that today is Alicia Ann's sixteenth birthday. She is also the first female to be born of this family since the curse was put into effect. Alicia has almost died twice. You can call it a coincidence, but I know that there's more to it than that."

The only sound that could be heard was the ticking of the grandfather clock out in the parlor and the sounds of the burning fire in the black cast-iron stove. "Like I said, my father told us to never speak of the curse after William Fick died. So it was forgotten over the years. But right now I feel like not a day has passed since the time William Fick rode up on his horse and told my father about the curse he and Doctor Troyer had hexed us with. At the time we nervously laughed and never gave it a second thought. That was over sixty-six years ago..."

Everyone remained silent until Russell spoke up, "I need another whisky."

"Not too much, Russell. Right now I need you with a clear mind." Catherine turned her head towards John, "Say that we believe you. How do we stop this?"

THOMAS A. RYERSON

"I don't exactly know, Cathy. I can only guess that to satisfy the curse, Alicia must die on her sixteenth birthday. If that is the case, we just need to simply keep her alive until this day passes." John rubbed his grey mat of hair and finished his whisky. "Well, I don't need a clear head. I'm having another whisky."

Samuel was the emotional one of the Murdock men. He had kept silent through the story; now it was time for him to have his say. He was visibly shaken up, and he still felt wronged. "You forgot all of this stuff, Pop? It just slipped your mind all of these years? A murder, Pop! A murder was committed here. A suicide and another death. A grave. A curse. I can't believe it!" Obviously, Samuel had accepted what his father had told him. Or, quite possibly, it was the only thing that made sense at this point. John just gave Samuel a blank stare. He felt that he had explained himself as best as he could.

Elizabeth then said something that was probably in the back of everyone's mind. "What is the connection between Roddy Fellows and the Reverend Sweetwater? Why would they try to kill Alicia? What would be their motive?"

"That part of the puzzle, I don't know," admitted John. "But again, if I had to guess, I would say that they were possessed by an evil spirit. It must be the evil spirit of William Fick. He has obviously waited for this moment for sixty-six years."

"Well, there is your demon after all, Pop. So you're saying that a demon possessed both Roddy and the Reverend and tried to kill my granddaughter?"

"It's crazy, Sammy, I know. But what else makes sense? Alicia Ann has lived a perfectly safe and healthy life for sixteen years. Never been seriously sick a day in her life. Then, today of all days, she is almost struck down—not once, but twice!"

"It's not so crazy, John," reflected Catherine. "Roddy was not himself this morning. It's so obvious now, as I look back and think about it. He was so full of pep and at the same time so unfocused...scattered."

"You're right, Cathy." Russell agreed. "Roddy was acting very peculiar when he came back to the farm after Alicia's fall from Holly. He must have been disorientated after having the demon inside him."

Catherine agreed. "I had a feeling that Roddy was out of sorts this morning, but it just wasn't enough for me to worry about it." Catherine then spoke to John, "What more can you tell us about the girl that was killed and her father?"

John rubbed his chin again and thought. He was searching his memory deeper for more answers. "Like I said, I remember very clearly the day William Fick came riding out to our home farm. It's the same farm that stands across the lake, now. That was when he had cursed us. I don't remember much about the daughter. She was older than my brother and I. We didn't associate with her much. She was snooty. The clearest thing I remember after William Fick cursed us was that his barn burned with him inside it. The authorities didn't call William's death a suicide though. I suppose they must have felt that enough shame had fallen upon the Fick family as it was.

William Fick was given a pauper's funeral and was allowed to be buried beside his daughter. I think a local charity may have paid for the stone."

"Where, Father? Where were William and his daughter buried?"

"They are up at the Roulston churchyard—buried somewhere in the back corner—in the old section."

Elizabeth joined back into the conversation. "Do we exhume him? Is that the answer?"

All four of the others looked at her in disbelief. Elizabeth was supposed to be the rational one of the group. John looked directly at Elizabeth, "I think the best answer is to just keep Alicia alive into the next day. If she's still attacked by something after tomorrow's morning light, then we will dig him up. How does that sound?"

Elizabeth defended herself, "That's how they do it in the stories John. They dig the body up and bless the bones or something like that."

Russell looked squarely at his mother. "Mother, we are not digging anybody up. Like Grandfather says, we will just stay with Alicia all night."

Then a horrified expression crept across Catherine's face.

"What is it, Cathy?" Russell asked.

"What if the demon enters into one of us? Or Robby or Johnnie? How will we know who it takes over next? How will we know who is the demon and who isn't?"

Elizabeth looked quite impressed at her daughter-in-law,

"Now that is a very good question."

"I suppose who the demon went into would depend on the method that he used to do so. If you were the demon, how would you move from one person to the next?" questioned Samuel.

"I think it would have to be by touch, Father. It's the only logical explanation. If someone physically touched the demon-possessed body, then it could easily pass from one person to the next."

John nodded his head in agreement. "That certainly makes sense, Rusty." Then, grinning, John turned to Elizabeth, "Have you read any books on the subject, Lizzie?"

Elizabeth looked up at John and didn't see the humor in his comment. "I am a teacher, John. I have read a lot of books. I was just trying to help."

Russell jumped into the conversation before continuing his current train of thought, "Mother, I think Grandfather John is just teasing you. Let's stay focused here. Obviously, the demon can't pass directly into Alicia..."

"Obviously?" questioned Catherine.

Russell turned to his wife. He was excited and was speaking quickly, "If the demon could pass directly into Alicia, she would be dead already. The demon would have traveled from Roddy or the Reverend right into Alicia if it could have. It would have had the chance time and time again. So I figure that the demon can only commit an act that will result in her death. It can't actually enter her and kill her in that way."

Samuel then added, "Just like my grandfather did. He committed an act that resulted in the death of that girl. It's like an eye for an eye. The life of sixteen-year-old Alicia Murdock for that of sixteen-year-old Lorra Fick. An event that originally occurred in 1821 is atoned for in 1888."

There was a heavy silence, and then Russell spoke his thoughts, "The question now is who did the Reverend Sweetwater come into contact with? How many people have touched him since he was questioned about the incident with Alicia at the church? Definitely the sheriff. There was the bailiff and the deputy, too. Maybe even someone at the church?"

Catherine spoke, "It would have to have been right after the attack on Alicia. Not before. It would be anyone who may have touched the Reverend after the church incident. You see, since the demon was not successful in the body of the Reverend, it would have passed into someone who could make another attempt." Catherine thought for a moment. "Russ, you were there when the sheriff took Reverend Sweetwater down. Did anyone get close to the Reverend right after he was shot?"

Russell didn't have to think long. He had watched the whole scene play out. He slowly articulated, "Colonel Bostwick was the first man to approach the Reverend. But after that there would have been the doctor, the deputy, and maybe even the sheriff. Who really knows?"

Catherine looked across the table at everyone, "Colonel Bostwick, eh? He should be our number one suspect, then. Do we tell the sheriff? And if so, what do we tell the sheriff?"

In unison, the others emphatically said, "No!"

"It's crazy enough that we believe this. But Alicia is our flesh and blood and we are all she has. If we go to the sheriff with this insane story, he will lock us all up and throw away the key. And then, who will protect her? We stay here. We watch her and shoot anyone that acts suspicious."

"Suspicious, but not crazy. Right?" Elizabeth added. She finished her second cup of coffee. "One of us should be in that room with her right now. Alicia should not be alone for the rest of the evening."

"That's a good idea, Lizzie. I will take the first watch. What time is it right now?" John asked.

"Six p.m., Father," said Samuel. "We just need to watch her for six more hours, and we will be in the clear, right?"

"God willing," John said.

"I'm going to get dinner started. We need to have full bellies so we can stay on our toes."

"I'll help," said Elizabeth.

John got up from the table and steadied himself. The whisky was having some effect on him.

"Are you going to be okay, Pop?" asked Samuel.

"Yes," laughed John. "I'm old and reliable, Sammy. I will be fine. I will go up and sit with Alicia. After an hour or so, we will switch." As he spoke, John took the last cookie from the plate of treats.

"I will bring dinner up to you John when it's ready. We're going to be having boiled beef with mashed potatoes and gravy."

"Simple but effective," spoke John as he walked out of the kitchen on his way upstairs, munching.

The women busied themselves with the dinner preparations and the two remaining men decided to clear out of the kitchen. Against his wife's request, Russell poured himself another whisky, and Samuel poured himself another cider. "Let's go back into the parlor, shall we, Father?" Russell suggested.

The two men stood up and made their way out of the kitchen. "We will be in the parlor if you need us, Cathy."

Russell's wife turned around as she was counting out potatoes and asked, "Please check in on your grandfather and Alicia for me." Russell could tell she was trying not to get overly emotional. He smiled, nodded, and then followed his own father out across the hall to the parlor.

Russell entered the parlor and pulled back a curtain that faced the west. There was still a fair amount of light outside and he didn't want to light the oil lamps yet if he didn't have to. He turned around and saw that his father was already getting comfortable in one of the Queen Anne chairs. "This is the life," Samuel said, smiling.

"I'm just going to check upstairs." Russell set his drink down on a side table and left the parlor. He was just about to make his way to the second floor when he thought about his sons. They should definitely be in the house for the evening. It was the only way to remain safe.

Roddy Fellows, a man who lived on this property and served the Murdock family, had been the first victim of the demon, as they had called it. Roddy was a man whom they had trusted. Next was the Reverend, the very person who had baptised both of Russell's sons in the name of God. Would Colonel Bostwick be the next person under the influence of the demon? How and when would they know for sure? Russell got a shiver as he thought about his boys outside all by themselves.

Instead of going upstairs as he had promised, Russell took a detour, leaving the house out the side door. He crossed over the courtyard to the barns and out-buildings.

Russell entered into the main barn and stopped. He stood on some loose straw on the dirt floor of the barn. The smell of the horses within the barn was reassuring. He cupped his hands around his mouth and yelled, "Boys! Robert! Johnnie!" Perhaps if he called Robby by his full name he would take him seriously.

Russell walked into the main hall of the horse barn. Directly in front of him was Holly's stall. This was the horse that had almost killed his daughter. Of course, it wasn't Holly's fault. She was just a tool of the demon. Russell turned to his left and continued to walk slowly down the hall which was actually quite dark. He called the boy's names again, but still there was no response. Then Russell thought he heard a whisper.

Or was it just his imagination? He walked ahead ten more feet, and noticed small traces of either hay or straw falling from the ladder opening above him in the ceiling. This was the ladder that led up into the mow on the second level of the barn. Again, he saw some movement. Russell slowly looked up to the mow opening. His attention was totally transfixed on what might be up there. In fact, he was so absorbed in what he was doing he did not see the stealthy figure come up from behind him.

The sudden shock of the two cold hands on his waist made Russell Murdock jump straight up and at the same time he screamed. And it wasn't a manly scream either. He jumped into the air so fast and high that he struck his head on the cross beam directly above him. Russell landed on his posterior with his body slamming into the wall of the main stall hallway. As he shook his head, trying to clear his thoughts, Russell began to hear hysterical laughing from above in the mow.

He realized that the laughing was from his son, Johnnie. "Father screamed like a little school girl!" Johnnie looked down at Robby who had come up behind their father. Robby was not laughing. He knew that he had genuinely scared his father. He had never seen a grown man jump or scream like that. Robby knew that his father wasn't going to be impressed at all by the prank. Once he realized that he was the only one laughing, Johnnie stopped. He lay with his belly flat on the floor of the mow. His head hung over the opening. The boy's father looked faint and his glasses had fallen off.

Russell Murdock continued to shake his head. He then got his bearings. He was a reasonable man and had been a kid once. He said sternly, "Robby, find my glasses now. If they are broken, God help you, son."

CASTLE LAKE

Robby began to shake nervously, knowing now that he had given his father a terrible scare. Johnnie climbed down the wooden ladder from the mow. "Careful!" Robby yelled at his brother. "Don't be steppin' on Father's glasses."

"I ain't no dummy. I won't crush them." Johnnie lowered himself to the floor of the barn and began to look in earnest for his father's glasses.

"There they are, boys. Over by the tack bucket." Russell was getting some of his composure back.

"Wow. You must have been scared father. They plum flew six feet."

"Are they bent or broken, Robby?" Russell asked. He leaned up against the wall and took a deep breath, "Don't ever do that again." Both boys shook their heads and understood. They had never thought that their father would react like that. Of course they had never scared him under these kinds of conditions before.

"What's all the commotion about," Catherine Murdock said as she entered the barn. She was wearing an apron and had flour on her hands. "Who screamed? Why?"

Russell took the glasses from his son and cleaned them with the bottom of his blue work shirt. He looked up at Catherine and blushed.

"It wasn't you, was it?" Catherine began to laugh. Both boys joined in with their mother. So did Russell. What else could he do? As he laughed both of his sons came to either side of him, giving him a bear hug.

"The boys play a little trick on you, did they?" Catherine accurately guessed.

"With everything that is going on right now, I guess I was just ripe for the pickings, wasn't I, boys?"

"We're sorry, Father. We had no idea you'd scare so badly," Robby apologized to his father.

"I'm sorry too, Papa," added Johnnie.

"Its okay, boys, maybe I needed a laugh. Let's lock the barn up for the night and get into the house."

Catherine gave her husband a knowing look and then headed back to the house. She reassured those gathered on the porch that everything was okay and that her sons had just played a harmless prank on their father. Catherine continued into the house and Elizabeth and Samuel followed her. Elizabeth and Catherine returned to their task of preparing dinner while Samuel sauntered back into the parlor to wait for his son.

Back in the barn, Russell, Robby, and Johnnie closed and secured all the doors. The boys were oblivious to anything demonic and bounded up and down the halls making sure everything was tightly shut. Johnnie scooted back up the ladder into the hay mow and secured all the doors that led to the outside. Once he had that task completed, he slid back down the ladder and joined up with his father and brother. The three of them closed the last door to the barn and made their way back to the house.

"Why did we lock the barn up so tightly, Father? We

don't normally do that unless we leave the farm for a spell."

"Well, Robby, today isn't normal. We have to take extra precautions until the morning comes. I'll explain it all to you both after supper." Russell didn't want to get the boys too riled up before they ate. He was sure there would be lots of talk at the supper table.

"How is Alicia doing, Papa?" asked Johnnie.

"She's gonna be okay. Right, Father?" interjected Robby, trying to sound grown up.

The three Murdock men were just approaching the steps leading up to the porch of the house. Russell stopped walking and turned to face his sons. He crouched down to Johnnie's height. His sons stopped, and wondered what their father was up to. Russell looked very seriously at his two sons. "Boys, I need you to act like men now. I can't say who or why, but someone is trying to hurt Alicia."

Both of the boy's mouths dropped open. "That's why the sheriff was here!" blurted out Robby. He turned to Johnnie, "That's what all the commotion was about when we came in from the field."

Russell nodded his head. "That's right, Robby. Your mother and I didn't want you worrying too much until we knew what we were up against."

"Why ain't the sheriff still here then, Papa?"

"The sheriff can't help us now. Only we can help Alicia. Your mother and I don't know exactly who is trying to hurt Alicia. All we know is that we just have to get through this night. I need men tonight, not boys. Can you do that for me?"

Robby spoke first. "Yes, Father. Whatever it takes, Johnnie and I will help protect Alicia." Robby gave his best stiff upper lip.

"Let's get in there then," added Johnnie. "Mmmmmm... something sure smells good up in the kitchen." Johnnie bounded up the steps and into the house.

Russell kept a hand on Robby's shoulder. "Son, I need you to go up to Alicia's room and peek in on her. Your great grandfather, John, is with her right now. Just make sure they are both safe, okay?" Robby gave his father a firm smile and then followed his brother up the stairs and into the house.

Russell Murdock looked up and gazed at the house. Was he sleeping within the domain of the enemy? He found it hard to fathom that this house had once belonged to William Fick. William Fick's daughter had lived within these walls and Russell's family was responsible for her death.

Lorra Anne Fick had actually died in this house! If Russell recalled right, the cold room used to be a bedroom. Could it have been Lorra Anne Fick's room?

Then Lorra Anne's own mother drowned herself in the very lake he and his children swam in. And to top it all off, William Fick burned himself alive in the barn that used to stand right behind where Russell now stood. Three Ficks. Three deaths. One grave. Would Russell have really wanted to know the history of this property before now? Maybe his grandfather had the right idea after all.

Russell Murdock kicked at the dirt in front of the step

and walked up to the porch. A wonderful aroma flowed out the cracks of the kitchen door.

Johnnie was right, something sure did smell good!

THOMAS A. RYERSON

11

Enter Colonel Bostwick

Colonel Barrington Wadsworth Bostwick had lived for almost sixty-five years and never once was sick. Today that had suddenly changed. He'd awakened feeling pretty good, but now he was strangely feeling ill. His entire body was cold. He had a chill that he just couldn't explain. The Colonel tried to think back to what he may have done differently today? Had he eaten something that may have made him sick? Did he catch some "bug" out of the blue? Or maybe it was simply just the excitement of the day catching up with him.

It had most certainly been an eventful day which, interestingly, seemed to revolve around young Alicia Murdock. First, the girl was almost killed by the stable boy and her own horse, and second, there was the mishap with Reverend Sweetwater. The Colonel was very glad he had been at the sheriff's station when Russell Murdock came looking for Sheriff Harris. The Colonel actually enjoyed assisting the sheriff in the apprehension of the Reverend. Just like back in the old days when he had been in the service.

The Reverend had obviously gone mad. Going on a rampage like that and attacking the sixteen-year-old girl with no apparent provocation. Colonel Bostwick was surprised by the fight that the Reverend had put up. It had taken two shots from the sheriff to take him down. The Reverend had gone unconscious after the shots, but the doctor was able to bring him back around. The Colonel assisted in getting the Reverend from where he had fallen into the manse. Sheriff Harris had decided that the Reverend would stay under house arrest at the manse until he was nursed back to health. The sheriff charged the Reverend with the attempted murder of Alicia Murdock. He had gone to the manse with little complaint. The fight was out of him at that point. The Reverend had seemed very confused and didn't understand what had actually happened. No further action would be taken until the Reverend was his old self again. The Colonel noticed the chill after the episode with the Reverend.

Colonel Bostwick was a large and bulky man. He was probably just a little larger than the Reverend. Of course, back in his prime, he had been in great shape. He had been in the service since he was a lad, and in those days he was a hundred pounds soaking wet. Life had been quite good to him since then and the Colonel's figure showed that, particularly the good food. He had gained a lot of weight since he had retired and become a successful investor.

Today, the Colonel wore a black three-piece suit with a black top hat. The suit had been properly tailored and looked very smart on him. The Colonel may have been a bachelor, but he didn't have to look like one. He didn't need a woman around to make sure he looked and smelled good. He took pride in his personal grooming, as well as in his personal property and possessions. His farm was very well attended to. The lawns were cut and everything had its place on the property. It was quite neat, especially for a farm.

The Colonel's carriage was also one of the most regal in the county. It had wide bench seats, one in the front and one in the back. The carriage could seat as many as five people, and the Colonel also saw that the carriage was always well polished. The carriage was pulled by two bay colored horses. He didn't really need two horses to pull it, but it just made him look and feel all the more important.

At the moment, he was riding in his carriage, and the clip-clopping of the two horse's hooves on the hard dirt road was very soothing and melodic. As he relaxed to the sound of the hooves, the chill came across him again. It was so very cold. The Colonel just wanted to get himself home and get warm. He would stoke his fireplace up and sit in front of the open fire with a brandy.

The Colonel waved to the occupants of an oncoming buggy as it approached him. The dirt road was narrow, and he had to coax the horses to the right. His horses and the horse of the oncoming buggy each wore blinkers over their eyes, so there was less of a chance of them getting spooked. The horses made no gestures or sounds to each other as they passed close by. The four people in the buggy returned the wave to the Colonel. As the buggy went past him, the Colonel kicked himself for not tipping his hat. He just was not feeling his old gentlemanly self at all.

Then the Colonel's stomach made some strange gurgling sounds. He could actually hear his stomach over the hooves of the horses and the wheels of the carriage. Maybe he just needed a good meal. He thought of the barreled salt beef he had back at home. "Mmmmmmm..." maybe he would cook that up with some cabbage and potatoes. That might make him feel better. And then he would sit in his rocker by the fire and relax with a brandy.

The soothing thoughts he was having were suddenly interrupted by strange pains in his head. With no warning, he was overcome by a sense of wooziness. His vision was also getting blurry. Nevertheless, all the Colonel could really do was soldier-on home to his farm.

Before he knew it, the Colonel was at the entrance way of his long laneway. He could see his very quaint and cosy two story house off in the not-so-far distance. He so craved to be home.

Moments later, the Colonel pulled the carriage up to the front of his house and motioned the horses to stop. The Colonel slowly made his way out of the carriage. He held the reins as he lowered himself down to the ground. He then led the horses several feet to the hitching post at the end of the stone pathway that led to the front door of his house. He secured the reins to the post. Content with that, he patted the snout of one of the horses and then made his way down the pathway.

The horses made some neighing sounds as he walked away. "Don't worry, boys. I'll be right back."

What was that? Had he changed his mind? He thought he had wanted some dinner, warmth, and a brandy, but now he wasn't so sure. The Colonel shook his head. He stopped halfway as he walked up to his door. He tried to focus his eyes on the brass door knocker in front of him. Then, he suddenly found himself walking, instead, to his drive-shed. He had this weird sensation like he was drunk—that he wasn't totally in control of his actions. It felt as though there was a little man in his brain who was calling the shots. Damn, he really thought he wanted to eat.

The Colonel approached the long, low drive-shed. He lifted the steel bar that crossed the front of the door, and let it swing free. He then pulled on the handle of the door and opened it. It was very dark inside building. Small fingers of light came in through a rear window and several cracks in the wooden walls. The Colonel stopped and let his eyes adjust to the darkness. It didn't help that his vision was still blurry. He turned to his left and was able to make out the center of the large, double doors in the front.

He purposely walked over to the double doors. Leaning down, he pulled the pin up that kept the double doors securely locked within the floor. As the steel pin lifted the Colonel pushed the doors out. They both swung open on their hinges which squeaked. The drive-shed now filled with the afternoon light, and the Colonel's eyes adjusted yet again. He then continued on with his quest.

The Colonel walked across the dirt floor of the shed to a multi-shelved wall. On the shelves were all kinds of different items. The center shelf was taken up by his horse tack. The rest of the shelves were covered in gardening tools, household tools, nails, wire, and such. But this wasn't what he was looking for. That much the Colonel knew.

He stood back for a better look, smiled, and clapped his hands together. He saw what he was looking for! On the top shelf were several tin containers of lamp oil. He counted four, and the Colonel decided to take them all. Reaching above his head, he retrieved the tins and set them on the floor. Once he had all four tins, he carried them two-at-a-time from the drive-shed to the carriage. The Colonel set the four tins on the front floorboard of the carriage and then went inside his house.

The house was a very impressive brick structure, and he had seen to the construction himself. He entered the front door which led into a very large foyer. On one side of the foyer was a rounded staircase that went up to the second floor. But the Colonel did not need to go up there. He, instead, walked down the main hall to the rear and proceeded into the kitchen.

Walking to a counter, he fumbled through several drawers until he found what he was after. A small box of wooden matches. He smiled as he stuffed the box into his suitcoat pocket.

The Colonel's stomach grumbled again, but he didn't really feel hungry. Possibly, just out of habit, he decided to take something to eat with him. As he left the kitchen, the Colonel grabbed an entire loaf of bread from a side table. He walked out of his house and didn't even bother to shut the front door behind him. He had left the doors to both his house and his drive-shed wide open.

The Colonel came to the side of the carriage and tossed the loaf of bread up onto the front seat. He walked back to the hitching post and untied the reins. His fingers didn't move too well; they were cold and hard to manage--a very strange sensation.

He held onto the reins as he climbed back inside the carriage and motioned the horses to back up. They did so, and he then directed them into the circle of his laneway and they headed out. He snapped the reins and the two horses trotted down the and to the concession road. They turned at the road and headed towards the Atlantic coast—and more important—Castle Lake.

The sun was beginning to set and the air was starting to cool. The Colonel felt even colder than he had before. He had really wanted to warm up; how had he forgotten that? It was like he was receiving mixed signals. He didn't even know where he was heading. The little man in his head did, though.

He knew exactly where they were going.

After traveling for thirty minutes down the dirt road, the Colonel saw his destination in sight. A broad smile came across his face. He could see the smoke rise from the multiple chimneys of the house. She would be in the house. He just had a feeling.

He imagined her sitting in the house just waiting for him to do what he had to do. If she were sleeping, his job would be even easier. No doubt her family would be there to protect her. That was why he had come up with his diversion plan.

About half a mile away from the house, the Colonel pulled the carriage over to the side of the road so that he could wait for nightfall. Deciding this would be an opportune time to eat, he picked up the loaf of bread off the carriage seat, broke the loaf in half, and pulled the soft, white bread from the center of the hard shell. He ate as though he were an animal. He just shoved the pieces of bread into his mouth, soggy chunks falling from his lips and landing on his lap as he chewed. He ate what he could and then waited for dark.

The Colonel woke up with a start. He had dozed off while he had been waiting. The sleeping had certainly helped the time pass. It was now dark. The Colonel realized that he shouldn't ride any closer to the farm. He would walk from here. Shaking himself awake, the Colonel got out of the carriage and walked around to the horses. He was still very cold, even colder than before.

For no apparent reason, he decided it would be a good

idea to let the animals go free. The Colonel realized that he would not be returning from his mission. He unclasped the leather straps that connected the shafts of the carriage to each of the horse's sides. As soon as the second clasp was undone, the shafts fell to the ground. The horses were unsure of what to do and one stepped forward. The Colonel moved to the horses' heads and led them around the front of the carriage in the opposite direction. He gave each horse a smack on their hindquarters. The first one bolted down the road, and then the other joined right behind him. The Colonel smiled. They were free. Just like he was about to be. Free of a very heavy burden he had been carrying for far too many years.

The Colonel collected his thoughts and turned his attention back to the carriage. He reached into the carriage and took out the steel tins of lamp oil. The thin steel handles should have dug into his fingers. However, he didn't actually have much feeling left in either of his hands. With two tins in each hand he walked towards the Murdock farm.

The Murdock farm. It was his farm, rightfully. Why did he think that all of a sudden? Were these the thoughts of the little man in his head? Not too far from the carriage, the Colonel saw a well-worn path which cut through the field. The Colonel had a feeling that this path would lead directly to the barn buildings on the Murdock property. The light of the moon allowed him just enough light to see where he was going. He just had to be careful of falling into the odd gopher or rabbit hole along the way. Hopefully, the Murdock's didn't have a dog. The Colonel was suddenly confused because he did remember a dog, but then the voice told him there was no dog. Time would tell.

He snuck up on the Murdock property. The two-story house looked very snug and comfortable. Smoke continued to rise from both chimneys; the light from the lamps shone through the windows. The Colonel stayed close to the edge of the main barn, and finding a door, he unlatched it. The door creaked open. Inside he could hear the horses stirring. He stopped and looked towards the house, comforted that no one inside had the slightest idea of what was going to happen. The Colonel edged slowly inside the barn where it was very dark. He continued to walk down what appeared to be the main hallway. Here the light was a little better as the moonlight seeped in from several windows located near the end.

The Colonel walked towards the light. As he did, he bumped into something soft. Upon further inspection, he realized that it was a pile of loose straw. Just what he was looking for. He set the four tins of lamp oil on the floor of the barn, bent down, and unscrewed the lids of all four tins. He let the lids fall onto the floor. He dumped the entire contents of one tin onto the pile of straw directly in front of him. The liquid gurgled as it flowed onto the porous material. As soon as the tin was empty, the Colonel simply let it fall to the floor. He picked up a second tin and walked down to the end of the hall and splashed this container all over the door and the floor. He let that container fall to the floor, as well.

Returning to the last two containers of lamp oil, he splattered each on the walls of the opposite end of the main hallway. He walked backwards as he sloshed the fluid onto the walls and the backs of the stall doors. The horses became more agitated as they stomped nervously in their stalls. They must have wondered what he was up to. He dropped the tins once they were empty and found the box of wooden matches in his pocket.

The Colonel then walked to one end of the barn and fumbled as he tried to get a match out from the small box. He managed to get one between his fingers and struck it on the mortar sill of the barn window. The match lit up, and the Colonel instinctively dropped it upon the floor. The lamp oil caught fire and began to burn hard. The Colonel walked quickly to the opposite end of the barn and lit yet another match. He held it next to the lamp oil soaked door of a stall. The flame leaped from the match to the flammable material. The old dry wood of the stall door burst quickly into flames. He went back to the center of the barn where he had poured the lamp oil on the pile of straw, and feeling that he had allowed the lamp oil enough time to soak into the dry material, he struck a final match on the steel clasp of a stall door and dropped it into the pile of straw. Three separate fires were now burning in the barn.

The Colonel exited the barn the way he had come in. He left the door slightly open, to allow the air to flow in and feed the growing fires. He circled around the barn and crept across the courtyard between the barn and the house. Moving as fast as his bulk would allow him, the Colonel slunk to a corner of the house. His breathing was labored from the slight sprint he had made. Even though he knew he needed to find a back entrance, he decided first to wait for a reaction to the fire from the occupants of the house. That was the diversion after all. From where he was standing at the corner of the house, the Colonel could observe both the house's side door as well as the main door of the barn.

Inside the Murdock home things had settled down. The entire Murdock family—minus Samuel's brother, James—were spending the night in Russell and Catherine's home. James was still out of the county. The Murdocks that were present, however, would do all they could within their power to save Alicia. Old John had stayed with her for almost two hours. This allowed the folks on the main floor to get supper made, get everyone fed, and then have the dishes cleaned and put away.

About 9 p.m. Elizabeth decided it was her turn to watch her granddaughter. Alicia had been sleeping soundly for over four hours by that time. Old John retired to the boys' room up in the attic. The boys would join him soon enough. At the moment they were downstairs in the living room in the middle of a nail-biting game of checkers.

Before anyone realized it, the grandfather clock in the parlor suddenly struck 10:30 p.m. Catherine instructed her two young men to finish their current game and then head up to bed. The boys moaned and groaned, and so in retaliation they slowed the game down to a crawl.

It was at that point their father walked up to the table and stated it was time for them to retire for the evening. Johnnie jumped several of Robby's red checker pieces. Robby began to protest, and his father said sternly, "Kiss your mother and grandparents goodnight, boys." The boys knew they were beaten and that it was time to give in. It was still kind of special having everyone over this night; it almost felt like Christmas. They couldn't remember the last time the Murdock family was under one roof together like this.

Robby and Johnnie said their goodnights and gave everyone kisses and hugs. They then dragged their heels upstairs to the second floor, each peeking into Alicia's room where their grandmother was. Elizabeth saw the heads of the boys around the corner of the door and raised her finger to her lips. "Shhhhhhh!" she warned.

Once Robby and Johnnie were content that their sister was in good hands, they continued up the set of much narrower stairs to the attic. Up there, at the top of the house was their room. They had the entire attic to themselves. With the exception of tonight. This was evident as they got to the top of the stairs and could hear the snoring sounds of their great grandfather. Robby opened the door at the top of the stairs and said to Johnnie, "Oh, great. Good luck sleeping tonight."

They entered the room and shut the door behind them. Through the dormer window, moonlight streamed into the room. Johnnie agreed with his elder brother, "Between his snoring and the moonlight, I don't think we will sleep a wink."

"Pull the curtain, Johnnie. That should help with the light at least."

"A pillow will take care of our great grandfather," Johnnie joked as he walked over to the dormer window. When he reached up to close the curtain, Johnnie glanced down on the courtyard. Johnnie rubbed his eyes. Was he seeing things? The longer he watched, the more convinced he was that he wasn't crazy. He turned around as though he had seen a ghost. "Robby, the barn is on fire. I'm sure of it!"

Robby wasted no time in racing over to the window and having a look for himself. Sure enough, he could make out the flickering flames within the structure. The tips of the flames cast eerie shadows inside the barn windows. "We have to tell Father!"

Both boys shot out of the room and almost fell down the steps as they each yelled at the top of their lungs, "Fire! Fire! The barn is on fire!" They turned from the narrow stairway and bolted down the wider stairway to the main floor. As the boys zipped past Alicia's room, Elizabeth got up from her chair to see what the commotion was all about. She turned and looked at the still sleeping Alicia as she left the room. Charlie didn't even stir on Alicia's bed. He was deep in his own puppy dreams. Elizabeth made her way halfway down the open staircase and peered into the living room.

Robby and Johnnie were standing in front of Russell, and both were talking at a very high rate of speed. Each had their own version of the same story. Russell held his hand up to silence them. "What exactly is on fire?"

"Our barn, Father! Our barn!"

Russell jumped up from his chair and made his way to the side door of the house. He, his wife, and father had been relaxing with coffee and brandies in the dining room. Russell unlatched the door of the house and flung it open. Sure enough, he could clearly see the flames inside the barn.

"The horses, Father, we have to save the horses!"

Russell knew that his son was right. "Come on, boys, let's see what we are up against."

Catherine had been sitting beside her husband and stood up with great concern. Samuel put a hand on her arm. "Stay here, Cathy, the four of us should be able to handle this."

Russell was out the door and halfway to the barn as his boys followed. Samuel slipped his boots on and made his way out, as well. Catherine stood at the open door and watched. Elizabeth came down the stairs and stood just behind her daughter-in-law. She held Catherine's arm, and the two of them stared into the darkness at the burning barn.

Russell was the first to get to the structure. He tore the door open towards him and a wave of unexpected heat poured out. He could hear the horses inside neighing in fear. Every thought in his head at that moment was to save his thoroughbred horses. There was Holly, too. The heat and air pressure was intense. He could see the wicked light of the flames ahead on either side of the entrance. The horse's stalls were ahead of him on the west side of the barn.

Russell stepped towards the main hall and grabbed a heavy linen riding blanket. Robby and Johnnie were behind him. "Boys, go around to the south end of the barn and unlatch the door there. The air should draw the fire back that way."

They both nodded and ran back out the way they had come in. Then Samuel was behind his son. "Father, go around to the north end and open the door, see if we can't draw the fire that way."

Like his grandsons, Samuel nodded and left the way he had come. Russell covered himself in the heavy riding blanket and pushed forward. The heat was overwhelming as the flames tore straight up into the mow. The fire seemed to have taken the easy way out and went up. That was good in a way. Russell's stomach turned as he smelt burning flesh. Somewhere a horse didn't make it. He sprung forward, straight to Holly's stall. The black mare was leaping up and down and making frightened neighing sounds. Russell opened her stall door and walked up beside her, "Easy, girl. It's going to be okay."

Russell grabbed her mane and led her back, around and out. She moved towards the hall full of flames. Russell used every ounce of strength he could muster, and pushed Holly straight out the side door. Once out into the cooler air, she turned away from the barn and trotted quickly towards the house. One down, many yet to go. Russell turned back. Suddenly, the heat of the fire appeared to dissipate somewhat as each of the end doors was opened. The flames, however, were shooting higher. Russell went to the next stall and repeated what he had done for Holly. Then the boys and Samuel were at the door, and with the four of them, they began to rescue the horses, one by one. There were still cattle and pigs. It was going to be a long night.

Minutes before, the Colonel had heard the commotion in the house. As soon as the men bolted out of the side door, the Colonel snuck around the corner of the house. He watched them for about fifteen minutes, as they hurriedly were trying to save all the livestock. The Colonel knew that they would remain occupied for quite awhile.

He walked around the part of the house which faced Castle Lake. The lake appeared very peaceful in the moonlight. The house looked very inviting. The porch seemed like a nice place to spend some time doing absolutely nothing. Two rocking chairs stood on either side of the main door. He continued around the front of the house and to the far side. There was another new addition to the house he didn't recognize. Hell, he barely recognized his own house as it was. It was hard to believe that he had built the original structure with his own hands so long ago. The Colonel thought about this and realized that these memories weren't his own. He cleared his mind and circled around the new addition of the house.

At the east side of this part of the house, there was a door. He turned the handle of the door with a cold hand. The door creaked as it opened. The room was dark, but he could see that

271

it was some sort of spare kitchen. He left the door open and entered the house with the aid of the moon's light. Fifteen feet ahead was another door. He opened that one slowly and saw that it led to the main hall of the house. Thirty-five feet ahead, he could make out the form of the dresses of two ladies who faced the courtyard from the open door ahead. No doubt these were the women of the house watching the barn fire from the side door. To the left in the main hall was the stairwell up to the next level. Even though their backs were to him, the Colonel still wouldn't be able to sneak up the main stairs without being seen. He knew somehow that Alicia would be on the second floor.

There had to be another stairway up to the second level. Of course, there should be one from the kitchen he was now in. He turned to his left and felt his way along the wall and found a door and opened it. Unfortunately, it just led into a small pantry. The Colonel returned from the way he had come and looked for a door on the opposite wall. There it was! Located in the same spot as the first door, but on the other side of the room. Somebody here liked symmetry.

The door was only about two feet wide and the Colonel found that he almost didn't fit within the door frame. The steps off the stairwell were small and crude. Ah, the joys of auxiliary stairwells. The stairs went up several steps and then turned hard to the left. He crept up each step slowly and was acutely aware as they creaked and moaned under the bulk of his weight. At the top of the dark stairwell, was another door. He opened it slowly and peered out.

Oil lamps lit the second floor. He found himself in a small hall with several doors branching off it. He turned and walked towards the largest source of the light. At the end of this short hall was a main hall. To his right a narrow stairwell led to what he assumed was the attic. Almost in front of him, a main stairwell led down. He had managed to get around the two women!

The Colonel walked into the main hall which was much better lit. Ahead of him, he saw a white bedroom door that was ajar. The Colonel was about halfway across the hall when he heard, "I should go check on Alicia. It's been over twenty-five minutes."

"You stay here, Lizzie, I can peek in on her. I'll be right back." The higher pitched of two female voices was coming up the steps from the main floor. The Colonel turned away from the top of the stairway and slipped down the hall to the next door. He entered the room and turned around. He kept the door open just an inch so he could monitor what was going on.

Catherine Murdock walked up the steps to the second floor. At the top, a foul odour suddenly caught her nose. It smelled of something rotten. Then at the same time she felt a breeze to her left. Curious, she walked down the narrow and dark hall to where the rear stairwell was located. To her shock and dismay somehow the little door that led down to the summer kitchen was open. Catherine peeked down the stairway and could see the fingers of the moonlight through the door at the bottom. That was very peculiar. She was going to bring that to Elizabeth's attention.

Then the damn smell started up again. It was foul and stank of rotted meat. She turned around and walked directly into Colonel Barrington W. Bostwick. His jowls looked more disgusting than usual, and his eyes had sunken into his head. He didn't look well at all. "Colonel Bostwick, what is the meaning of this? Why are you in my home?" Then suddenly the realization hit her, but it was much too late.

The Colonel said nothing, but gave her a dreadfully sinister sneer. Both of his hands shot out. Before she knew it, Catherine Murdock was falling backwards down the narrow stairway. There was no room to go anywhere but down. Pain shot from every part of her body. Elbows toes forehead fingers knees bottom. She hit the small landing with a thud and then continued to fall the five steps out onto the floor of the summer kitchen. Catherine hadn't made any other noises other than the natural sounds of her falling down the steps. She lay sprawled unconscious on the floor. Blood trickled from the corners of her mouth and her forehead.

Elizabeth Murdock spun around and looked behind her as soon as she heard the noises coming from somewhere in the house. The thud, thud, thud sound had originated somewhere behind her. She crossed over to the bottom of the steps of the main stairwell and shouted up the stairs, "Catherine. Catherine!"

Elizabeth became panic-stricken and returned to the door of the house where she and Catherine had been watching

274

the fire. The men were still negotiating the livestock out from the barn. The courtyard of the farm was now full of horses and cows. She stepped out of the house and onto the porch. Elizabeth cupped her hands around her mouth and was just about to shout for the men when she stopped. There were more sounds from behind her.

Elizabeth turned around to face the hallway again. She then realized that the sounds she was hearing were coming from the summer kitchen. The men outside were busy enough. Elizabeth was sure she could handle this situation and convinced herself to investigate the sound on her own.

Elizabeth made her way slowly down the hall looking to the left and to the right. She was waiting for something to jump out at her. Visions of bogeymen danced in her head. How old was she again?

As she reached the end of the hall, Elizabeth noticed right away that the door to the summer kitchen was ajar. She stepped forward, took a breath, and pushed the door open. She looked straight ahead and saw that the exterior door of the summer kitchen was open to the outside. Then her instincts told her to look down. She gasped. In front of her, Catherine lay on the floor, bleeding. Elizabeth scooted down the two steps into the summer kitchen and crossed over to Catherine. She knelt down and checked Catherine's pulse. It was still fairly strong. So Catherine was okay. But what had happened that put Catherine into this state? Alicia!

Elizabeth left Catherine's side and tore back into the main

part of the house. Once she was at the side door, Elizabeth bolted out into the night. She almost fell down the steps of the porch while running. She ran hard across the courtyard while holding up the bottom of her dress with her hands. Elizabeth had to run around horses, cows, and now she noticed pigs. "Russell! Samuel! Boys!" Elizabeth yelled out as she ran towards the burning barn.

Back up on the second floor of the house, the Colonel was smiling. That had actually been fun. The look on Catherine's face just before he had pushed her down the steps was priceless. Ah, the power of the element of surprise! There was no more time to waste. It was getting close to midnight, and he still had a job to do.

The Colonel returned back to the main hall of the house's second floor. He boldly crossed the hall and flung the door open to Alicia's bedroom. He entered the room and without hesitation approached her bed. At the foot of the bed a puppy sat up and began to yawn. An oil lamp in the far corner of the room cast a little light that strained against the darkness.

The Colonel looked across at the head of the bed. His face dropped. There was a down-filled pillow, sure enough, but the layers of sheets and the comforter covered no body. He bent forward and felt the top of the bed to make sure. She couldn't be too far away. He turned to leave the room, but it was now his turn to be surprised. Shakily standing there in her bedclothes was the birthday girl.

Alicia's shoulder length auburn hair was quite messy and

stood up in places. There was sleep in the corners of her deep brown eyes. Her lips were dry. She seemed unsteady on her feet. Strangely, both of her arms were raised above her head. He looked up above her head to see that she was holding onto a square mirror that was eighteen inches from corner to corner. Alicia suddenly swung the mirror down with all her strength. It caught the Colonel on the temple and then shattered into hundreds of pieces. He reeled back and fell onto the edge of her bed.

As he fell, Alicia clumsily made her way out of the room. She fell out into the hall and headed for the stairs. Hanging onto the handrail, she slowly made her way down the steps. With only four steps to go, Alicia lost her footing and tumbled down the remainder of the stairs onto the floor. Instinctively, she put her hands out to break her fall, but one leg got caught under her. As Alicia hit the floor, she could feel her ankle give way, and she fell onto the hard oak plank floor so hard that her chin snapped back up. Alicia saw stars.

The Colonel pulled himself up with the aid of Alicia's night stand. He staggered out of her room and into the hallway. Blood trickled down his face as he made his way to the top of the stairs. When he looked down, he was pleased with what he saw. The girl was at the bottom of the stairs, crumpled up in a pile. He edged his way down step-by-step. Shards of broken mirror protruded from his scalp. His head was spinning. Only three steps to go!

Alicia lifted her head up slowly. Just feet ahead of her, the door to the outside was wide open. She pushed herself up and then stopped. She heard a creaking behind her. Afraid as she was, Alicia turned her head around to see that the Colonel was almost at the bottom of the steps. In a sudden burst of energy, she dashed through the hall into the dining room, crossed the floor in three hopping steps, and then burst into the parlor.

Alicia had decided that she was safer in the house where she could find a weapon. The open door had been inviting, but she didn't want to go out into the unknown darkness. Especially in her present condition. The interior of the house was her terrain; although the parlor was quite dark. The flames from the barn fire offered a little light, but not much. Alicia wondered about the strange light, she had no idea yet that the barn was actually on fire.

Alicia's first instinct was to hide behind some furniture. Maybe the grandfather clock would be a good place, and she could push it over on the fat, old bastard at the last minute. Alicia was good on her left foot, but when she transferred her weight to her right foot, the pain shot up her leg. With her last step, the pain was so great that she fell forward and landed on the edge of a cushioned, Queen Anne wing chair. Her face hit the bottom corner of the chair and a small upholstery tack caught her cheek. More pain to endure.

The Colonel slowly entered into the parlor and pulled the door from the dining room shut. Momentarily, he faced the door, saw a key in the keyhole, and turned it, locking the door. He turned back and faced Alicia. Now, it was just the two of them.

Alicia began to crawl towards the grandfather clock. The clock was getting closer and closer. Just a few feet more.

Suddenly, Alicia felt herself being squashed, and she gasped desperately for air. It was then that she realized the Colonel had actually dived upon her back. His bulk was literally squeezing the life out of her. His hands went to the back of her neck. Alicia somehow managed to roll herself from underneath the Colonel and onto her back. She now faced the crazed fat man. His hands were still firmly around her neck.

Foam appeared on both sides of the Colonel's mouth. He was possessed. He didn't seem human. And he was so cold. His ice-like hands squeezed harder and harder around her neck. Alicia Murdock had nothing left, and her body went limp.

Life began to leave her body. The grandfather clock ticked away behind her. She tried hard to turn and look at the clock, but her eyes saw double, and she was sure she could feel her throat filling with blood. All she could make were weak, choaking sounds as the cold hands tightened even further around her neck. Alicia somehow got herself turned to one side, and she was able to see the clock. Her last vision before she lost consciousness was the face. Three minutes before midnight...then darkness.

Suddenly, rapid, heavy pounding shook the parlor door. "One, Two, Three!" The solid timber door broke free of its hinges and fell into the parlor. Russell Murdock charged into the room just in time to see Colonel Bostwick choking the last bit of life from Alicia. Right behind Russell was Samuel, and behind him, Robby and Johnnie.

Russell was only ten feet away from the Colonel, but he didn't hesitate. He stood back up and aimed his great grandfather's Joseph Manton double-barreled shotgun at the Colonel's back. Russell Murdock had been too sorely vexed and burdened for one day. This was going to end now. He offered the Colonel no warning. No mercy. Russell pulled his finger on the trigger twice, and both barrels blew off, one right after the other. The recoil took Russell by surprise and sent him reeling back into a lamp table beside the door. The cabriole legs of the table crumbled under Russell's weight and and he lurched sideways, his head smashing into the plaster lathe wall. The sudden jolt knocked Russell out cold.

Russell's last conscious thoughts were of the shotgun. What tales that old shotgun could tell. What things had it shot during its long life? Russell Murdock definitely knew of two. Then everything went black.

Part 4—August 14, 1888

THOMAS A. RYERSON

12

A grand funeral

Many people had gathered at the Roulston Community Church. They had all come out to the funeral today to show their respect for the passing of someone they saw as a significant loss to their community.

Jeremiah Kenzie had actually cut the entire lawn of the church property for the funeral. He had his scythe sharpened to its fullest and sharpest and didn't miss one blade of grass. He had also collected all the sticks and refuse from the entire cemetery, including the old section, loaded it into a wagon, and taken it back to his farm for disposal. Jeremiah had also pulled the weeds from the sides of the church foundation and collected all the spider webs that had built up under the wooden awnings over the entrance of the church.

In addition Jeremiah had replaced the broken door that led up the church steeple. The hallway of the church smelled of fresh paint from the newly painted door and trim, which was just done the night before. No one was really prepared for this funeral.

He had taken a straw broom and swept the cobblestone walk from the church doors down to the area where all the buggies and carriages were tied up. Today was the fullest he had ever seen the parking area. In fact buggies and carriages lined up on either side of the concession road for several hundred feet.

The Reverend Sweetwater was still recovering from his two gunshot wounds. He was doing better. Because of how things had turned out, the attempted murder charges had been dropped. He felt badly that he couldn't attend the funeral, but it was felt that it was too soon for him to be moving about. Actually no one knew how the people who attended the funeral might react if the Reverend was in attendance. Sheriff Harris wanted the Reverend to remain at the manse for a while longer. Reverend Egerton Sweetwater insisted that he still had no memory of the attack on Alicia Murdock.

Bandages still covered the Reverend's chest where he had received the gunshots. Miss Ira Jenkins, Doctor Feeney's assistant, remained at the manse with the Reverend, and they were becoming fast friends. Sheriff Harris had instructed Miss Jenkins that under no circumstances was the Reverend to leave the manse.

Roddy Fellows was still in the Roulston jail; although, he too denied remembering anything about cutting the girth of Alicia Murdock's saddle. He stood his ground and declared that he had absolutely no memory of the event. His story was eerily similar to that of the Reverend's. Neither man knew of the other's evil acts towards young Alicia Murdock. That made it all the more strange.

That left Colonel Bostwick of the three attackers of Alicia Murdock. Three men whom she had little or no contact with had suddenly all attempted to kill her. And on her sixteenth birthday of all days! There was absolutely no motive that the sheriff could see.

Russell and Catherine Murdock had remained mum about the Fick curse. There was no point now in mentioning it. Curses and ghosts were the stuff of stories, not real life. Some folks did, in fact, believe that Roddy Fellows, the Reverend Sweetwater, and Colonel Bostwick had all been possessed. However, the Murdock's did not encourage this line of thinking. The general consensus of the people in the county was that all three men--for what ever reason--had all gone temporarily insane.

There was no other explanation. The community of Roulston simply did not believe in ghosts. This was 1888, for heaven's sake, not the bloody stone-age!

An expensive mahogany coffin lay at the front of the church. It was intricately decorated with carvings of angels and flowers. Fresh-cut flowers covered the entire polished coffin. Other bouquets of dried flowers stood on either side of the coffin and were held in shiny metal frames. Cards adorned the many flower arrangements stating the condolences for the family of the deceased.

The deceased would not be soon forgotten, that was for sure. They were well respected no matter what people may have thought of them at this particular moment.

The Reverend Wilber Ignace, who had ridden in from Evanston for the day, was the stand-in minister. Reverend Ignace had a connection with the deceased and wished to be a part of the service. He was a short and portly man who appeared to be in his fifties. His faded, brown suit was a size too small for him, but no one seemed to care. There were more important matters at hand.

The Reverend Ignace cleared his throat. The wooden frame church was packed with people who were out to pay their last respects. Both Wendy Birch and Marianne Myers stood near the back of the church. They craned their heads around people standing in front of them in an effort to see the action up front. The Reverend Ignace was sure that not another living person could fit inside the building. He spoke to the congregation, "Friends, family, and the many members of the community of Roulston. I humbly welcome you to the funeral service of a well-esteemed and beloved member of our county."

Crying could be heard within the church. The Reverend Ignace continued, "Colonel Barrington Wadsworth Bostwick was a very important member of this community. It shows from the turnout today. He was also my cousin." There was a hush over the crowd.

Sitting in the front row of the pews was the entire Murdock family of Roulston. Eighty-one year old John Murdock sat at the far end of the pew. He was sure that some people here might think that it was strange that the Murdock's would sit in the front row of the church. But John had no issue with Colonel Bostwick *per se*. He knew the Colonel was not acting of his own volition. For that reason, John and his family were here in the front row paying their last respects to a once great man.

John's thoughts then turned from Colonel Bostwick to that of his own family. John turned his head and glanced down the row to the group of people that made up his unique and special family. To his right was his son, Samuel, and Samuel's wife, Elizabeth. Next to them were John's grandson, Russell, and his wife, Catherine. A white bandage covered Catherine's forehead, and her arm was in a sling. Beside Russell and Catherine sat John's younger son, James. James had missed all the excitement by being out of town the night of the ghostly attack. None-the-less James was here today to show his support.

Beside James were John's great grandsons, Robby and Johnnie. They were fine looking young men and had made their great grandfather very proud. But the greatest reward that old John Murdock saw at that moment was that of his great granddaughter, Alicia Ann Murdock. She was sixteen years and three days old.

She had been scarred. That was for sure. Her face was

visibly bruised and there was a white bandage around her neck. Like her mother, her arm was also in a sling, and she had a thick, white cast around her ankle. But old John Murdock knew her physical wounds would heal in time. At least she was alive. His great granddaughter was alive.

Alicia felt her great grandfather's gaze and turned her head towards him. Their eyes locked for a moment, and they smiled at each other. His smile warmed her from inside, and reassured her that everything was going to be all right.

It seemed strange to be smiling at a funeral, but Alicia knew that she was a very lucky girl. Not that she ever intentionally took them for granted, but now Alicia really understood the importance of her family. They were the sole reason that she was alive and here today. Alicia would be in their debt for quite awhile.

Thanks to their courage, quick thinking, and faith in themselves as a family, the Murdock's of Roulston had triumphed over the curse set in motion so many years before.

Even so, the Murdock family never breathed a word to anyone outside their circle about beating the curse of Doctor Troyer and saving Alicia from the evil spirit of William Fick.

Who would have believed them anyway?

Printed in the United States
203910BV00001B/103-324/P

9 780980 037708